A GRINCH STORY

The GRINCH TAKES a VACATION

Also by Kaeti Vandorn

Monster Friends

Crabapple Trouble

The GRINCH TAKES a VACATION

KAETI VANDORN

RH GRAPHIC
NEW YORK

This is a work of fiction. Names, characters, places, and incidents either are the product of the author's imagination or are used fictitiously. Any resemblance to actual persons, living or dead, events, or locales is entirely coincidental.

 Published in the United States by RH Graphic, an imprint of Random House Children's Books, a division of Penguin Random House LLC, 1745 Broadway, New York, NY 10019.

RH Graphic with the book design is a trademark of Penguin Random House LLC.

Visit us on the Web!
Seussville.com
RHKidsGraphic.com
@RHKidsGraphic

Educators and librarians, for a variety of teaching tools, visit us at RHTeachersLibrarians.com

Library of Congress Cataloging-in-Publication Data is available upon request.
ISBN 978-0-593-70306-9 (trade)
ISBN 978-0-593-70307-6 (lib. bdg.)
ISBN 978-0-593-70308-3 (ebook)

Editor: Whitney Leopard
Designer: Bob Bianchini
Copy Editor: Stephanie Bay
Managing Editor: Katy Miller
Production Manager: Jen Jie Li

Printed in Canada
10 9 8 7 6 5 4 3 2 1
First Edition

A comic on every bookshelf

FOR GRANNY JEAN, WHO TAUGHT ME HOW TO SAY SEUSS THE GERMAN WAY

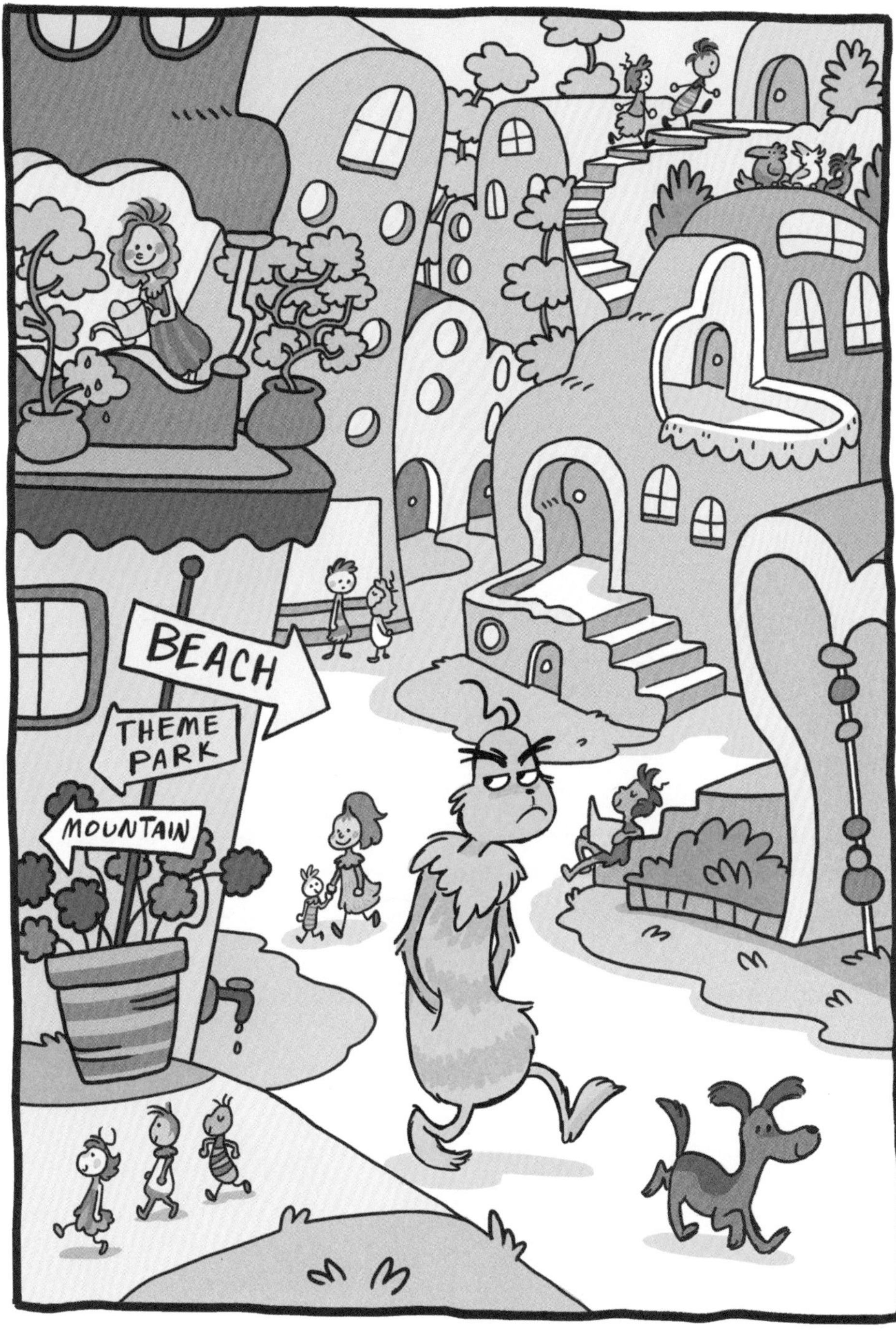
BEACH
THEME PARK
MOUNTAIN

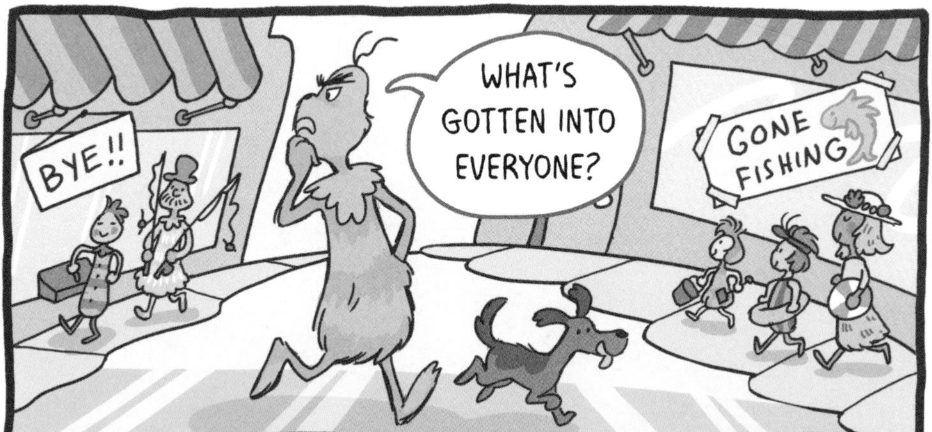
BYE!!
WHAT'S GOTTEN INTO EVERYONE?
GONE FISHING

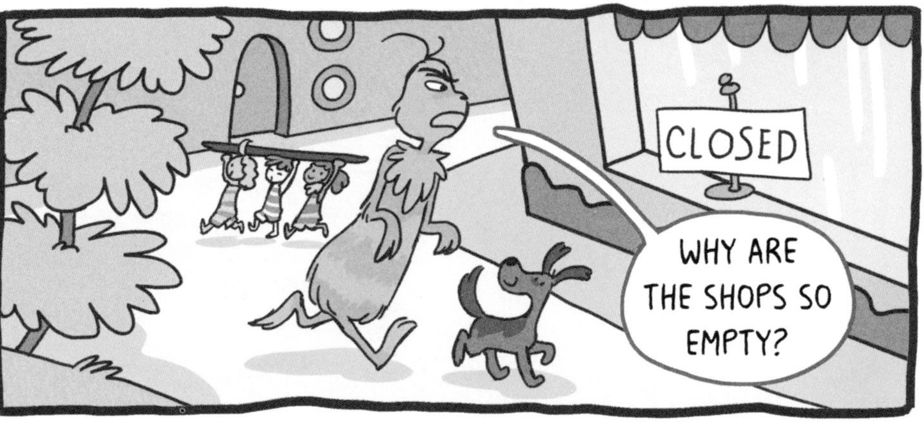
CLOSED
WHY ARE THE SHOPS SO EMPTY?

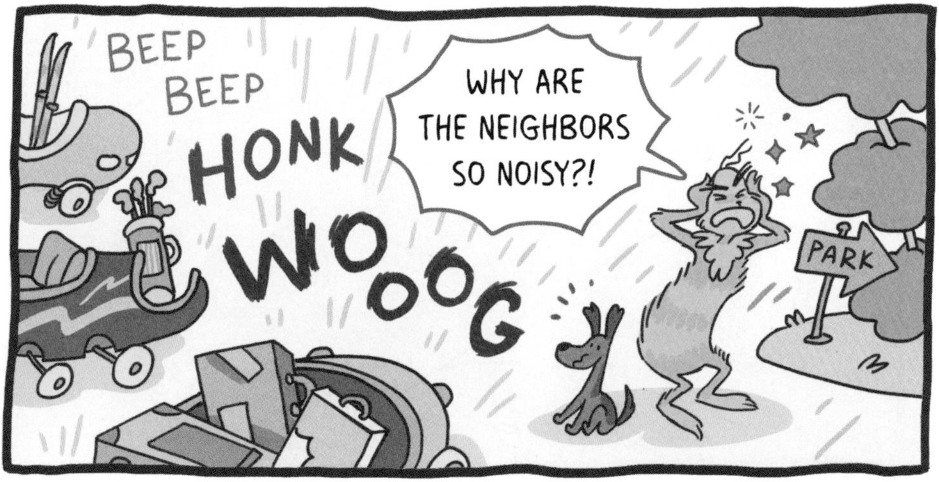
BEEP BEEP
HONK
WHY ARE THE NEIGHBORS SO NOISY?!
WOOOG
PARK

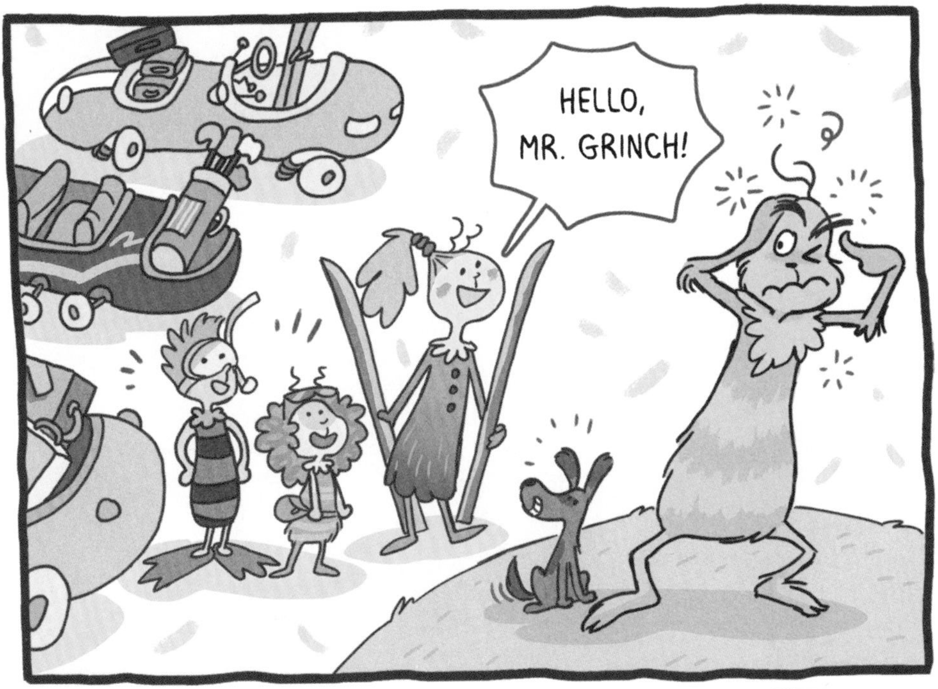
HELLO, MR. GRINCH!

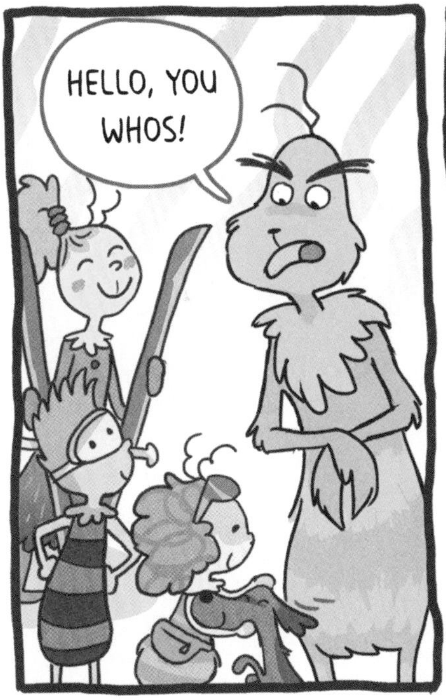
HELLO, YOU WHOS!

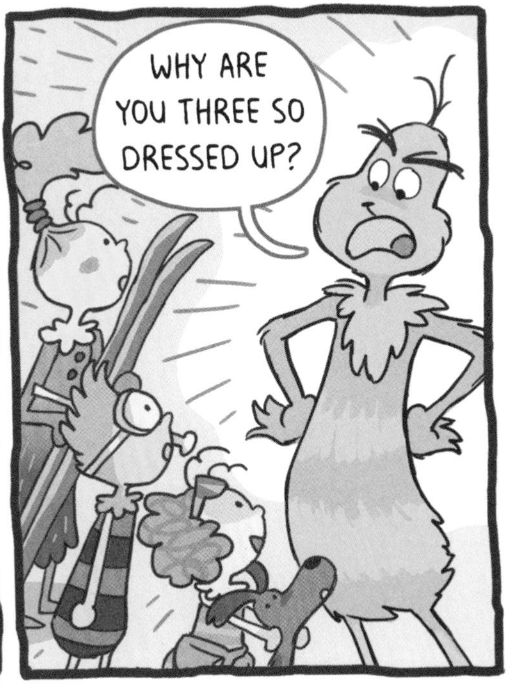
WHY ARE YOU THREE SO DRESSED UP?

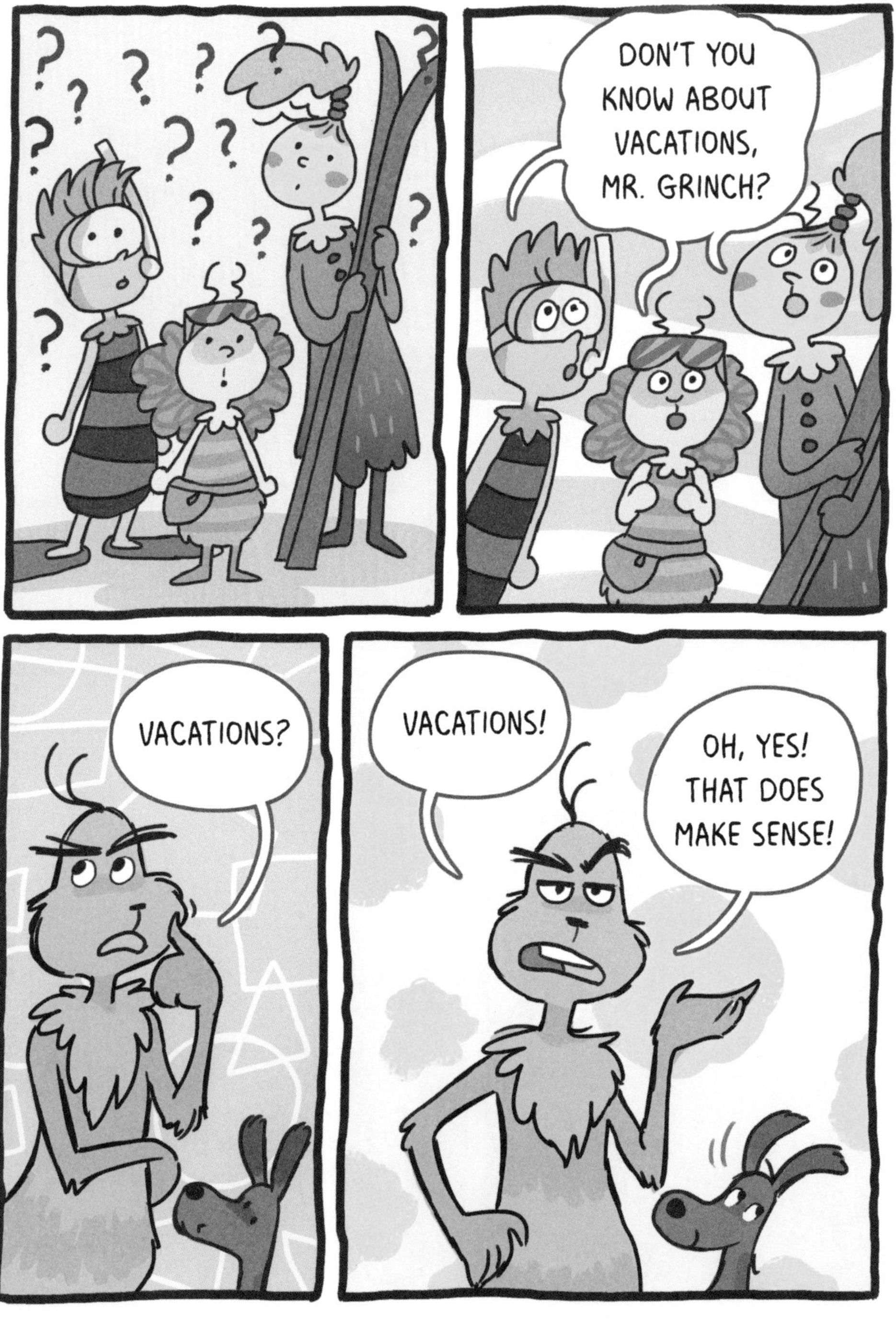
DON'T YOU KNOW ABOUT VACATIONS, MR. GRINCH?
VACATIONS?
VACATIONS!
OH, YES! THAT DOES MAKE SENSE!

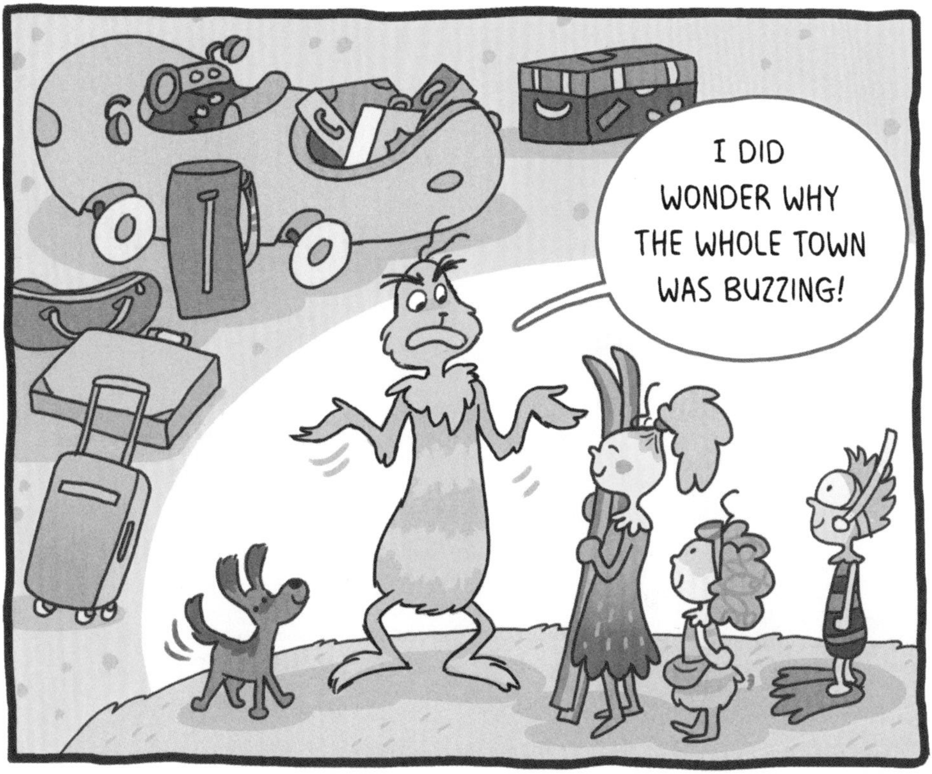
I DID WONDER WHY THE WHOLE TOWN WAS BUZZING!

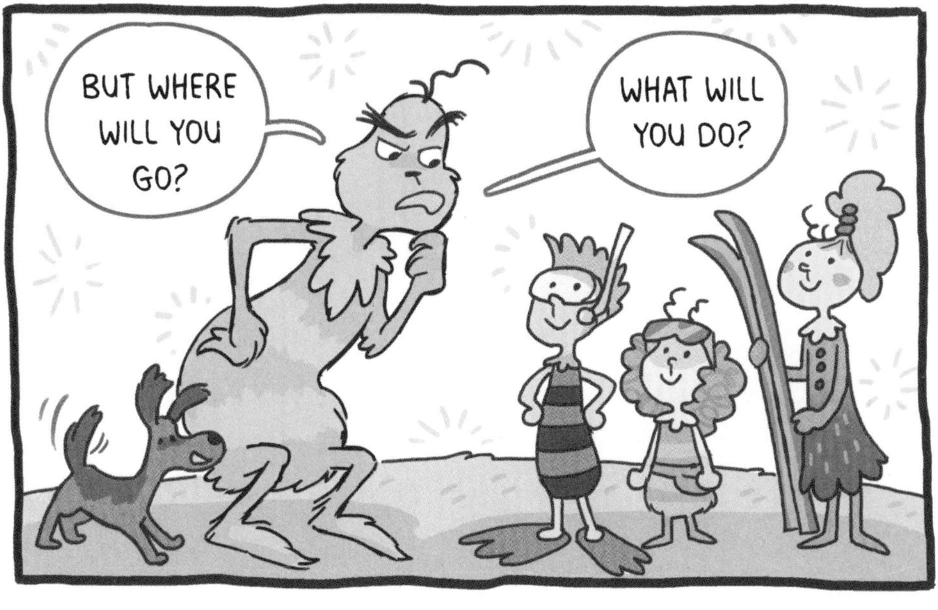
BUT WHERE WILL YOU GO?
WHAT WILL YOU DO?

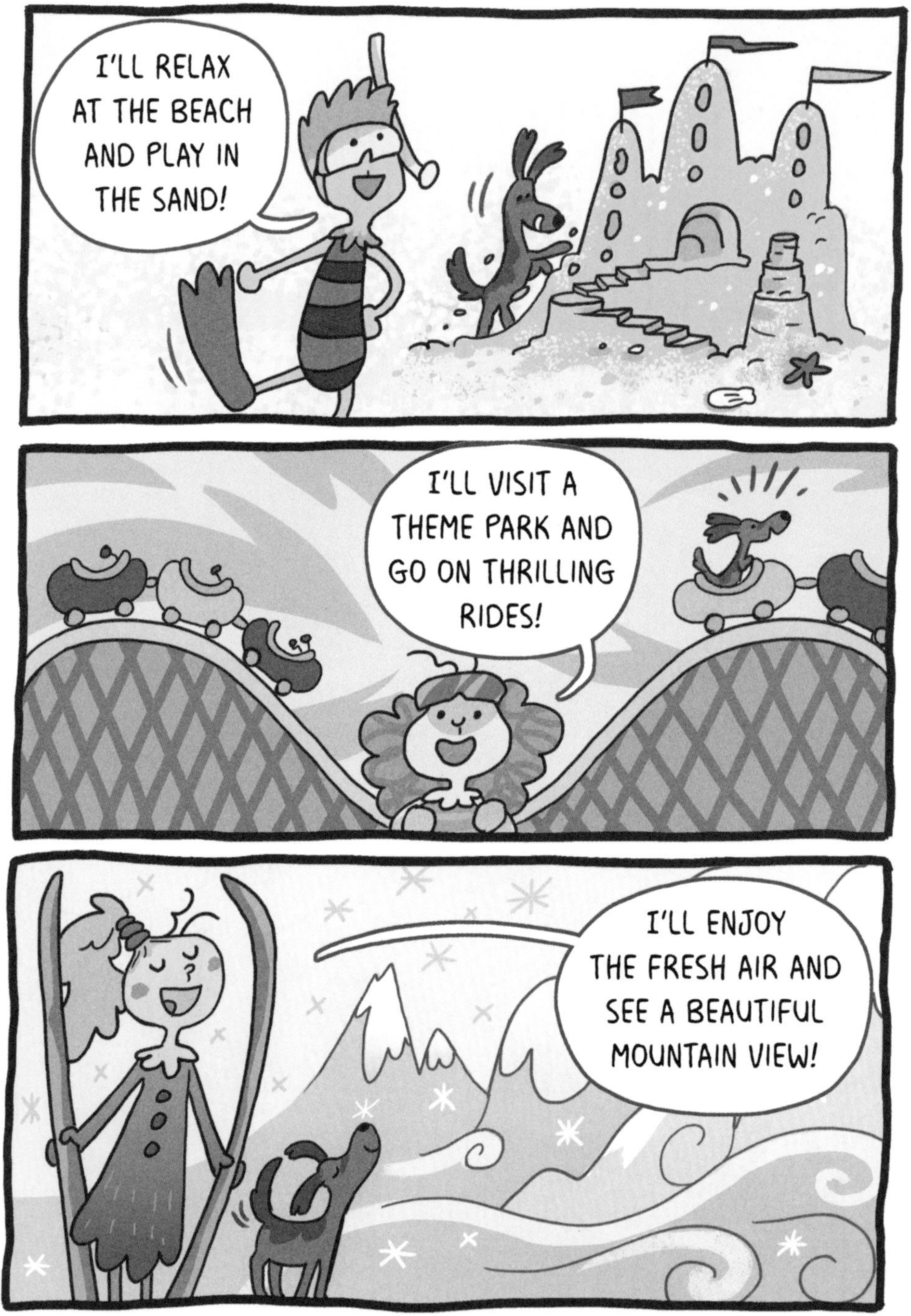
I'LL RELAX AT THE BEACH AND PLAY IN THE SAND!
I'LL VISIT A THEME PARK AND GO ON THRILLING RIDES!
I'LL ENJOY THE FRESH AIR AND SEE A BEAUTIFUL MOUNTAIN VIEW!

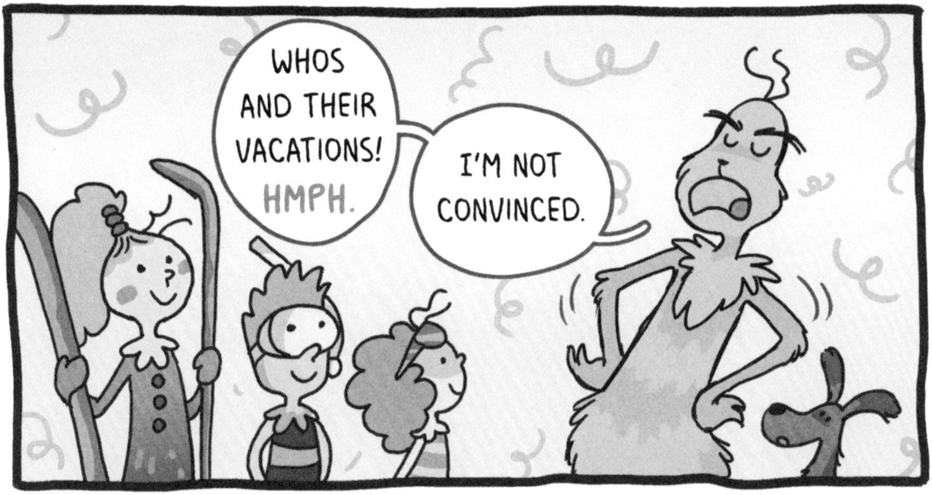
WHOS AND THEIR VACATIONS! HMPH.
I'M NOT CONVINCED.

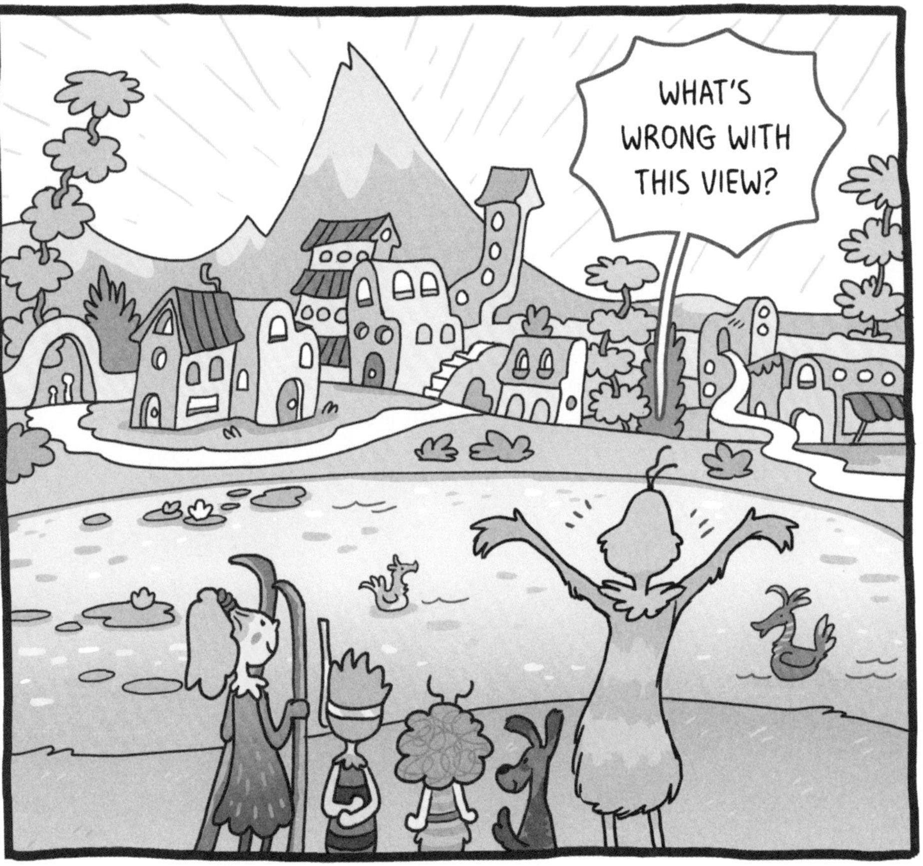
WHAT'S WRONG WITH THIS VIEW?

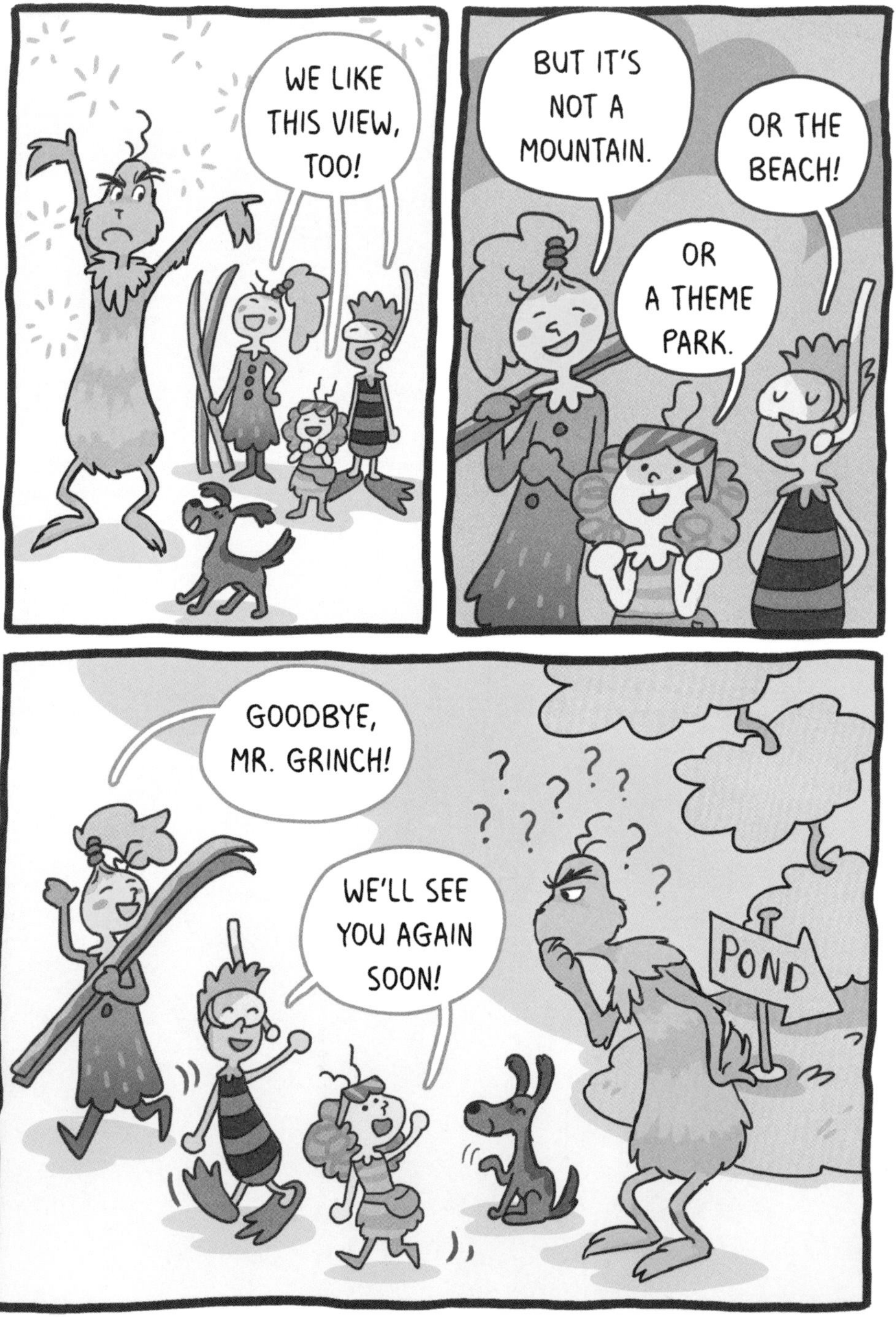
WE LIKE THIS VIEW, TOO!
BUT IT'S NOT A MOUNTAIN.
OR A THEME PARK.
OR THE BEACH!
GOODBYE, MR. GRINCH!
WE'LL SEE YOU AGAIN SOON!
POND

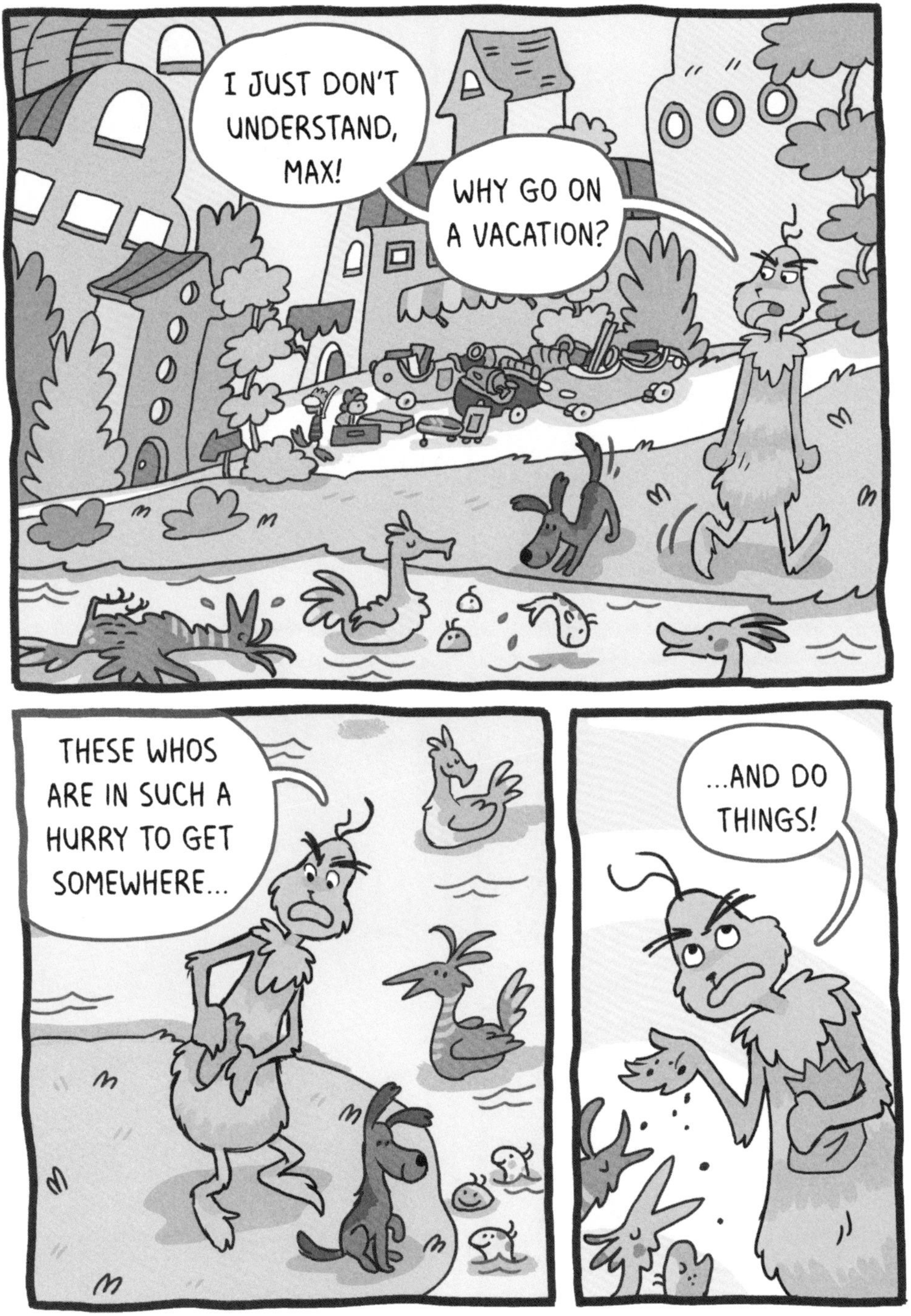
I JUST DON'T UNDERSTAND, MAX!
WHY GO ON A VACATION?
THESE WHOS ARE IN SUCH A HURRY TO GET SOMEWHERE...
...AND DO THINGS!

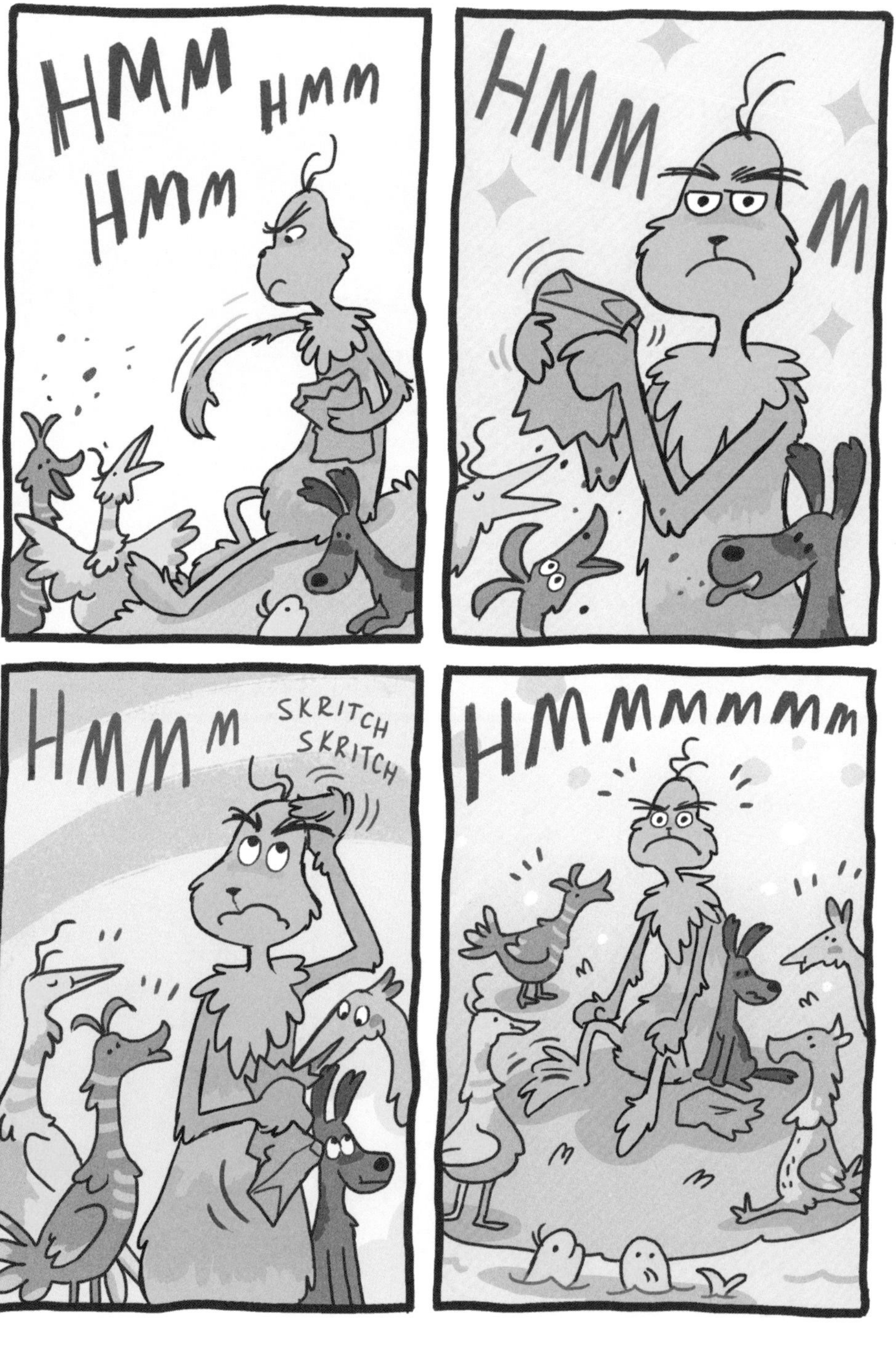
HMM
HMM
HMM
HMMM
HMMM
SKRITCH
SKRITCH
HMMMMMMM

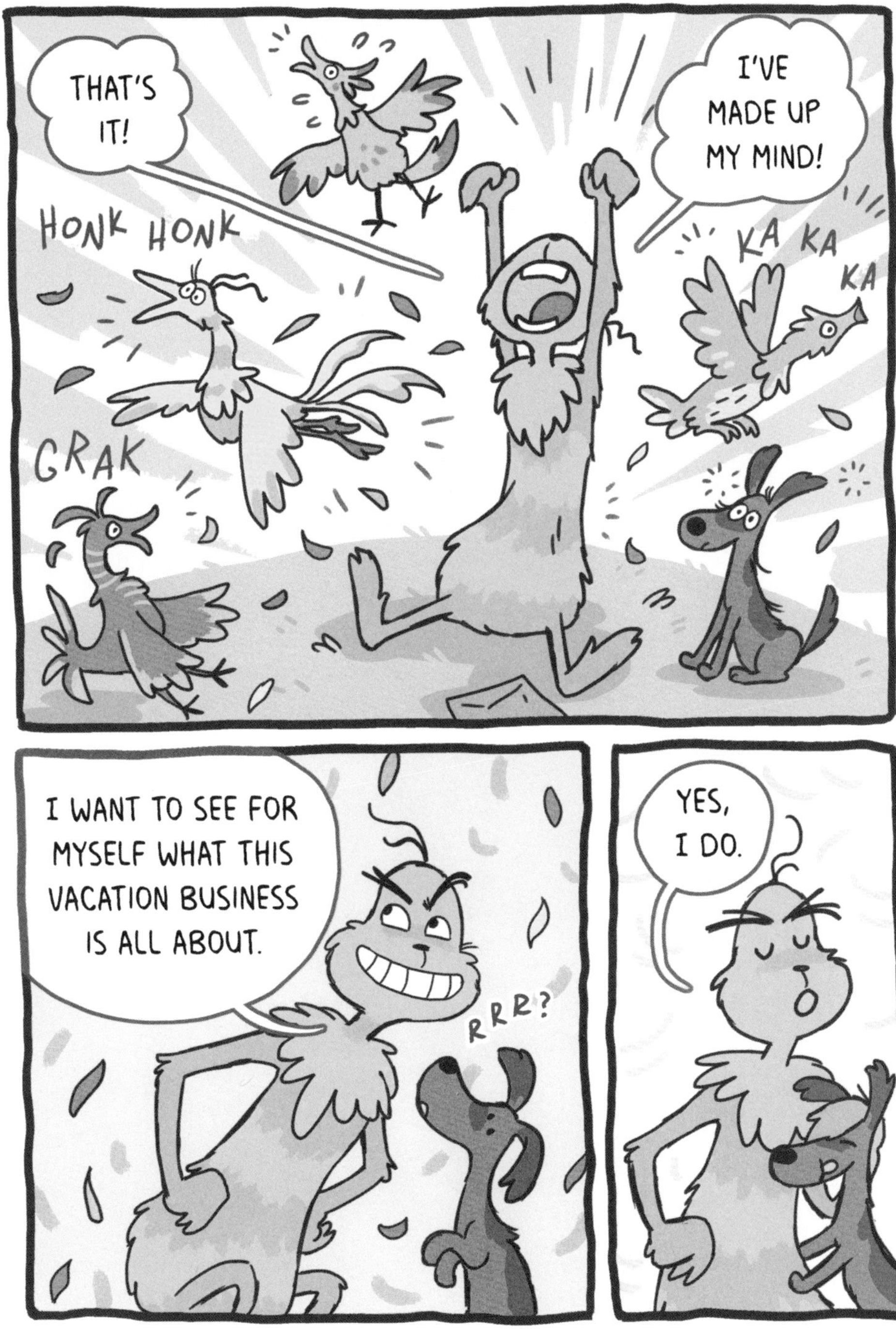

THAT'S IT!
HONK HONK
GRAK
I'VE MADE UP MY MIND!
KA KA KA
I WANT TO SEE FOR MYSELF WHAT THIS VACATION BUSINESS IS ALL ABOUT.
RRR?
YES, I DO.

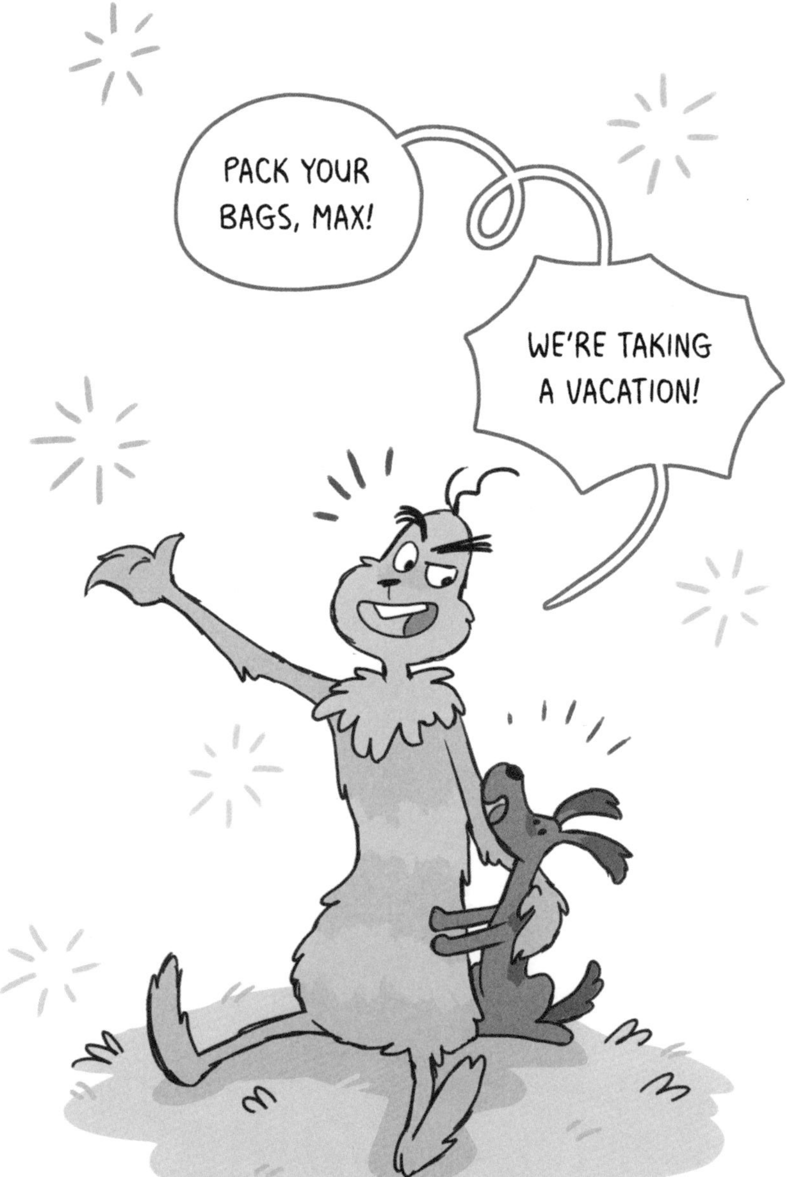
PACK YOUR BAGS, MAX!
WE'RE TAKING A VACATION!

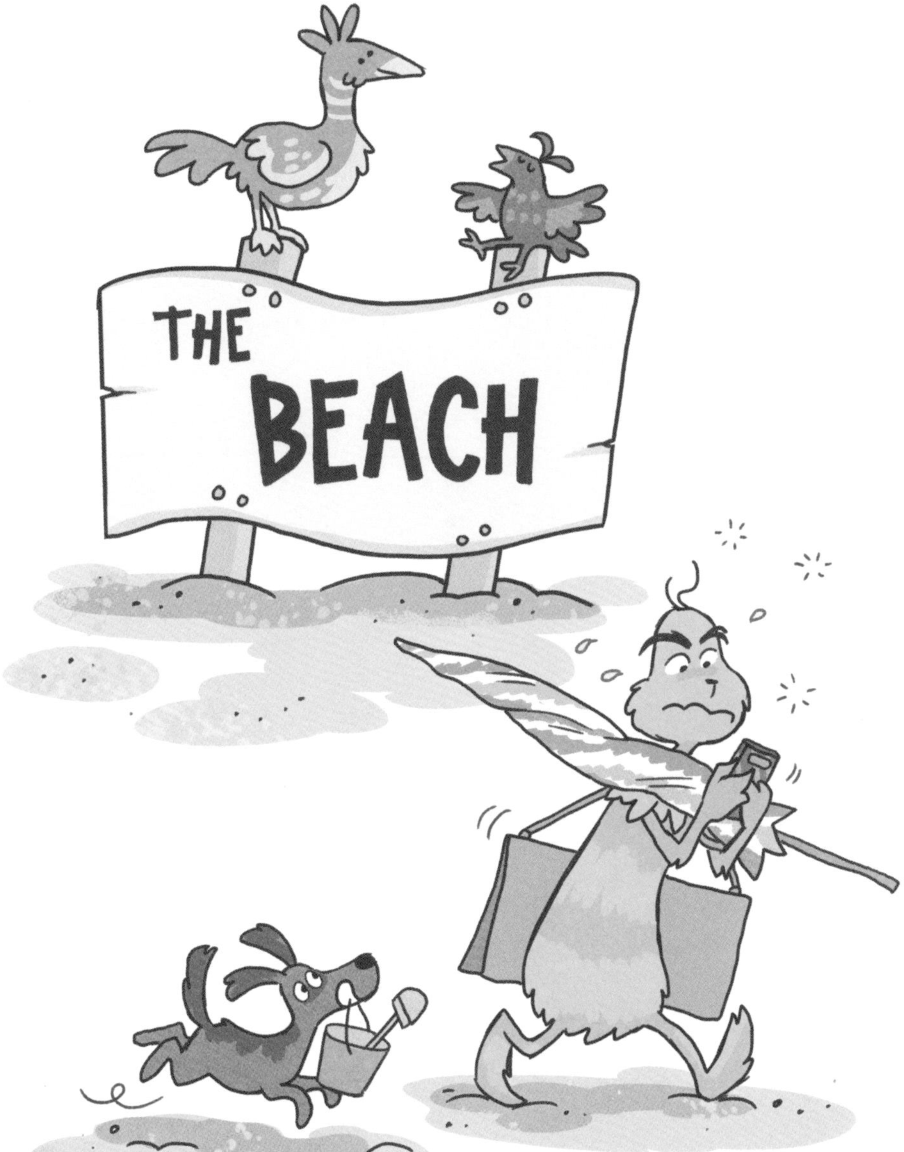
THE
BEACH

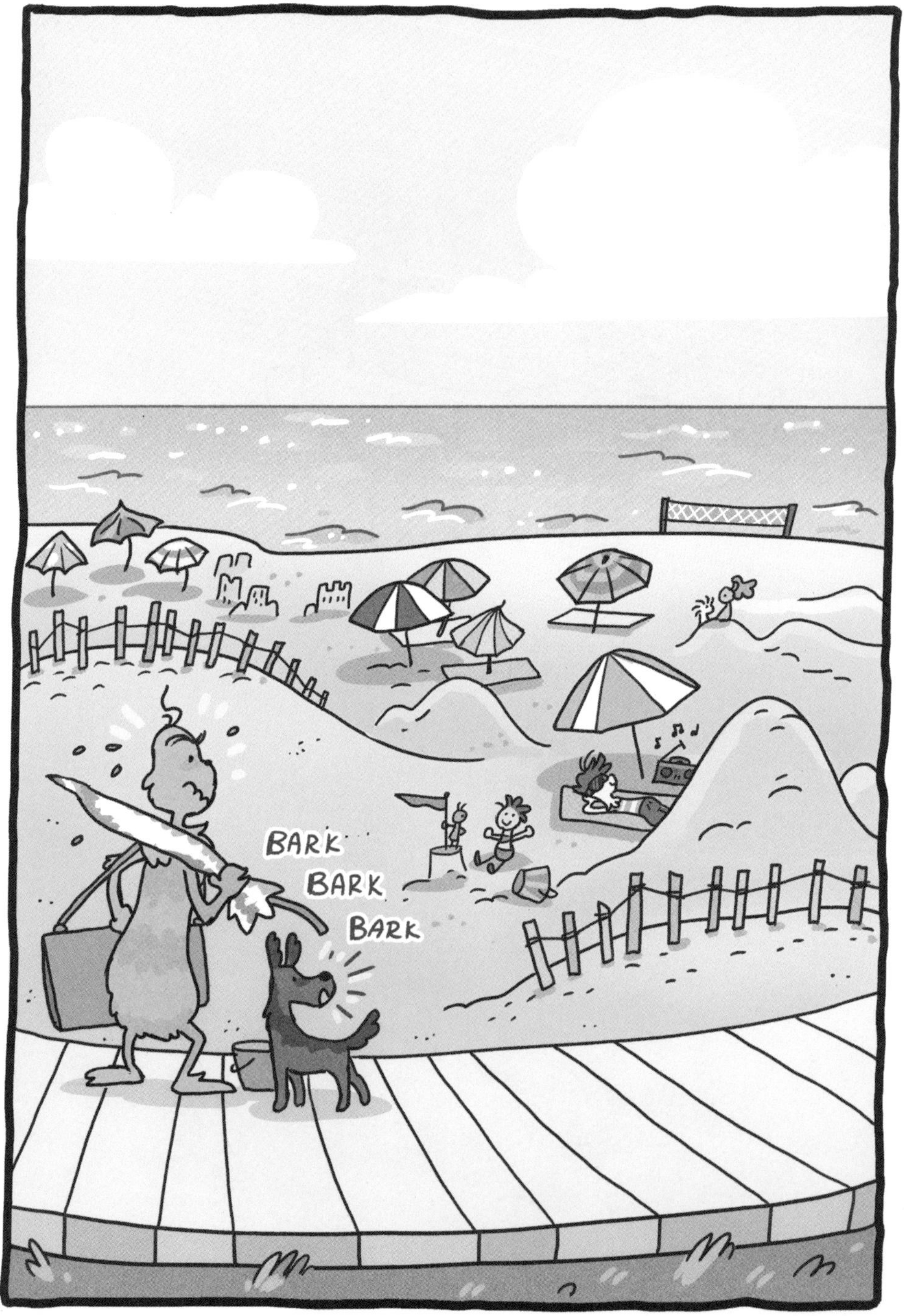
BARK
BARK
BARK

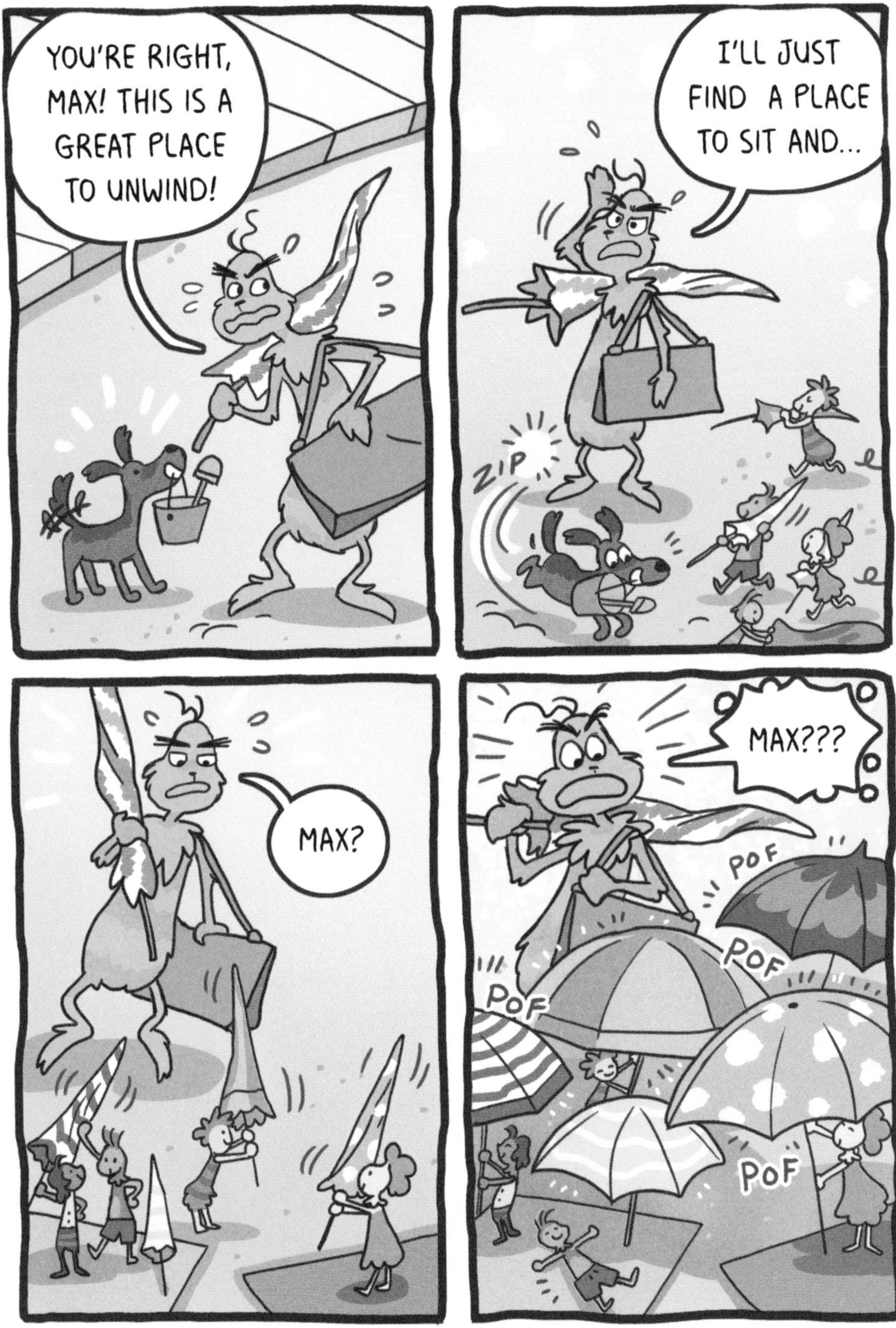
YOU'RE RIGHT, MAX! THIS IS A GREAT PLACE TO UNWIND!
I'LL JUST FIND A PLACE TO SIT AND...
ZIP
MAX?
MAX???
POF
POF
POF
POF

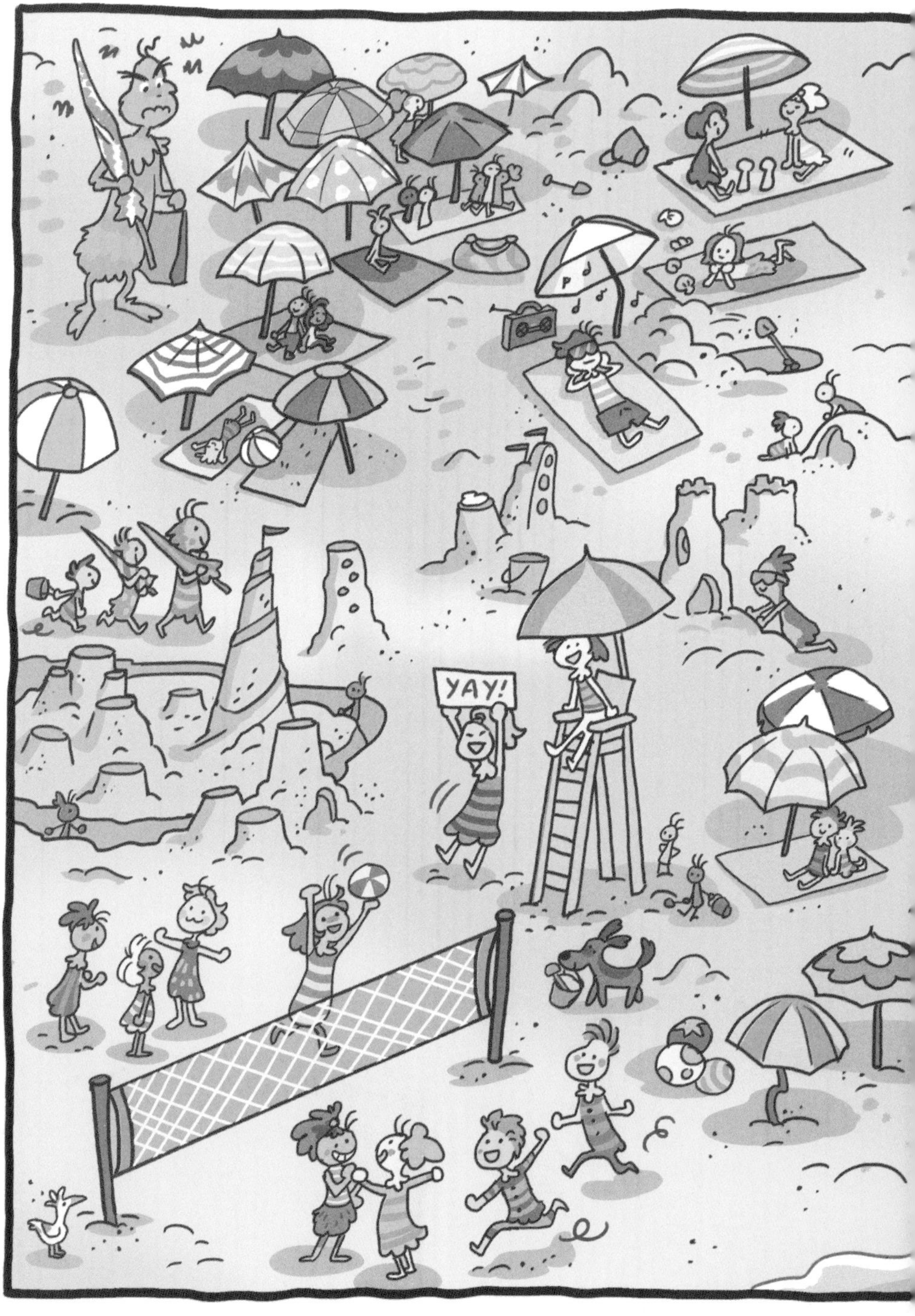
YAY!

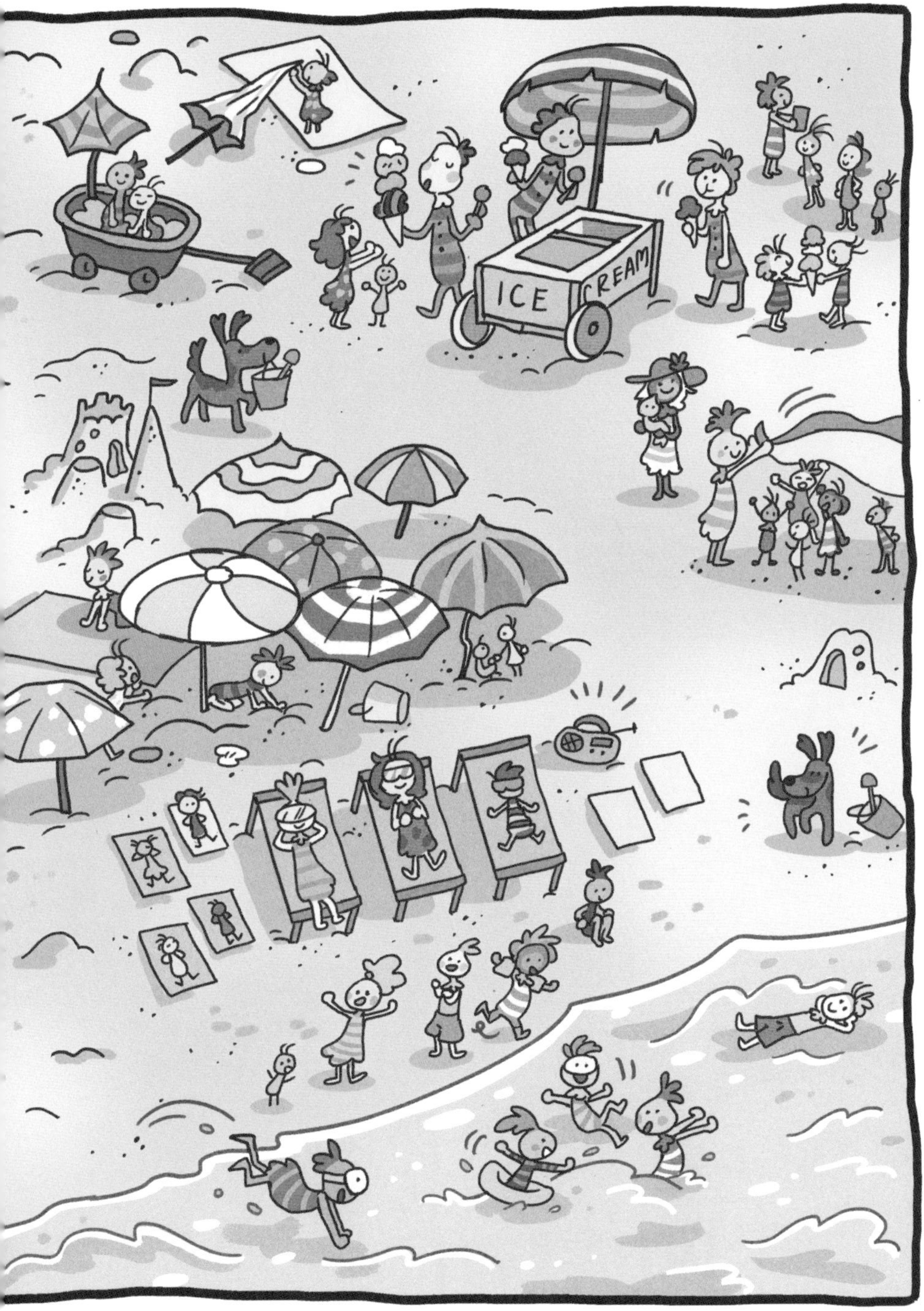
ICE
CREAM

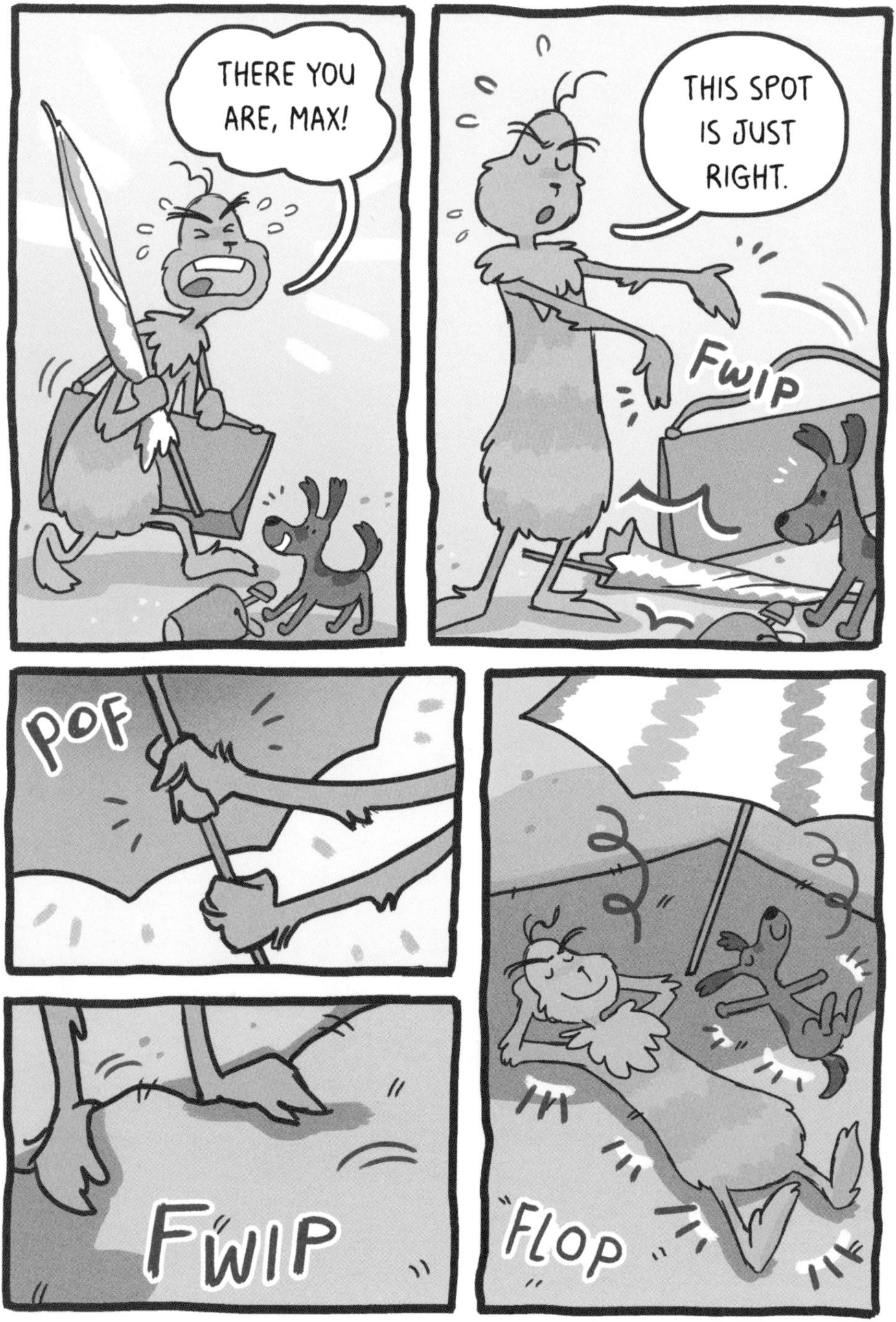
THERE YOU ARE, MAX!
THIS SPOT IS JUST RIGHT.
FWIP
POF
FWIP
FLOP

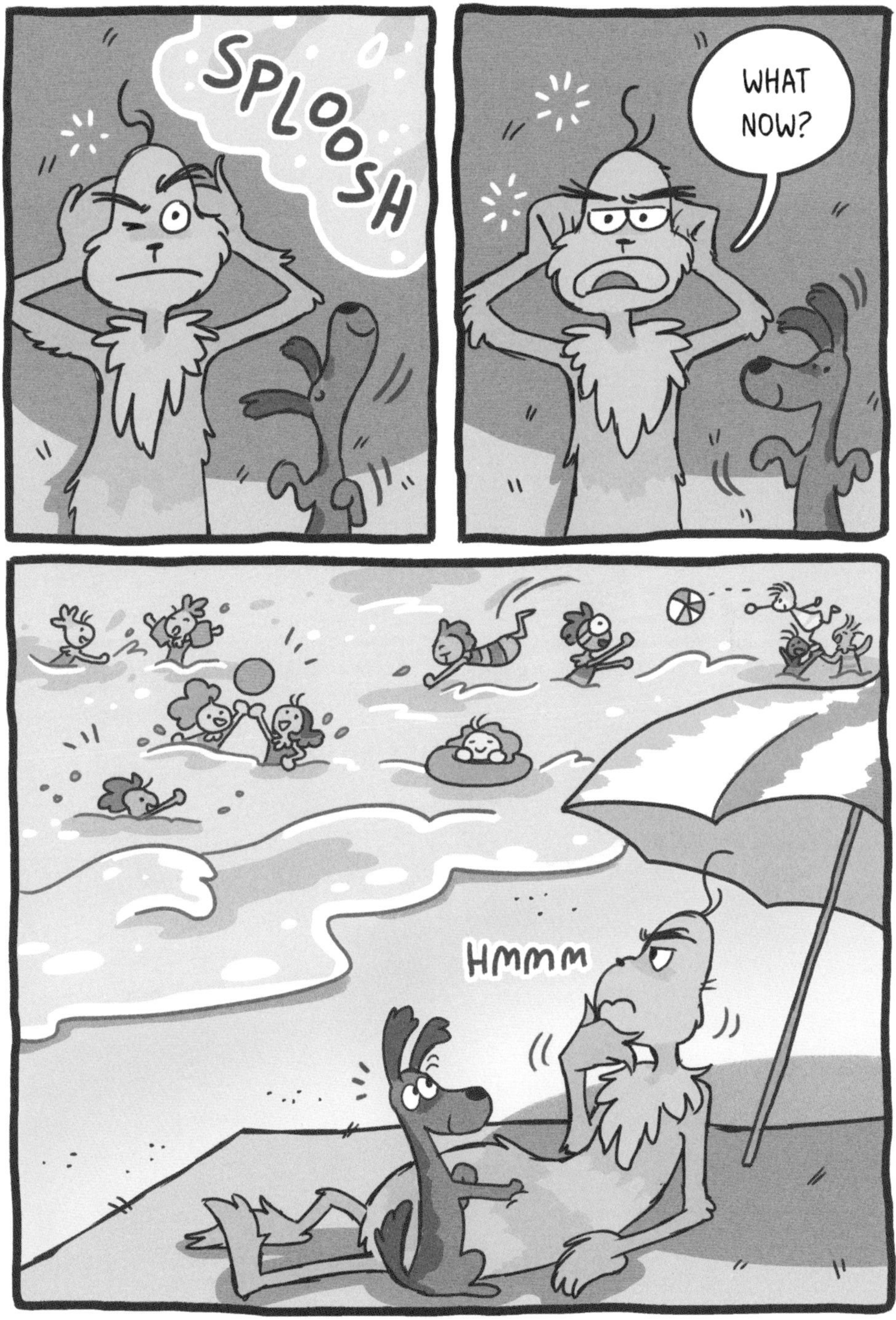
SPLOOSH
WHAT NOW?
HMMM

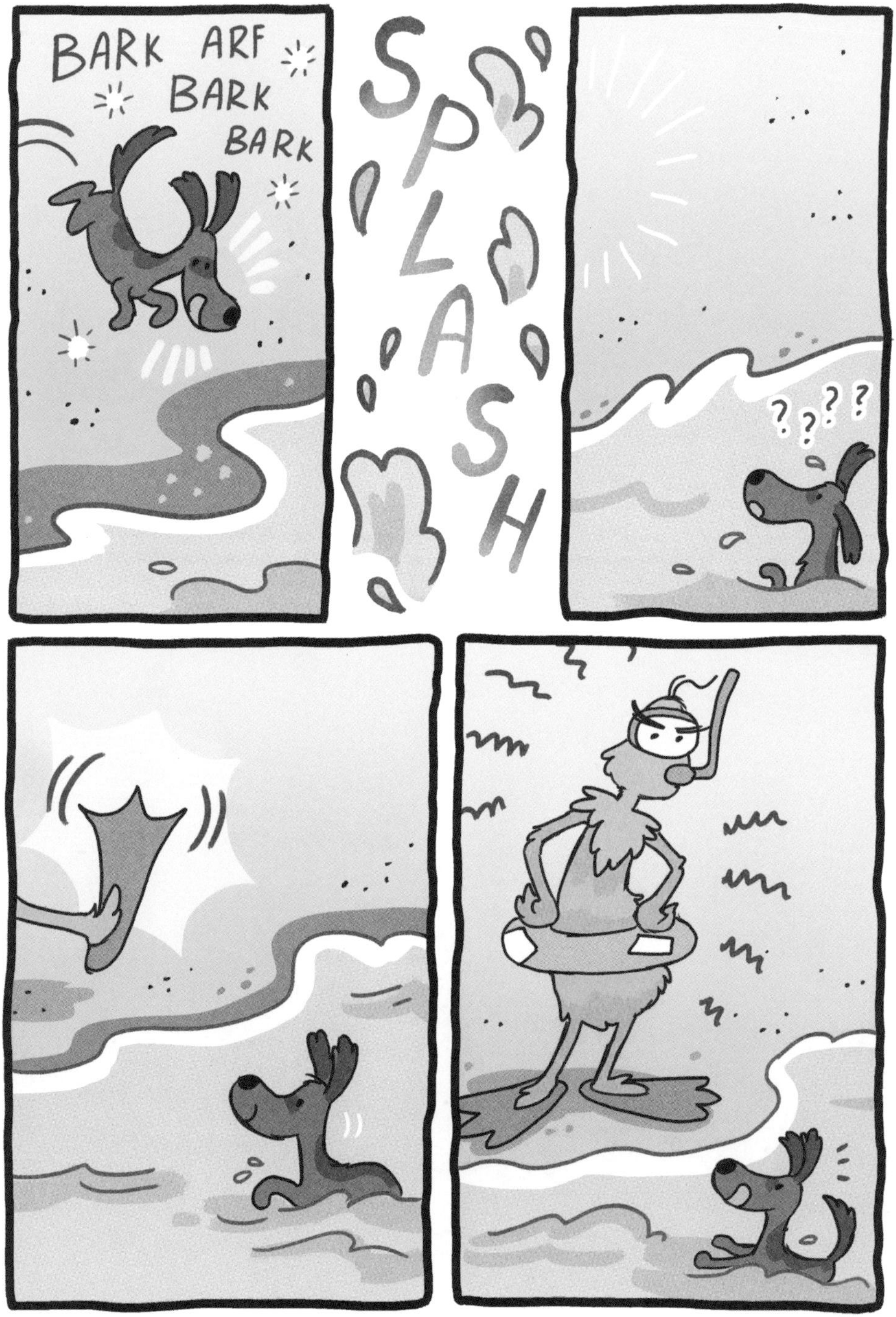
BARK ARF
BARK
BARK
SPLASH
????

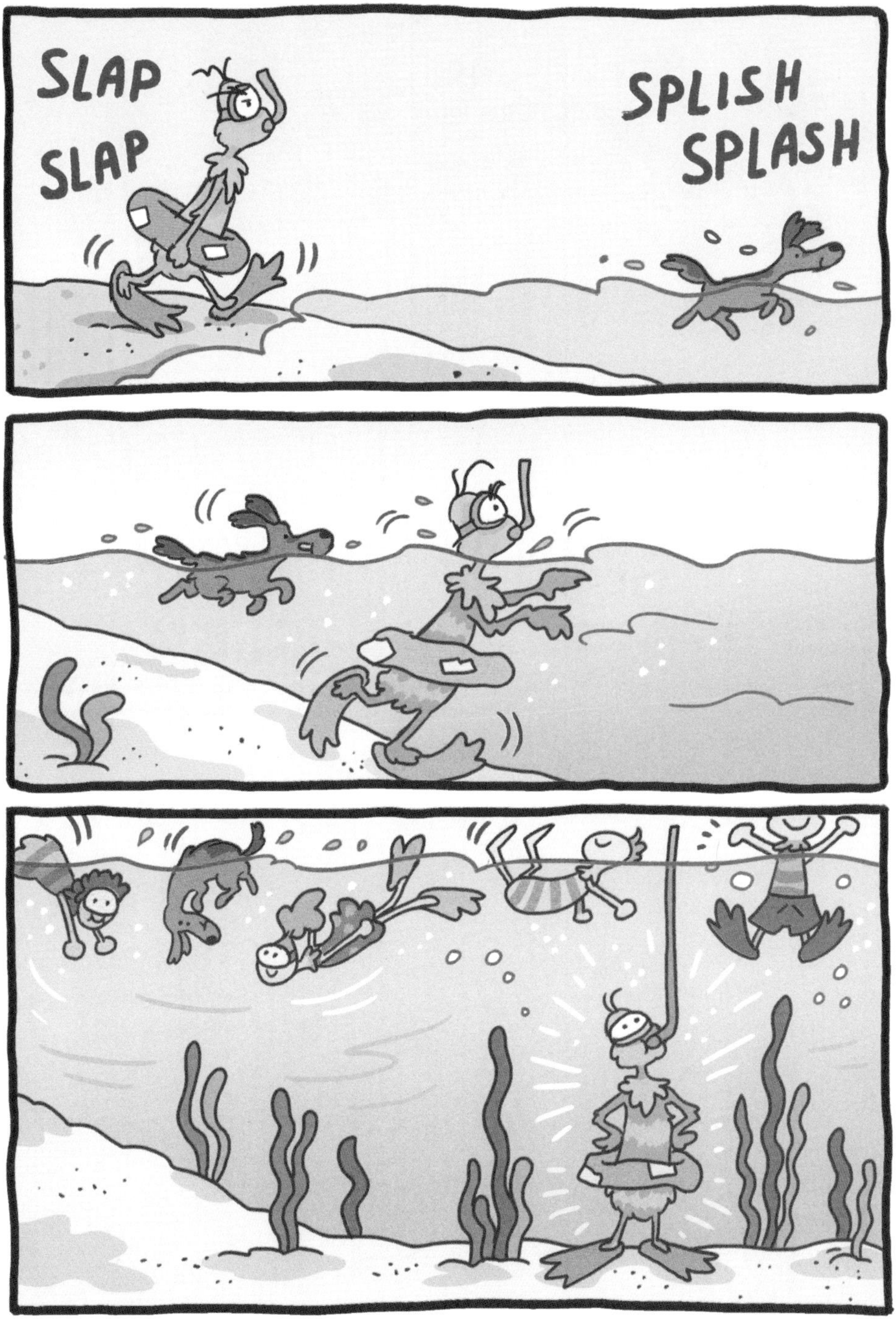
SLAP
SLAP
SPLISH
SPLASH

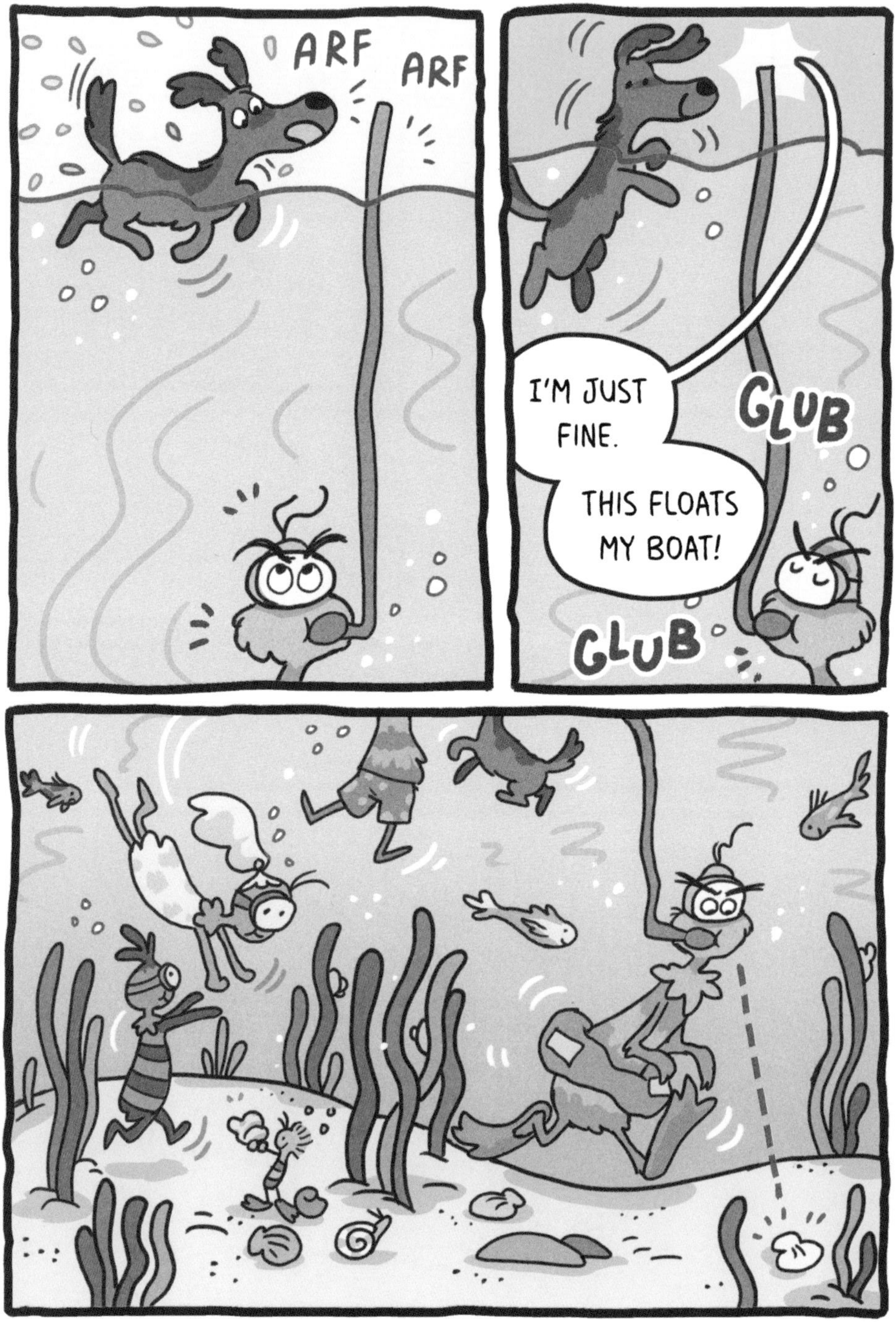

ARF
ARF
I'M JUST FINE.
THIS FLOATS MY BOAT!
GLUB
GLUB

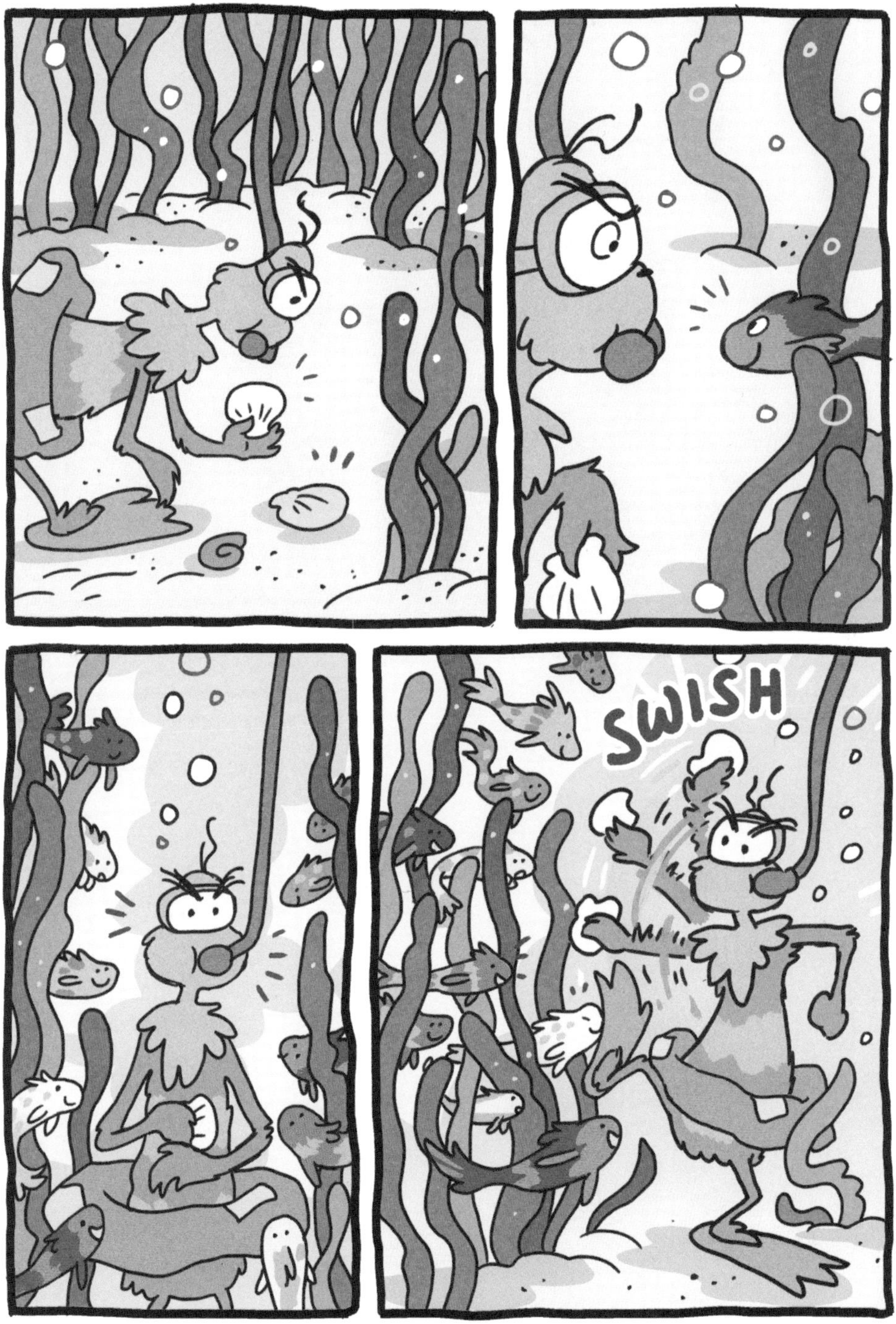
SWISH

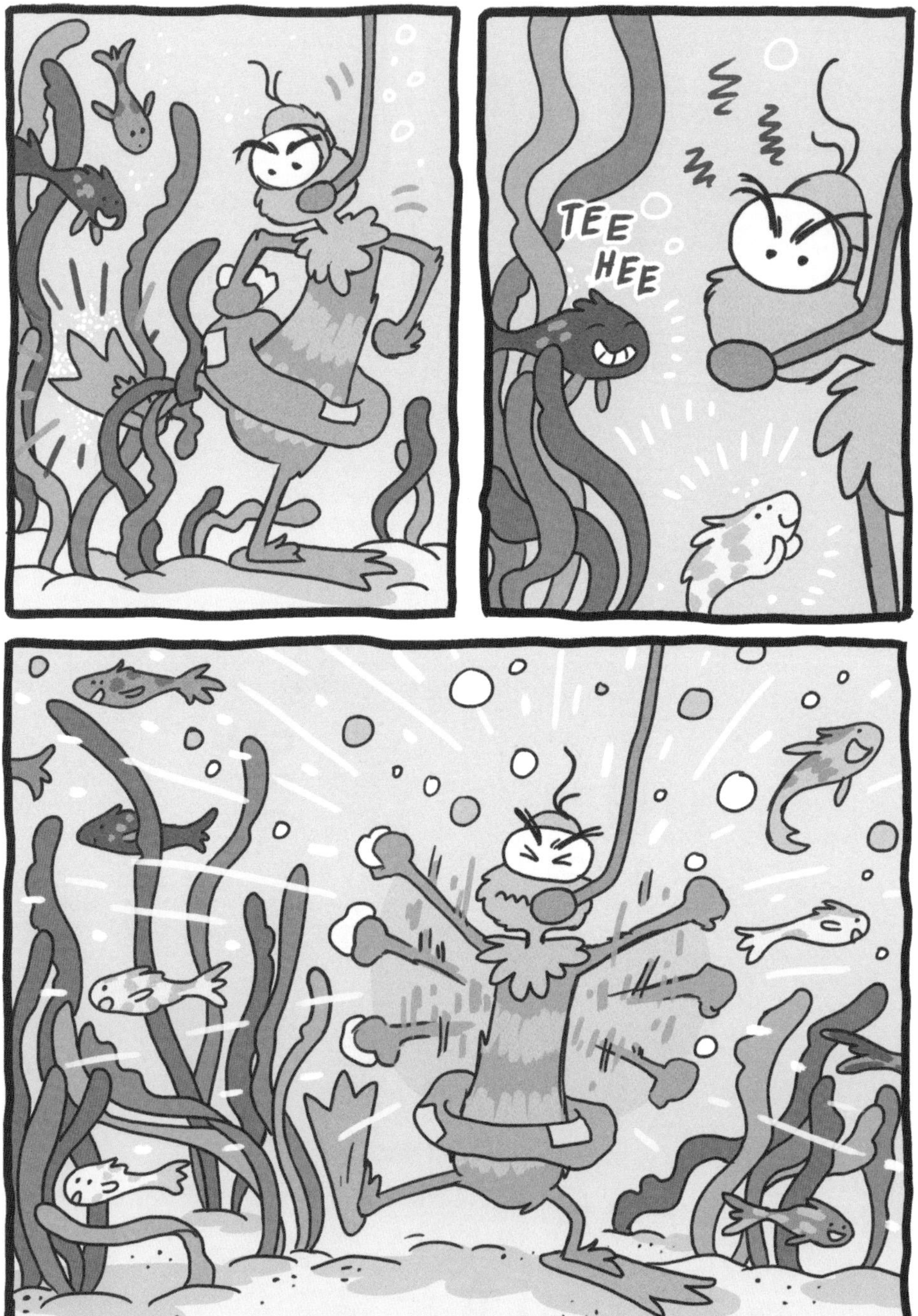
TEE
HEE

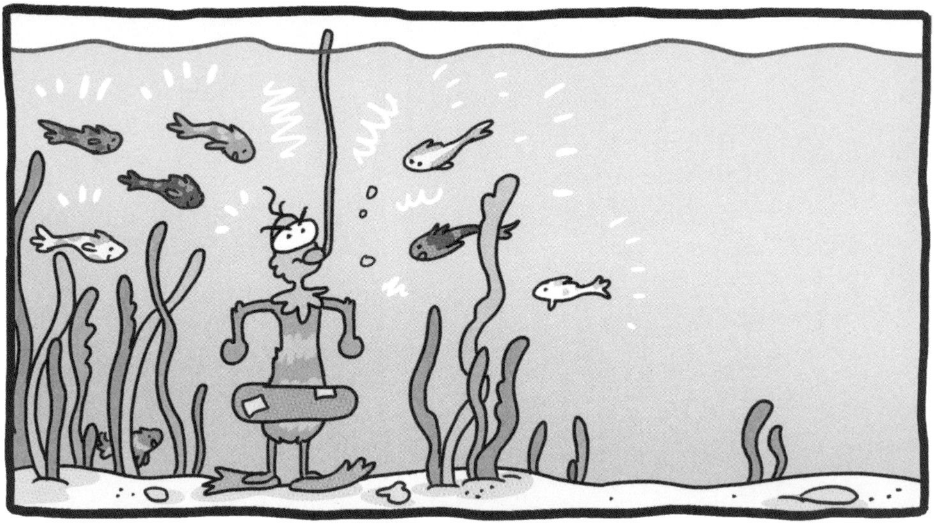

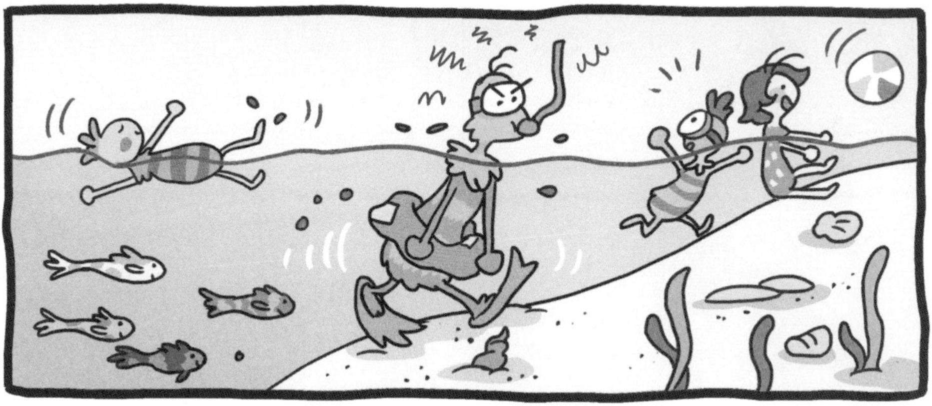

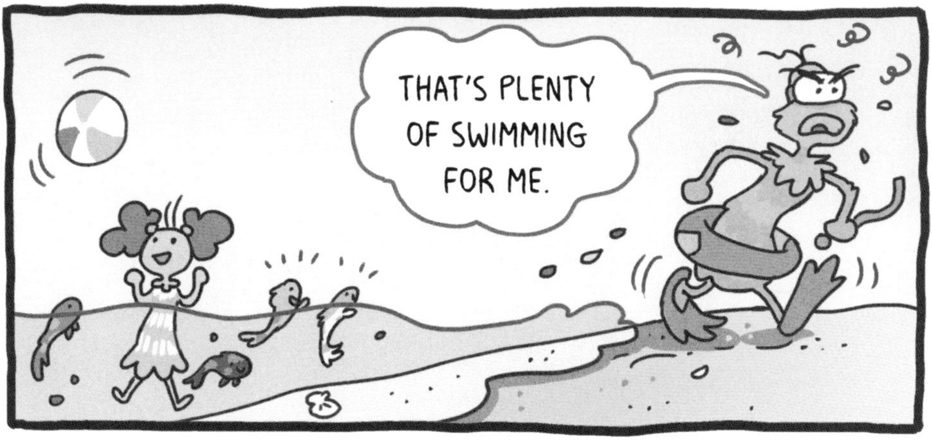
THAT'S PLENTY OF SWIMMING FOR ME.

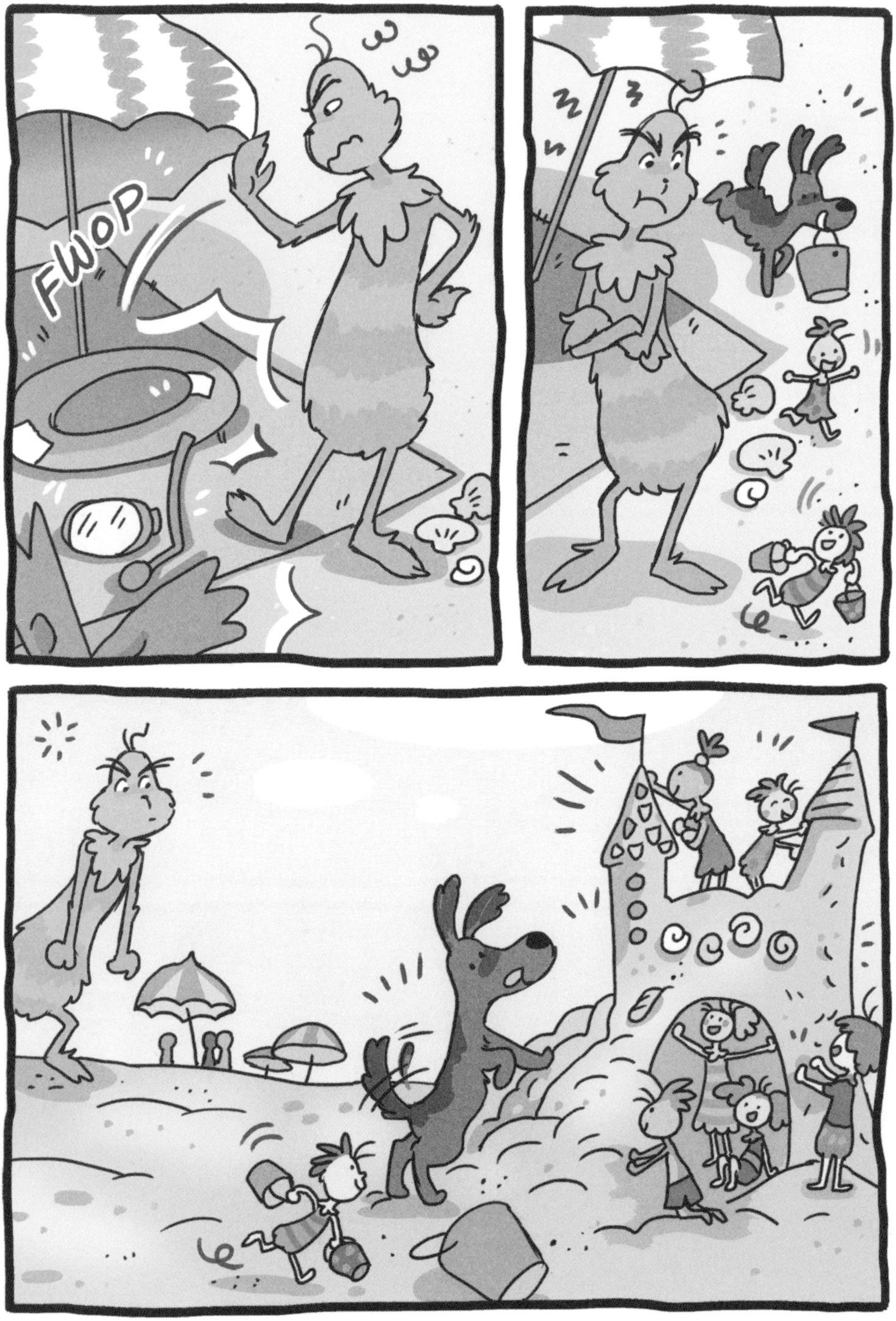
FWOP

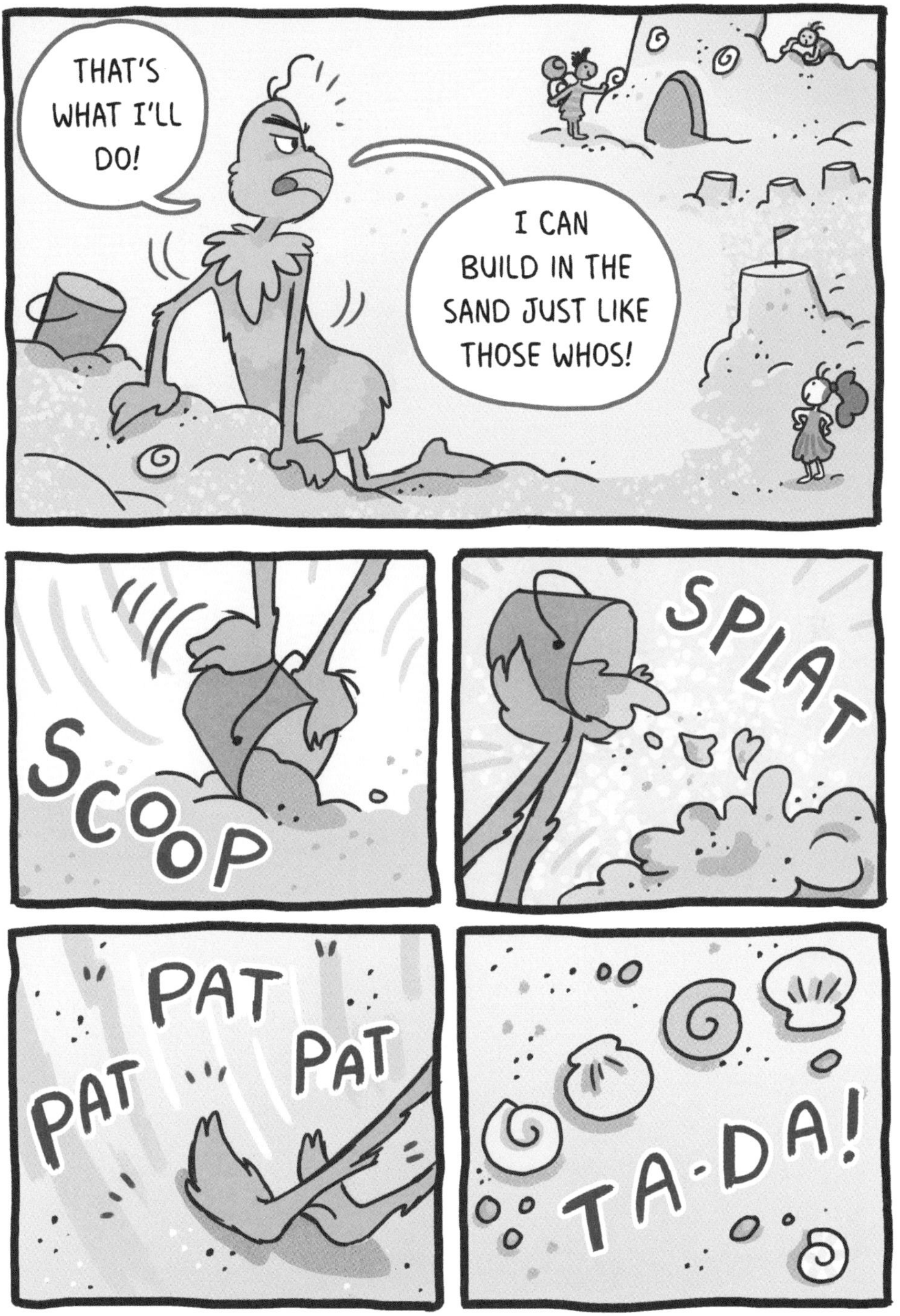
THAT'S WHAT I'LL DO!
I CAN BUILD IN THE SAND JUST LIKE THOSE WHOS!
SCOOP
SPLAT
PAT
PAT
PAT
TA-DA!

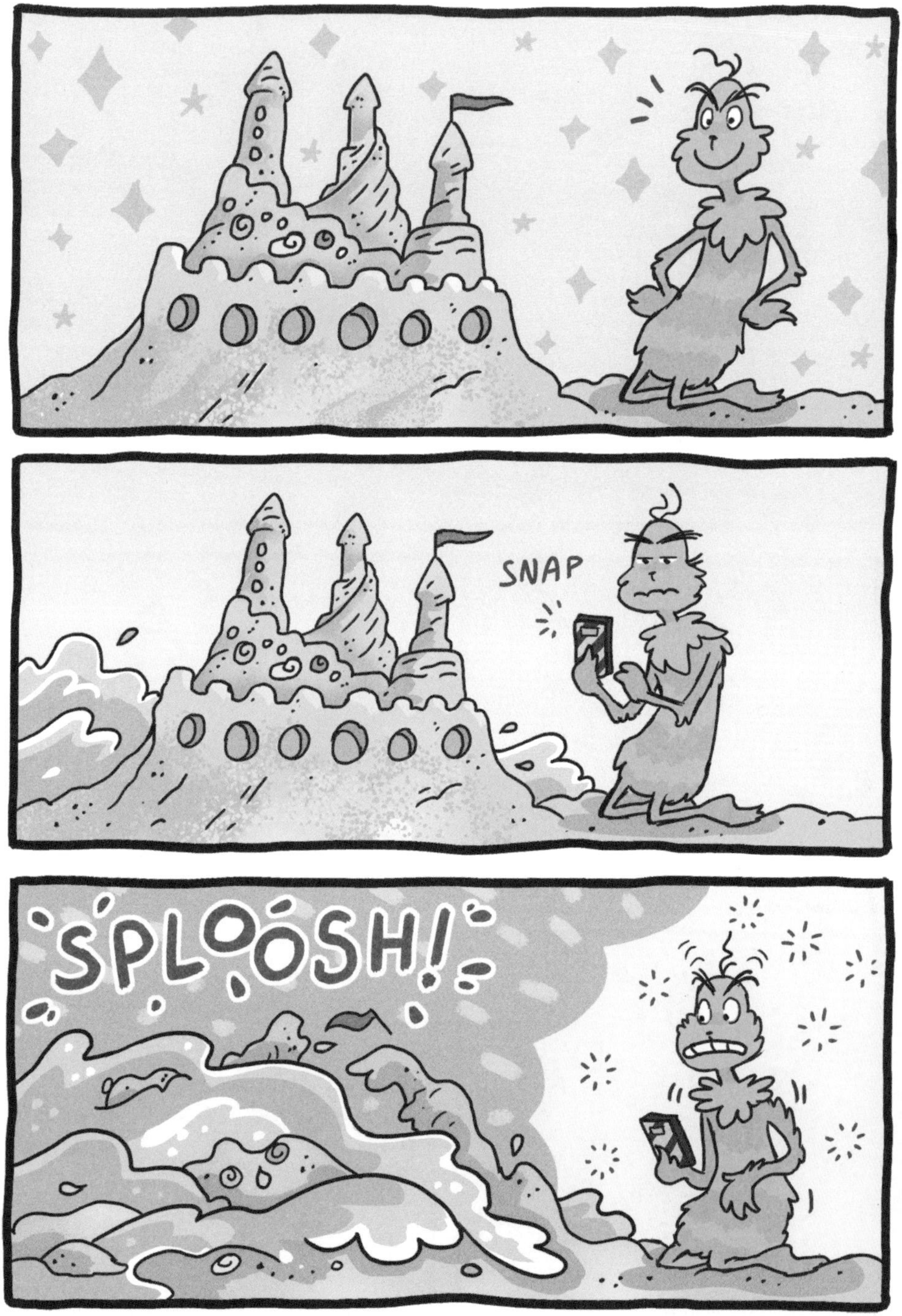
SNAP
SPLOOSH!

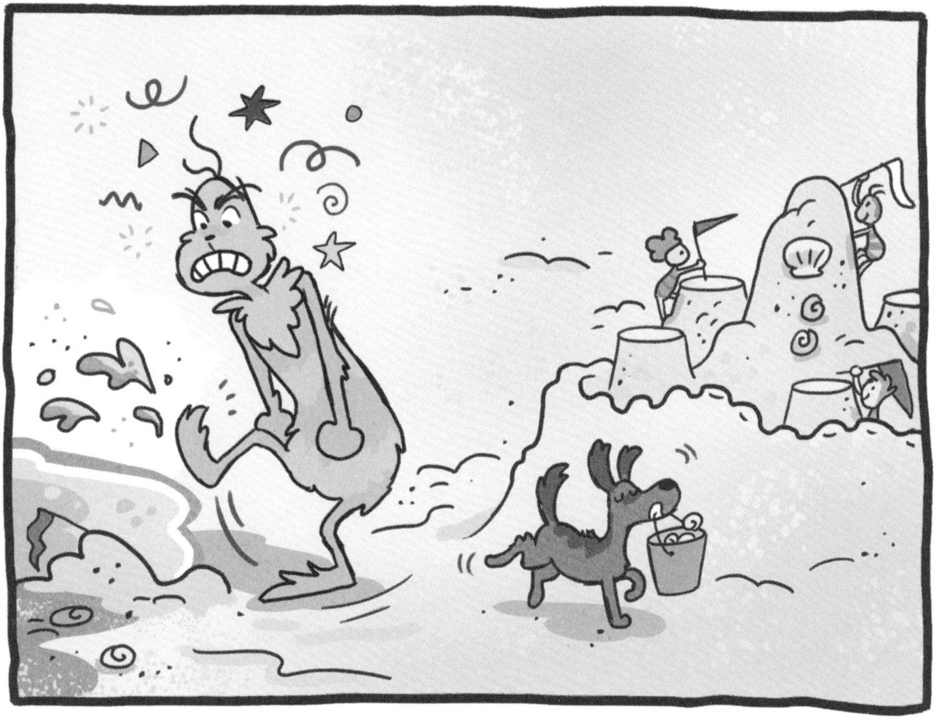

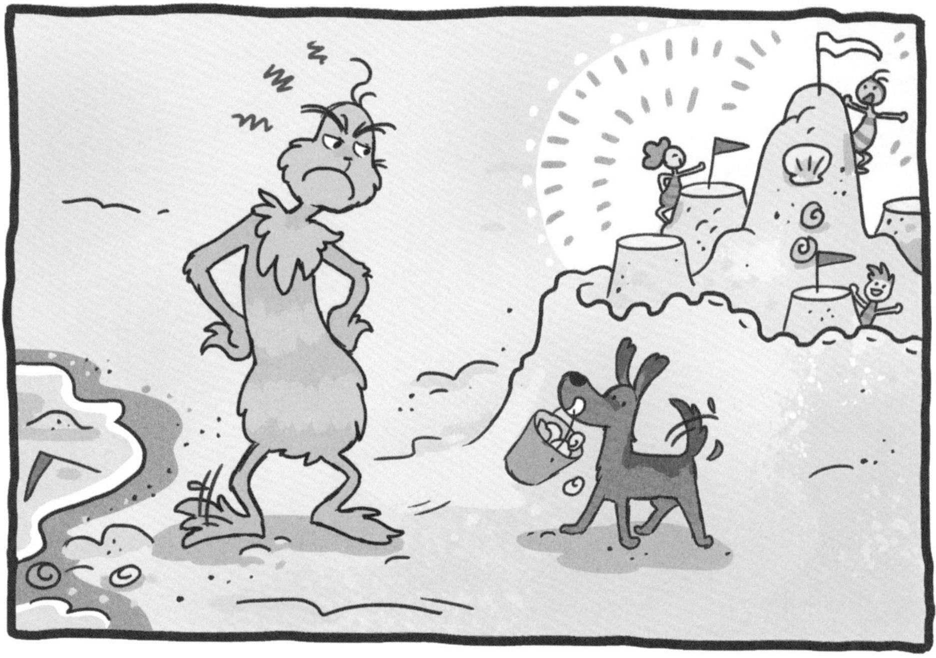

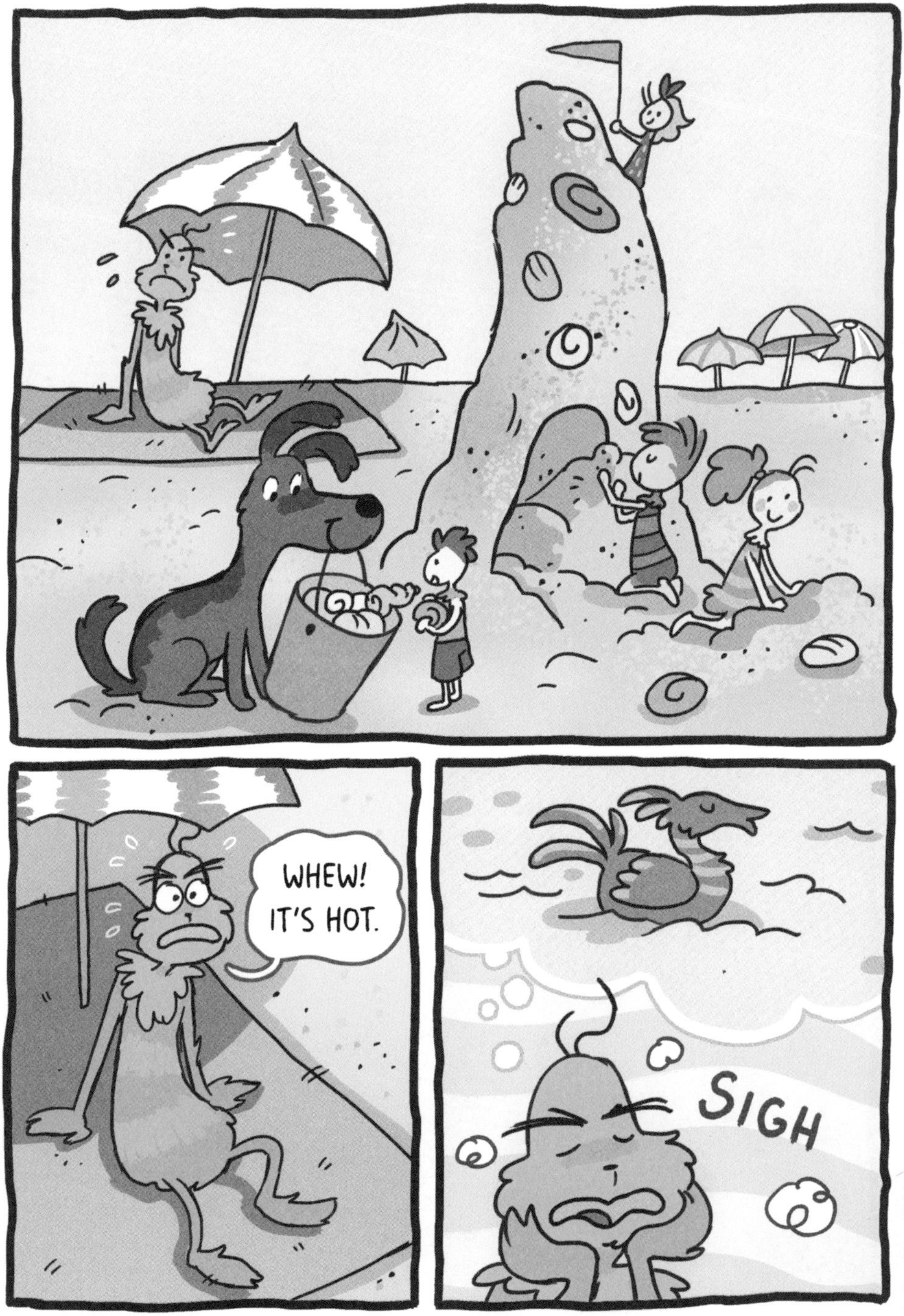
WHEW!
IT'S HOT.
SIGH

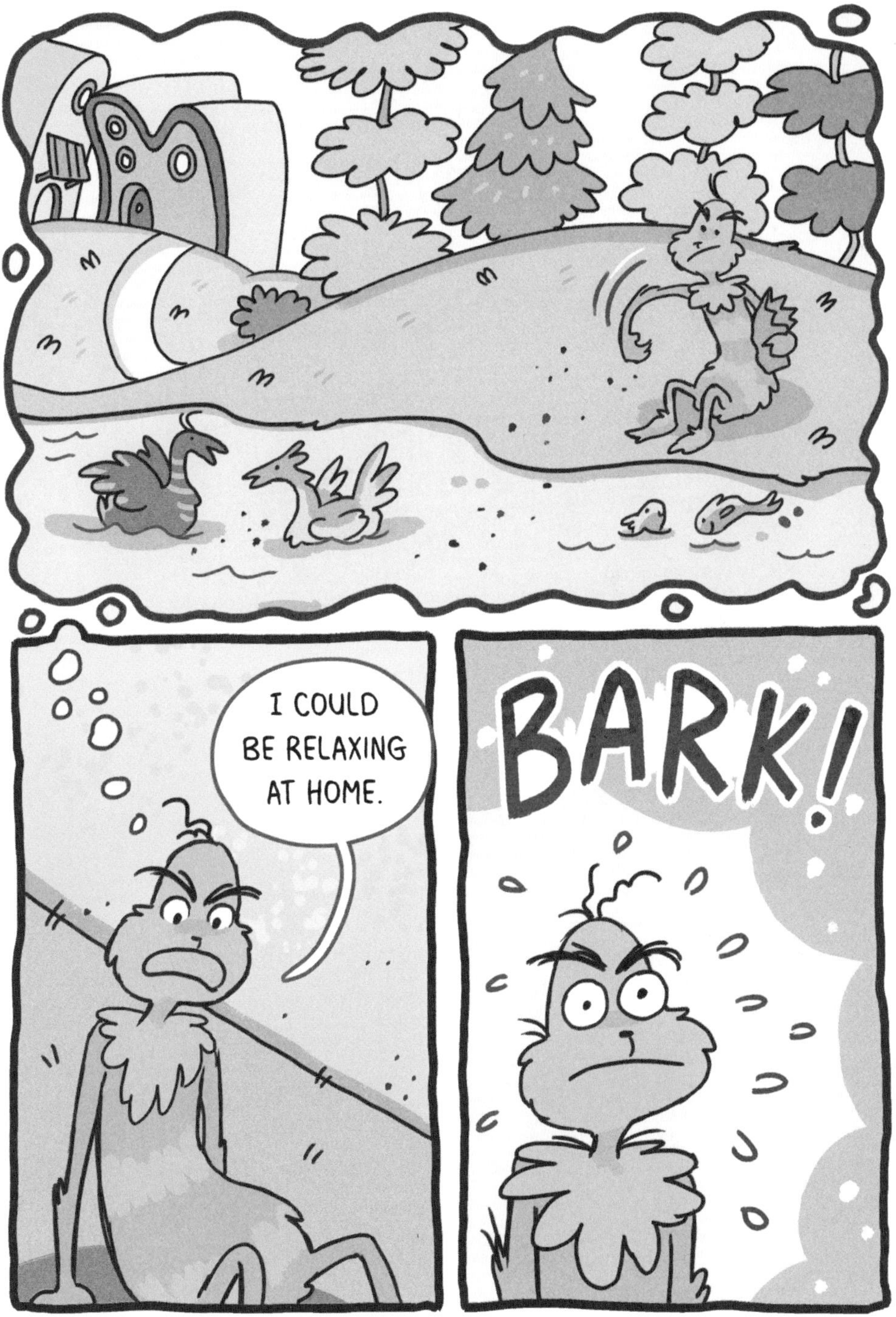
I COULD BE RELAXING AT HOME.
BARK!

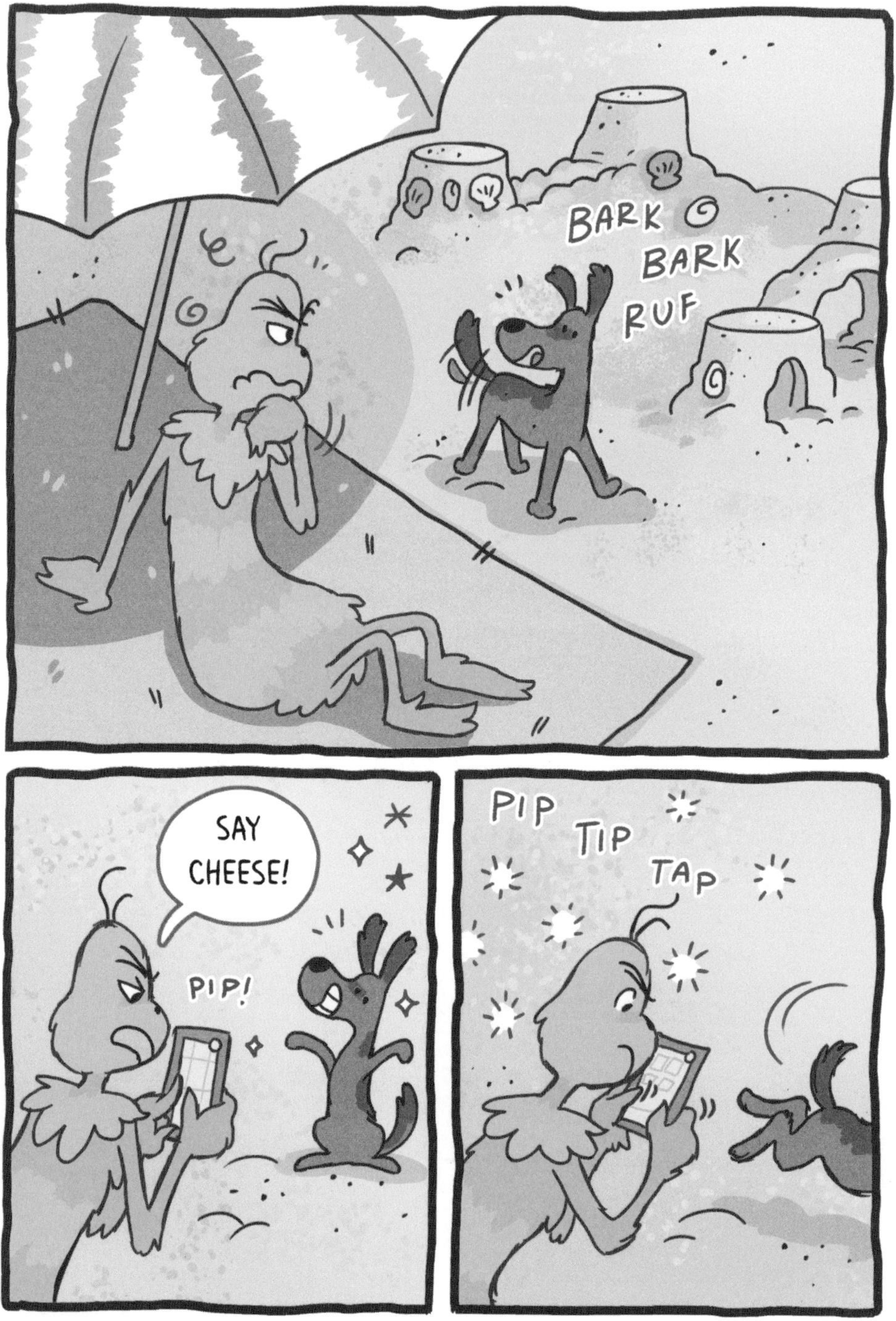
BARK
BARK
RUF
SAY CHEESE!
PIP!
PIP
TIP
TAP

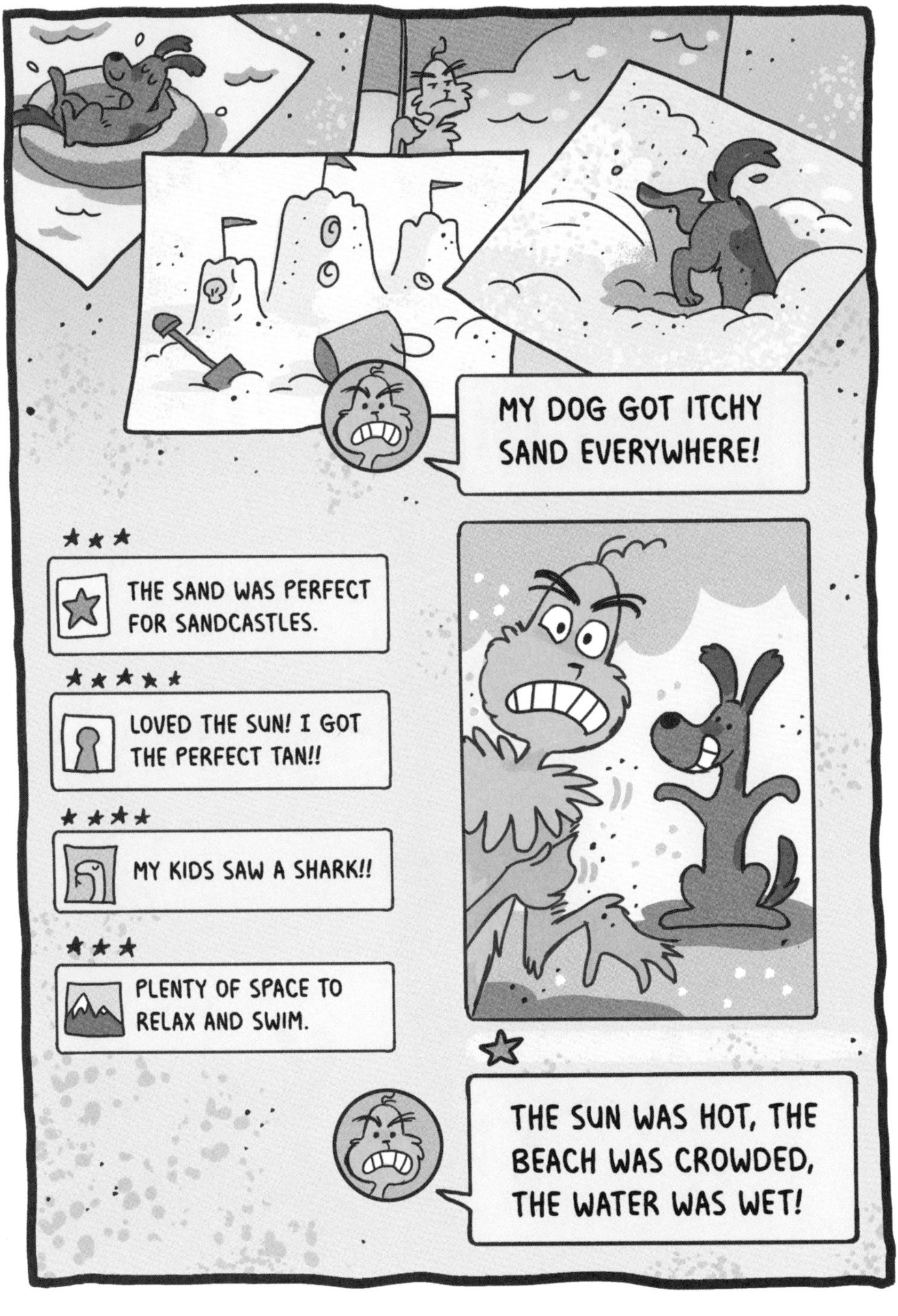
MY DOG GOT ITCHY SAND EVERYWHERE!
★★★
THE SAND WAS PERFECT FOR SANDCASTLES.
★★★★★
LOVED THE SUN! I GOT THE PERFECT TAN!!
★★★★
MY KIDS SAW A SHARK!!
★★★
PLENTY OF SPACE TO RELAX AND SWIM.
★
THE SUN WAS HOT, THE BEACH WAS CROWDED, THE WATER WAS WET!

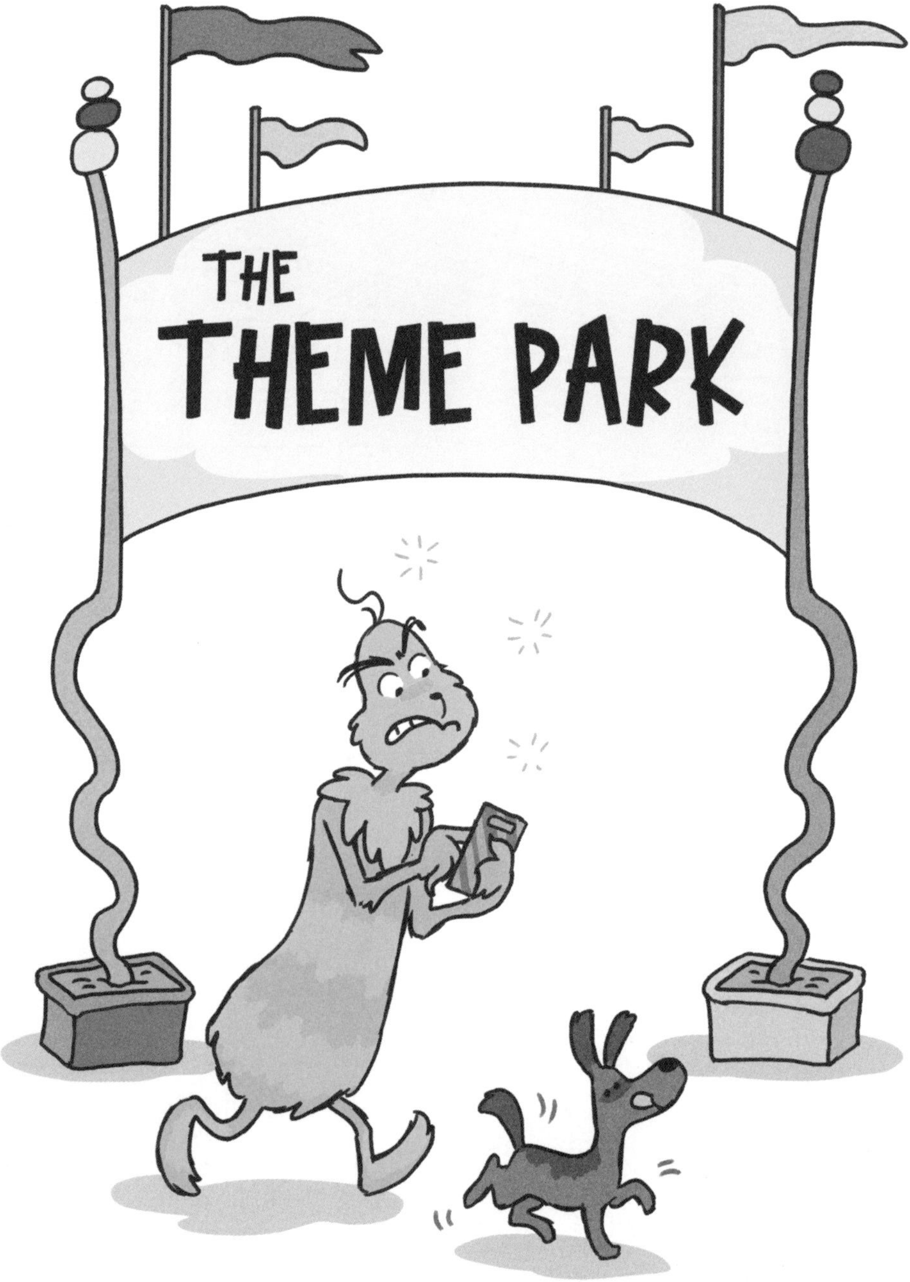
THE
THEME PARK

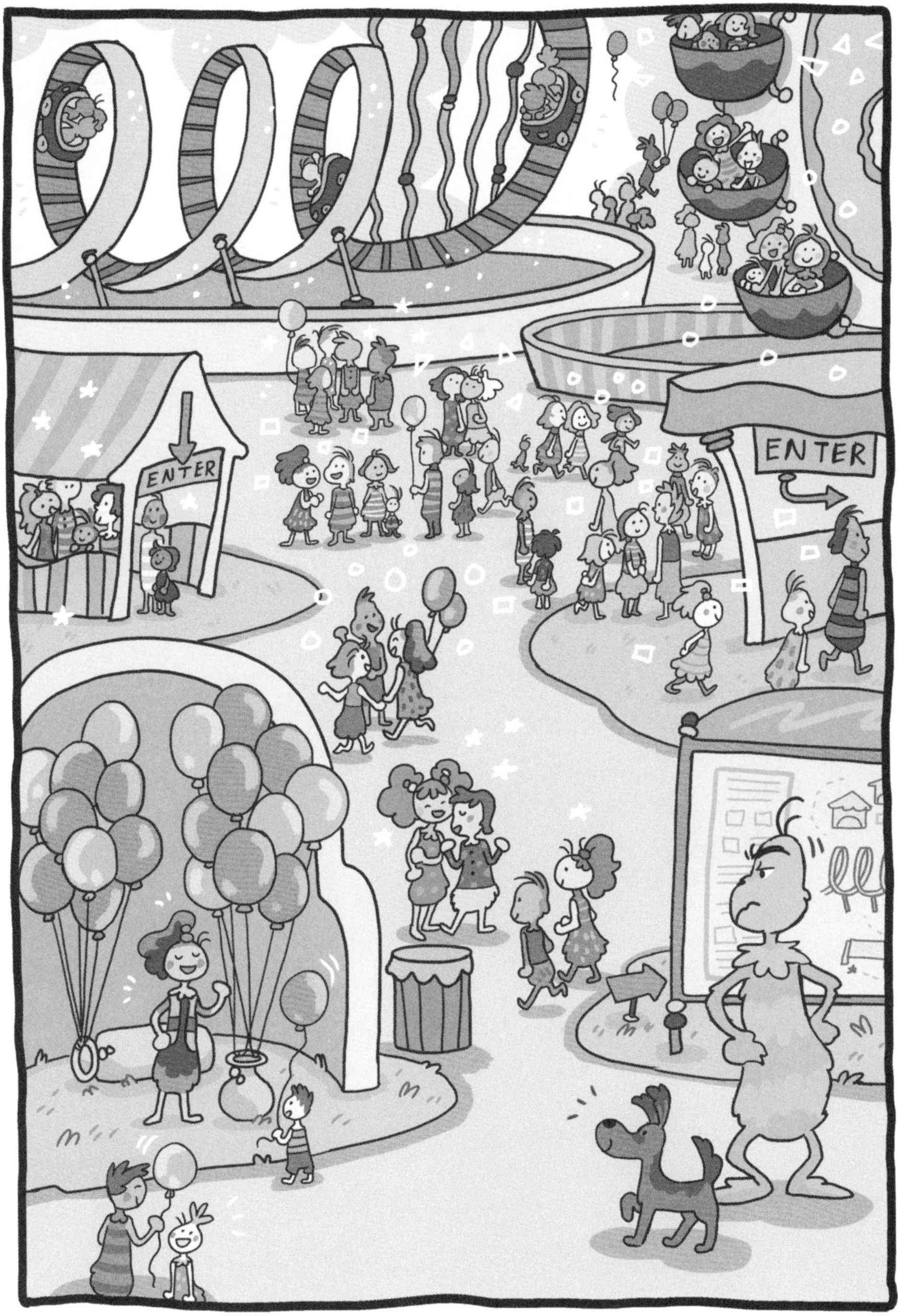
ENTER
ENTER

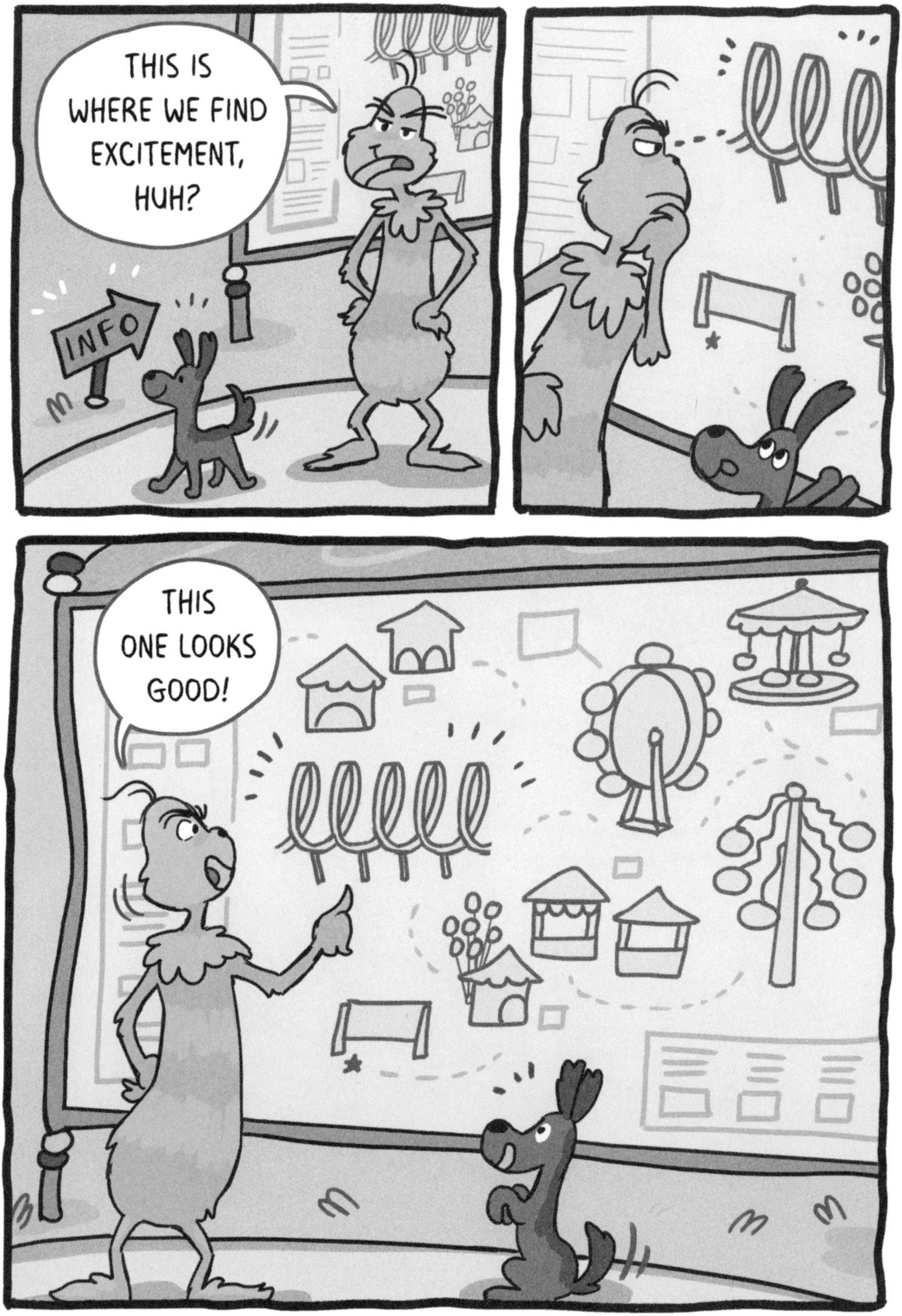
THIS IS WHERE WE FIND EXCITEMENT, HUH?
INFO
THIS ONE LOOKS GOOD!

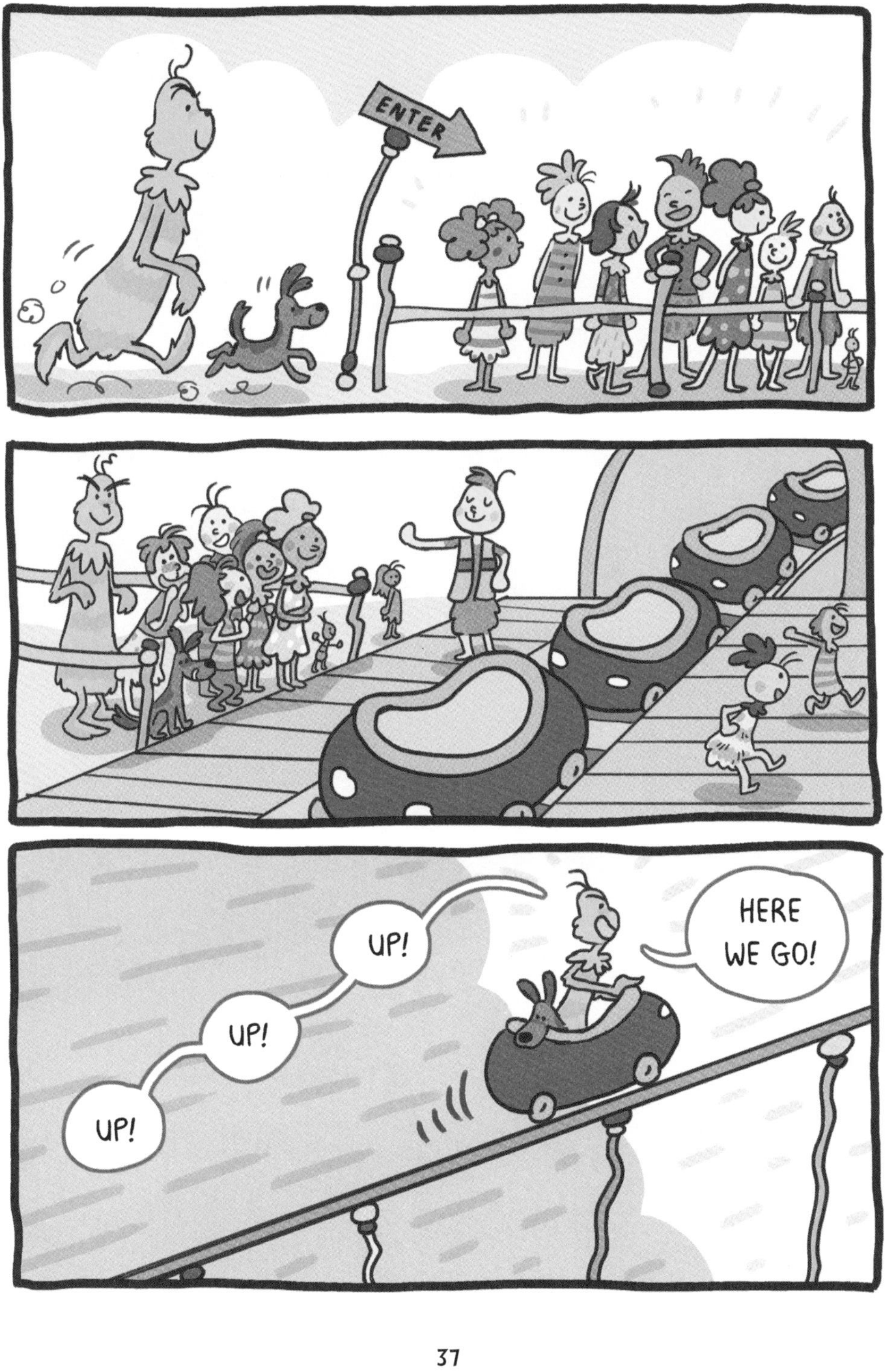
ENTER
UP!
UP!
UP!
HERE WE GO!

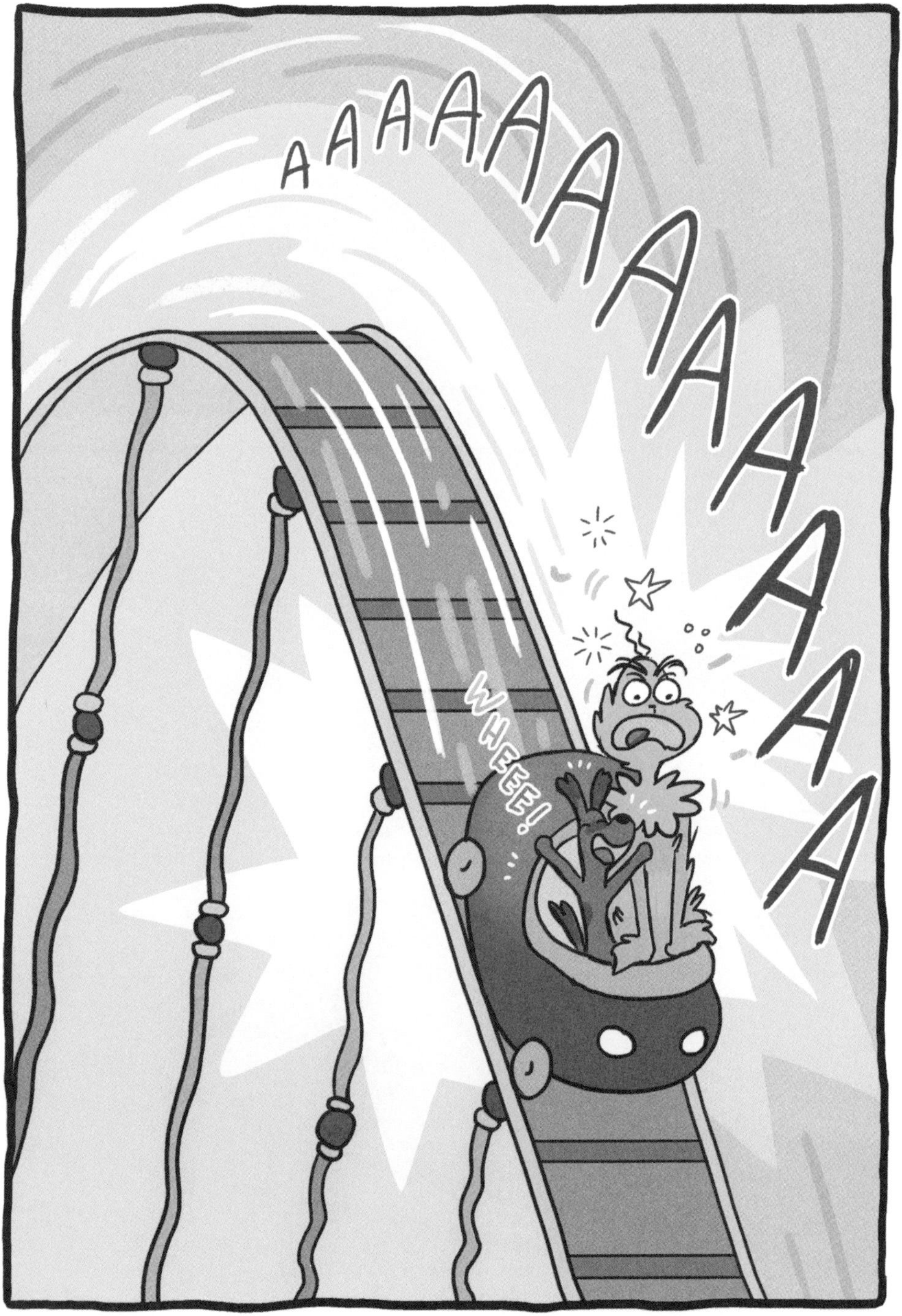
AAAAAAAAAAAA
WHEEE!

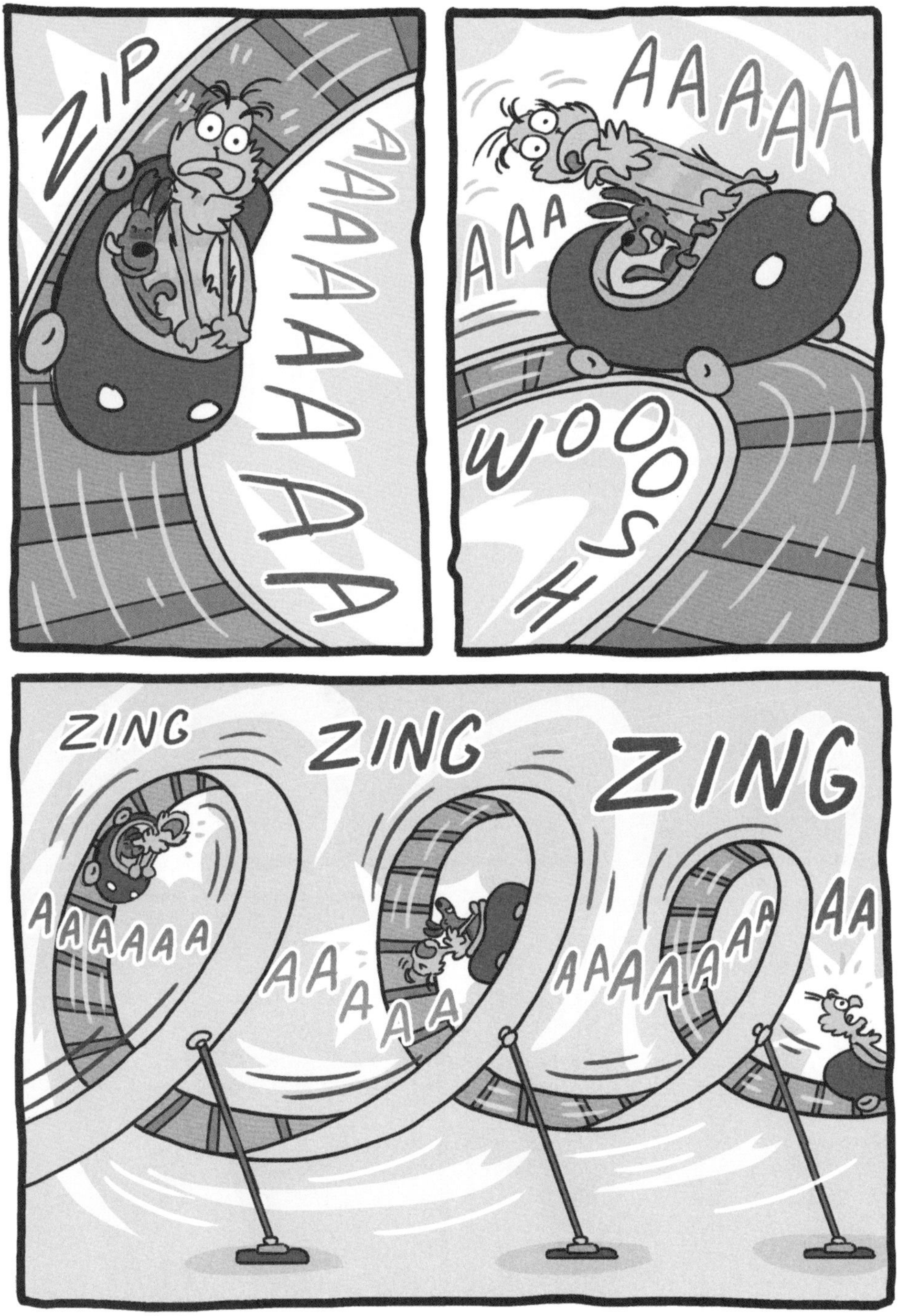
ZIP
AAAAAAAAAA
AAAAAA
AAA
WOOOSH
ZING
ZING
ZING
AAAAAA
AA
AAA
AAAAAAAA
AA

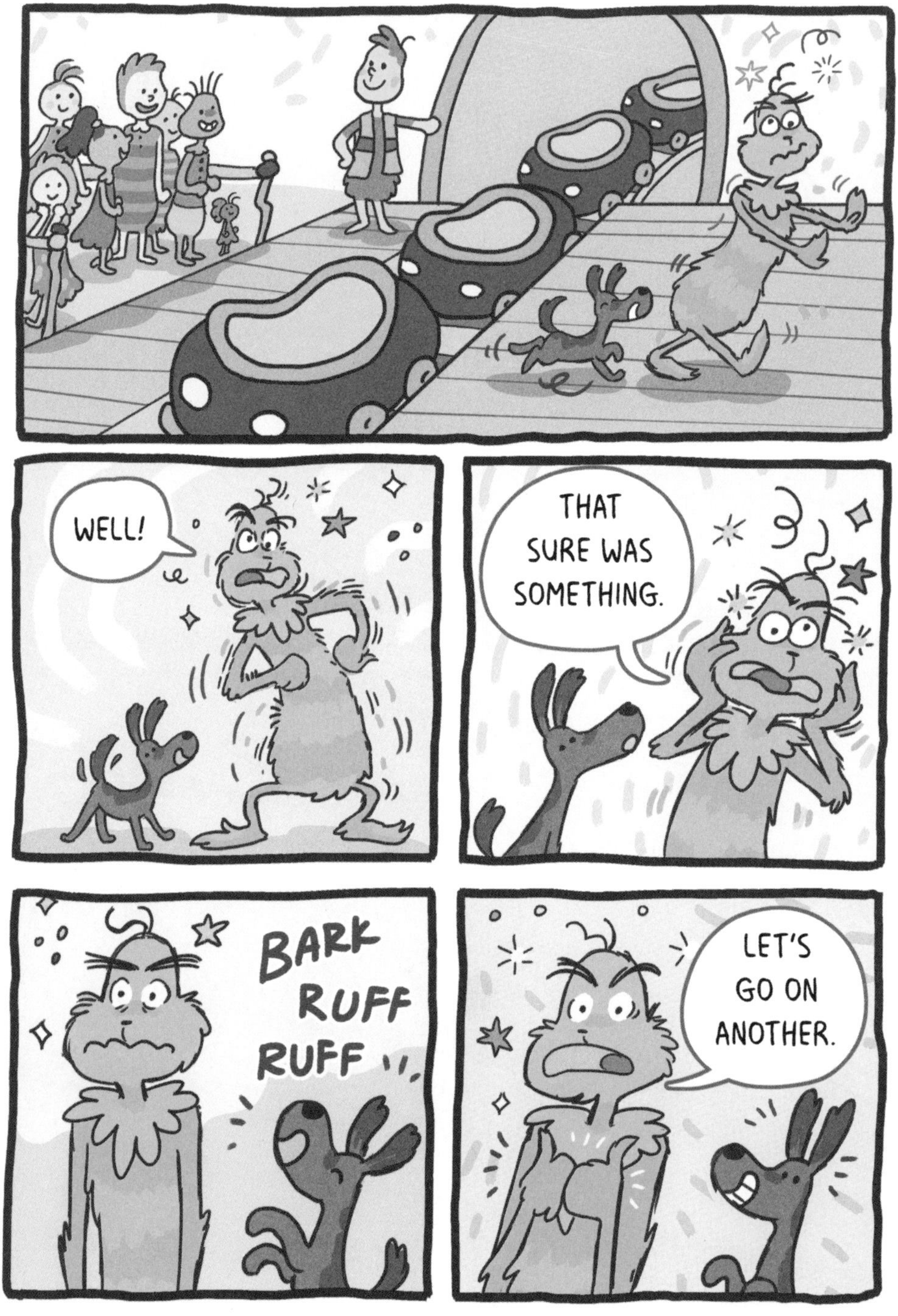
WELL!
THAT SURE WAS SOMETHING.
BARK RUFF RUFF
LET'S GO ON ANOTHER.

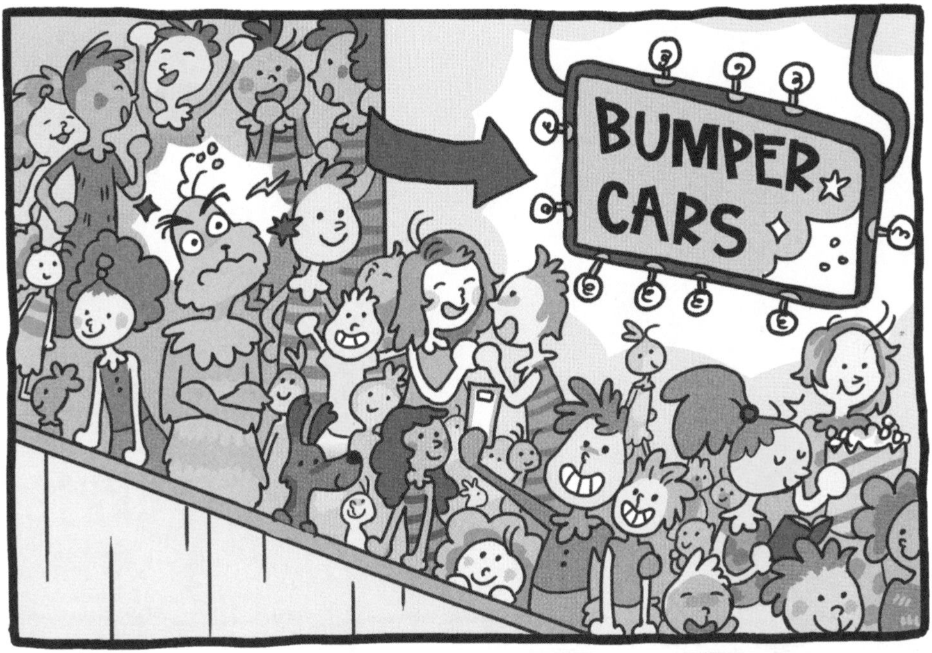
BUMPER CARS

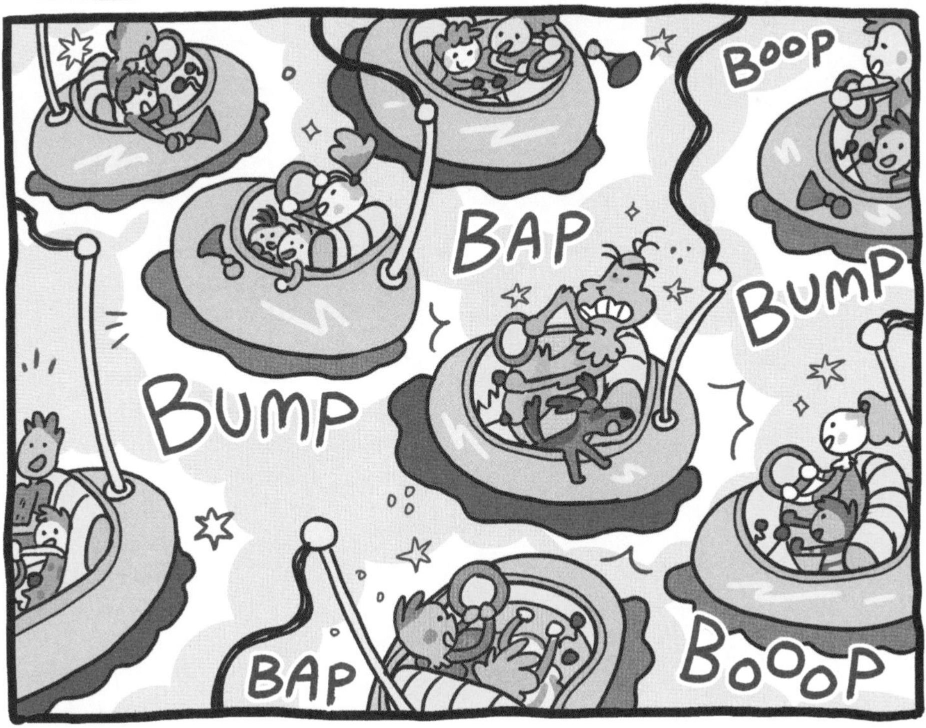
BOOP
BAP
BUMP
BUMP
BAP
BOOOP

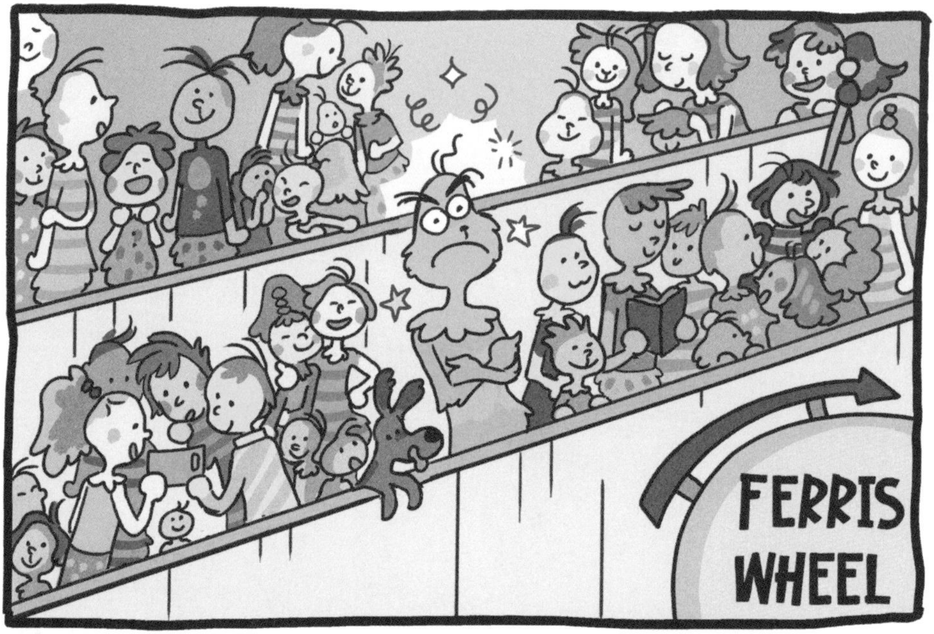
FERRIS
WHEEL

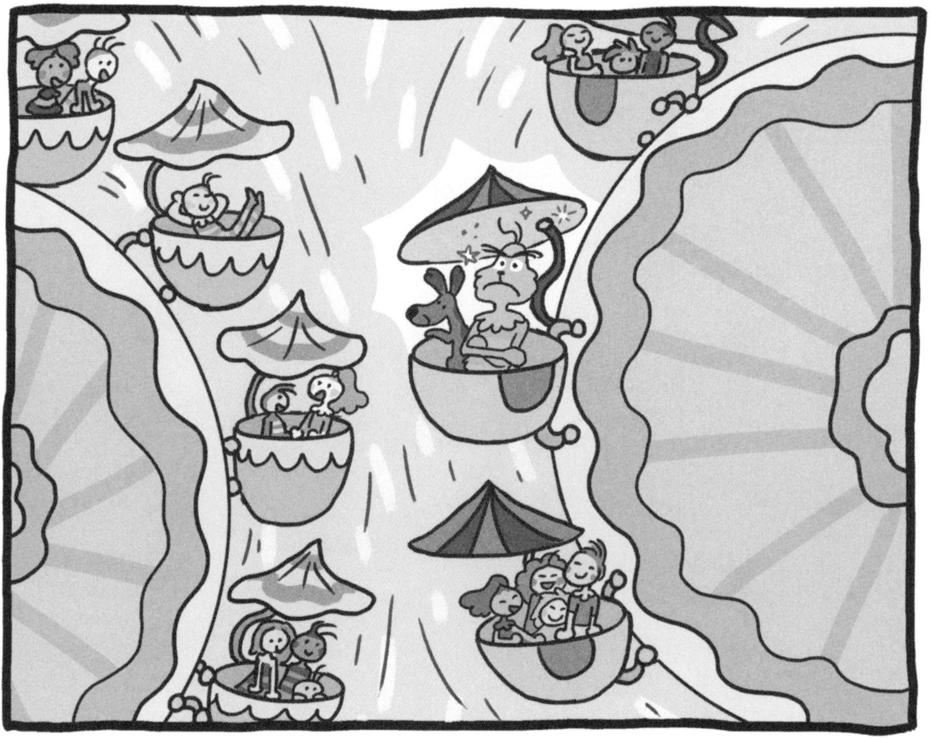

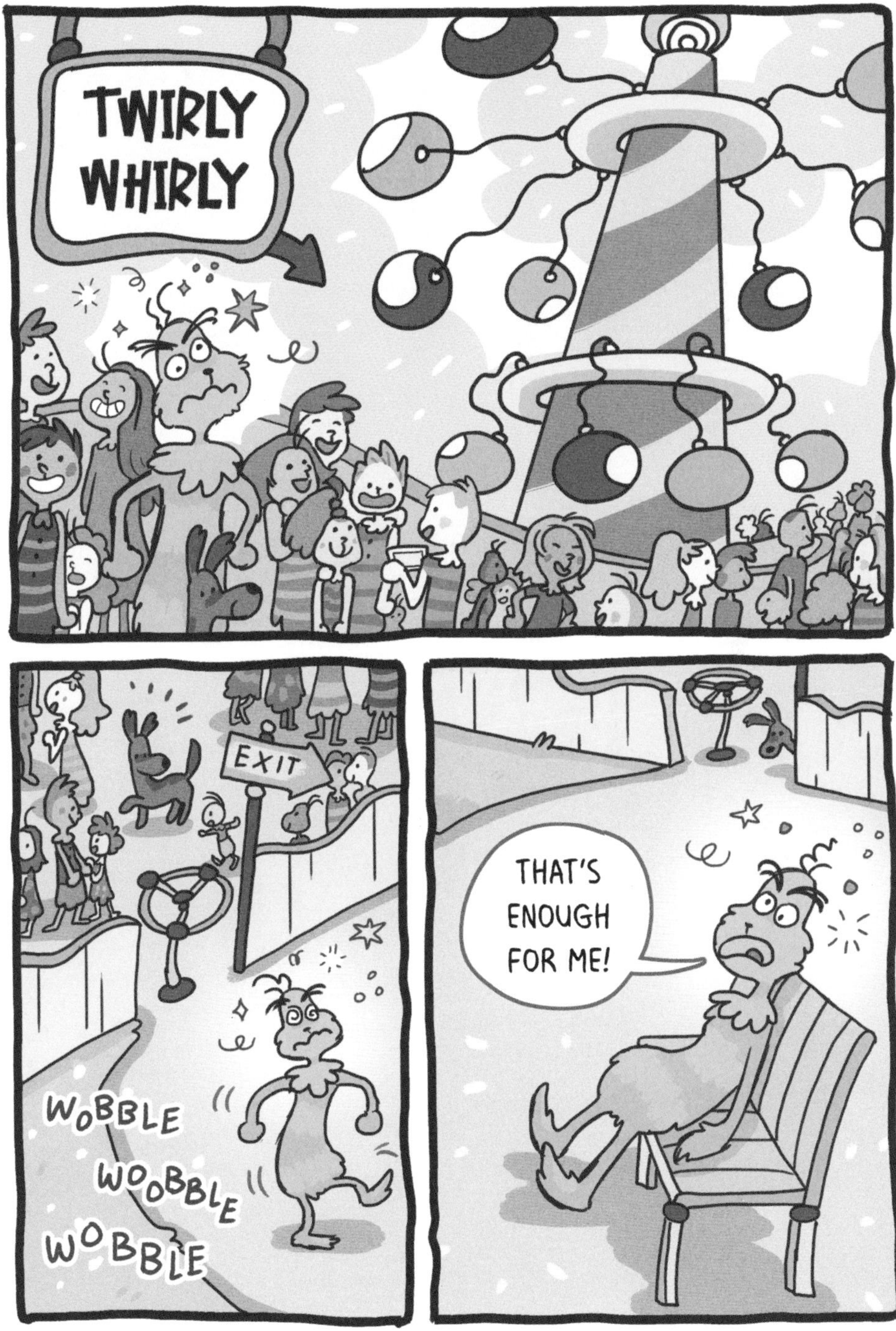
TWIRLY
WHIRLY
EXIT
WOBBLE
WOOBBLE
WOBBLE
THAT'S
ENOUGH
FOR ME!

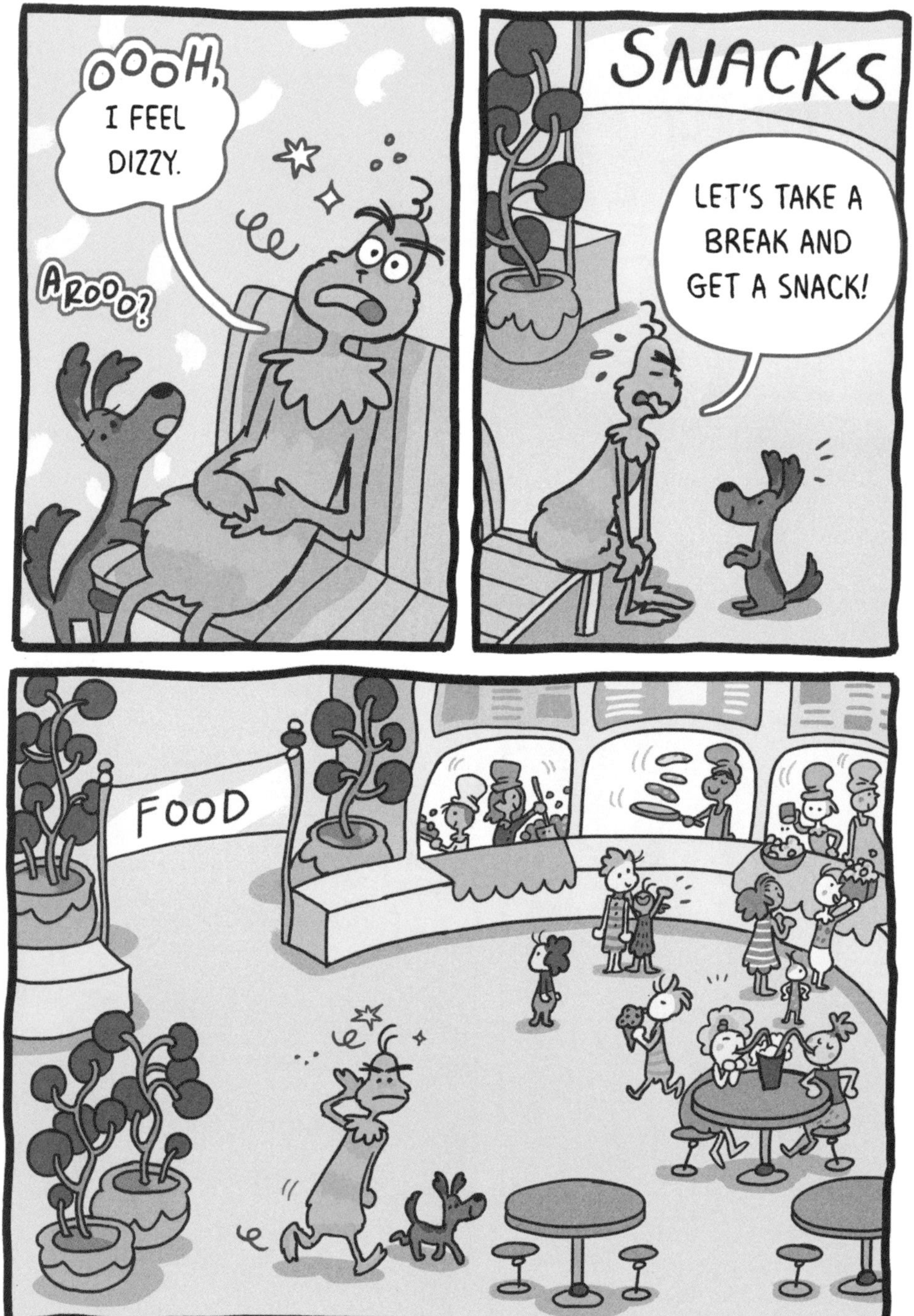
OOOH,
I FEEL
DIZZY.
AROOOO?
SNACKS
LET'S TAKE A
BREAK AND
GET A SNACK!
FOOD

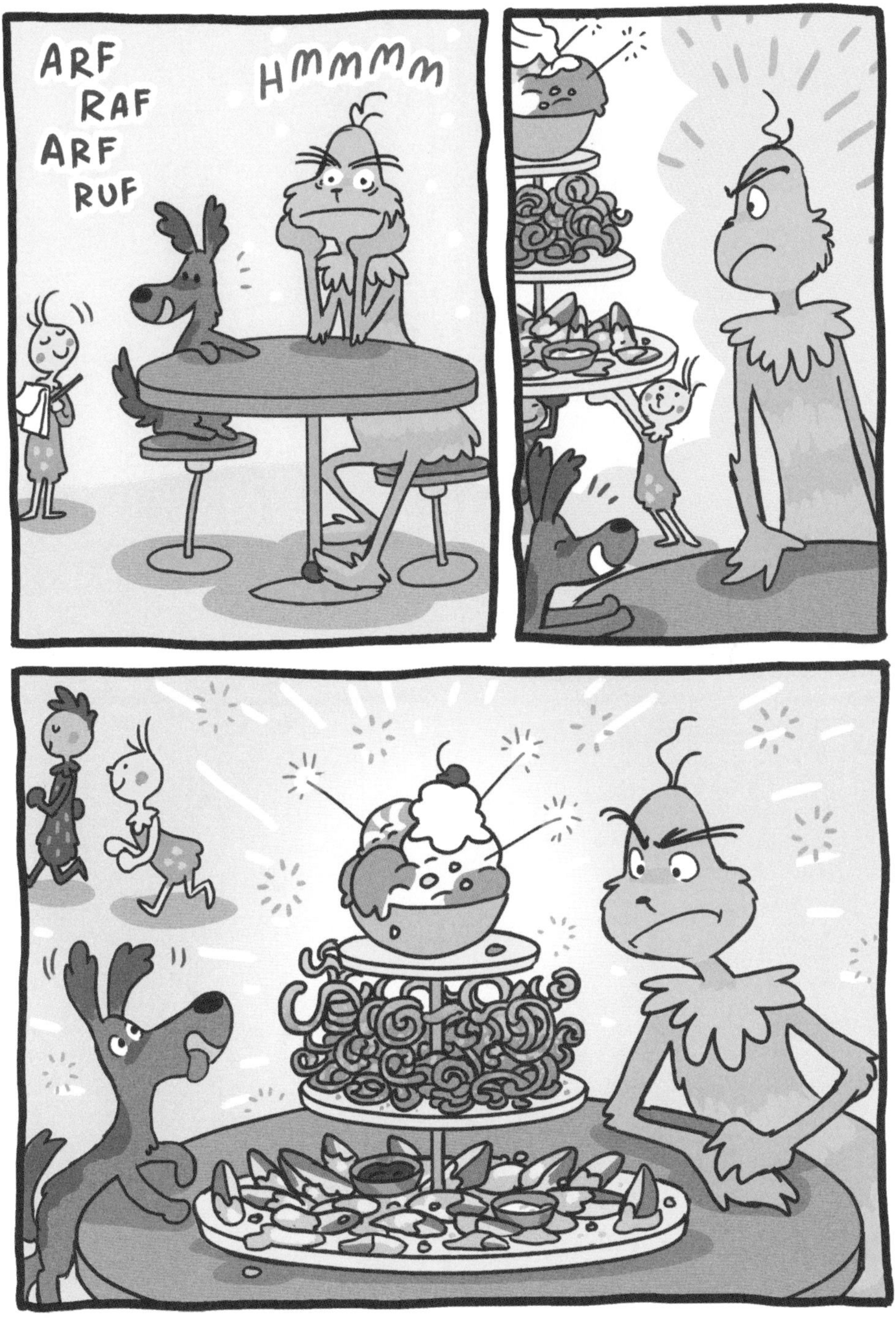
ARF
RAF
ARF
RUF
HMMMM

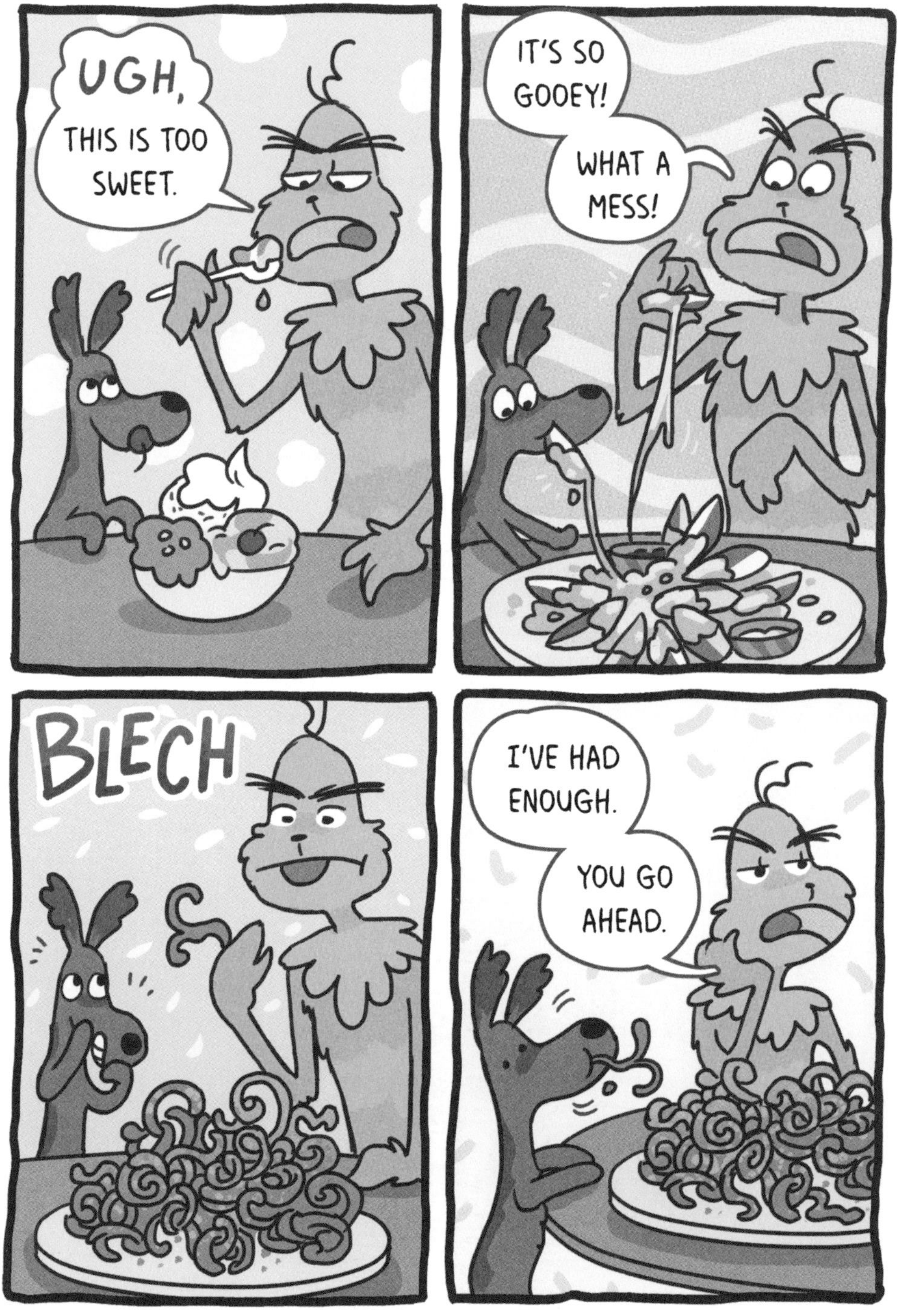
UGH,
THIS IS TOO SWEET.
IT'S SO GOOEY!
WHAT A MESS!
BLECH
I'VE HAD ENOUGH.
YOU GO AHEAD.

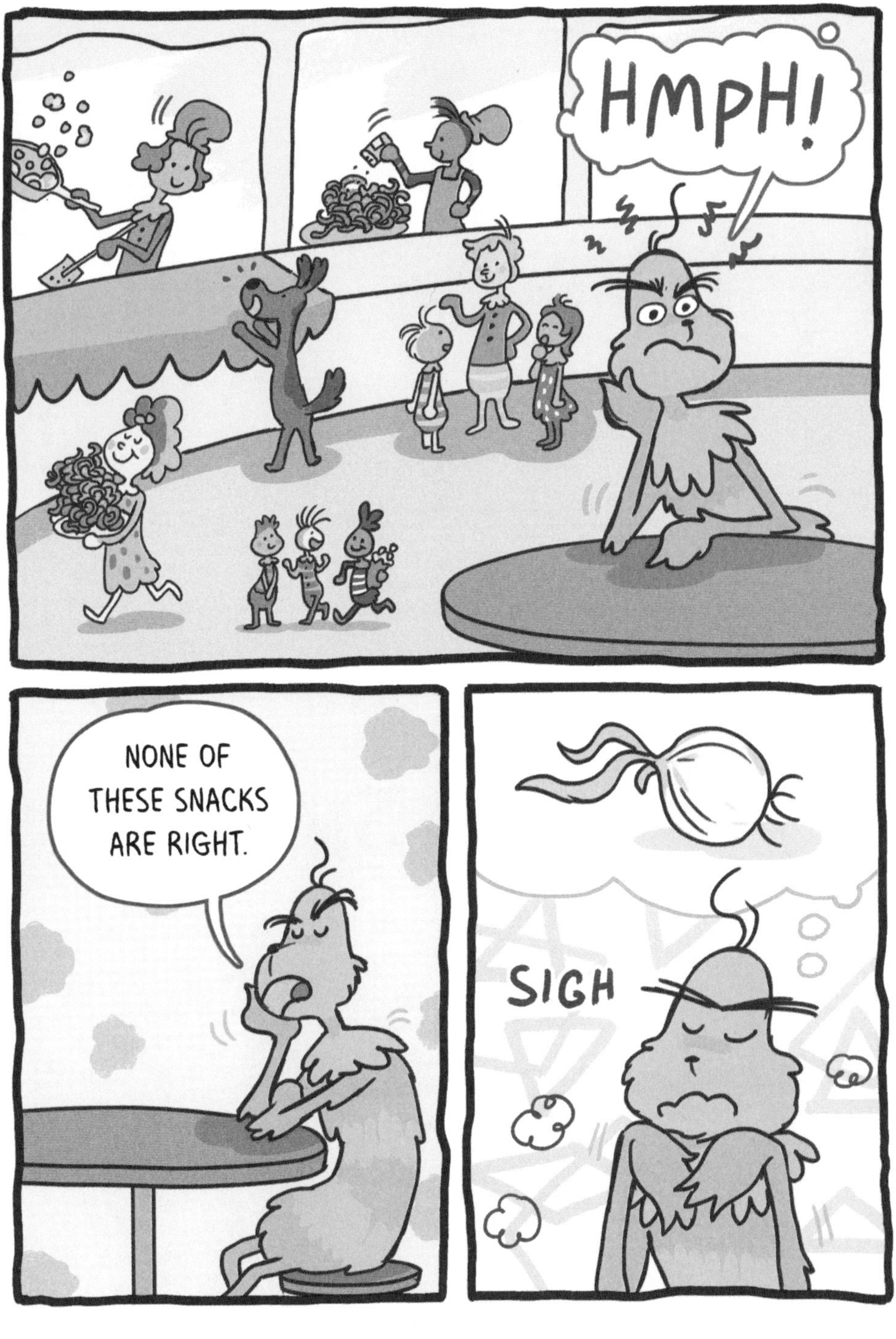
HMPH!
NONE OF THESE SNACKS ARE RIGHT.
SIGH

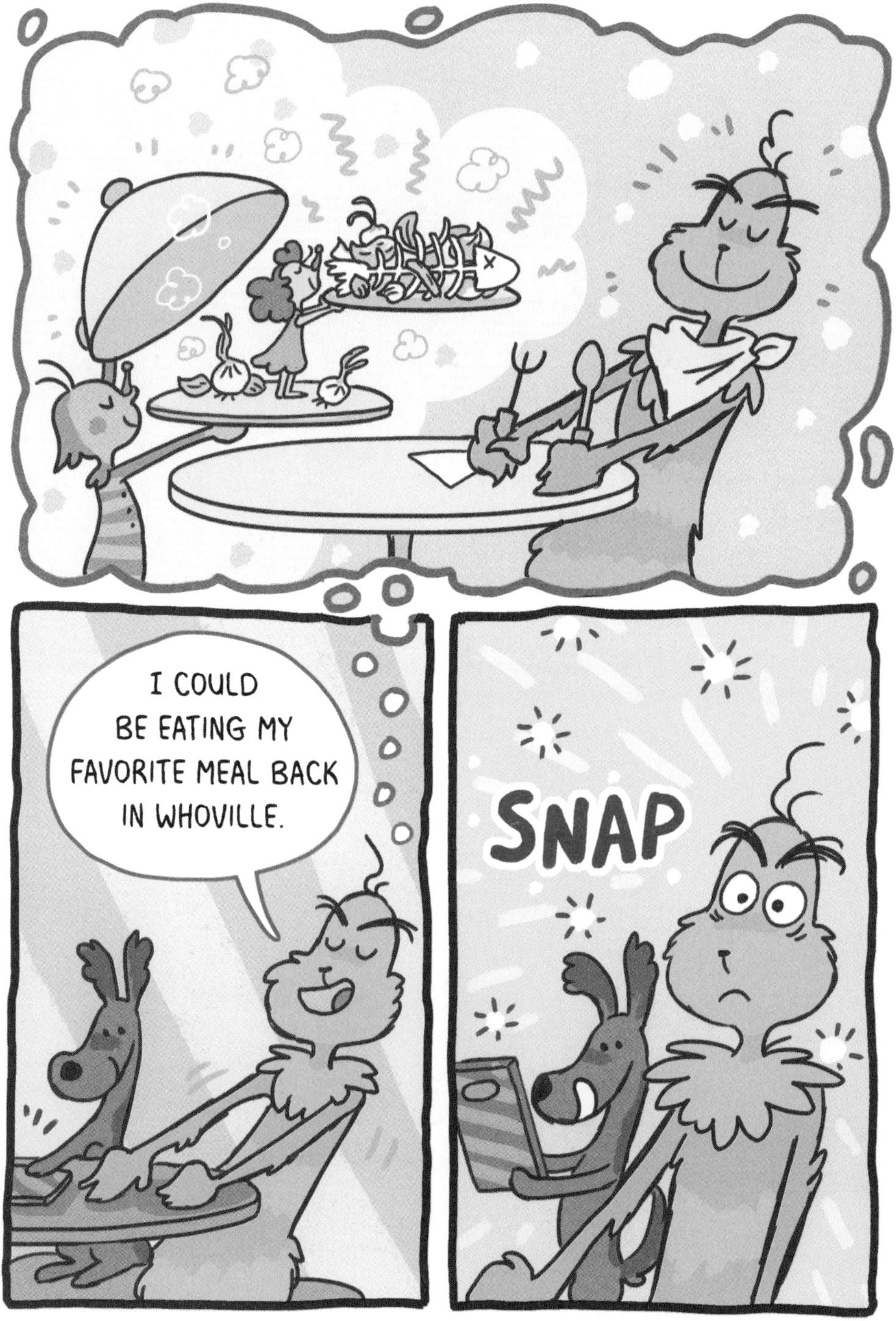
I COULD BE EATING MY FAVORITE MEAL BACK IN WHOVILLE.
SNAP

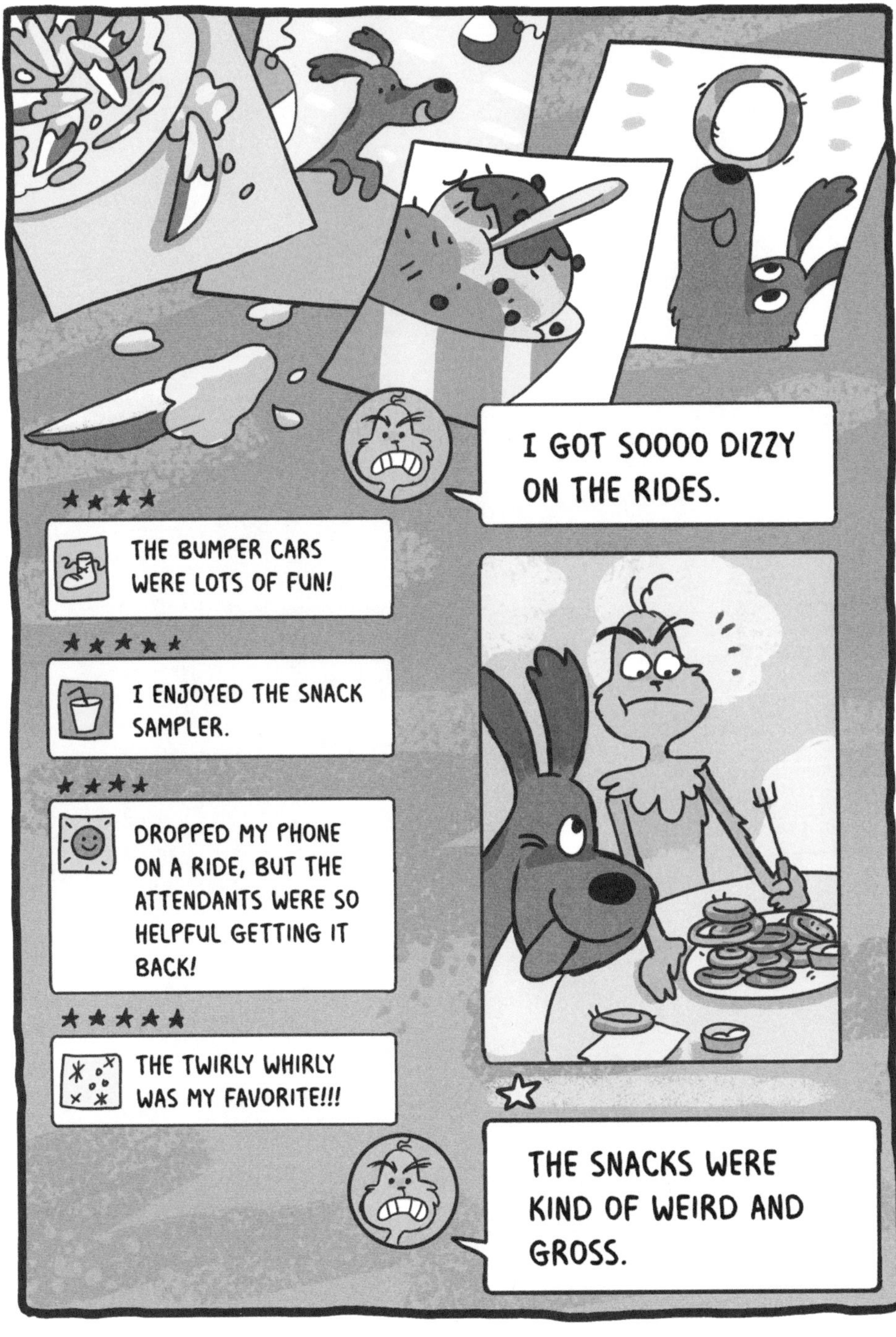
I GOT SOOOO DIZZY ON THE RIDES.
★★★★
THE BUMPER CARS WERE LOTS OF FUN!
★★★★★
I ENJOYED THE SNACK SAMPLER.
★★★★
DROPPED MY PHONE ON A RIDE, BUT THE ATTENDANTS WERE SO HELPFUL GETTING IT BACK!
★★★★★
THE TWIRLY WHIRLY WAS MY FAVORITE!!!
☆
THE SNACKS WERE KIND OF WEIRD AND GROSS.

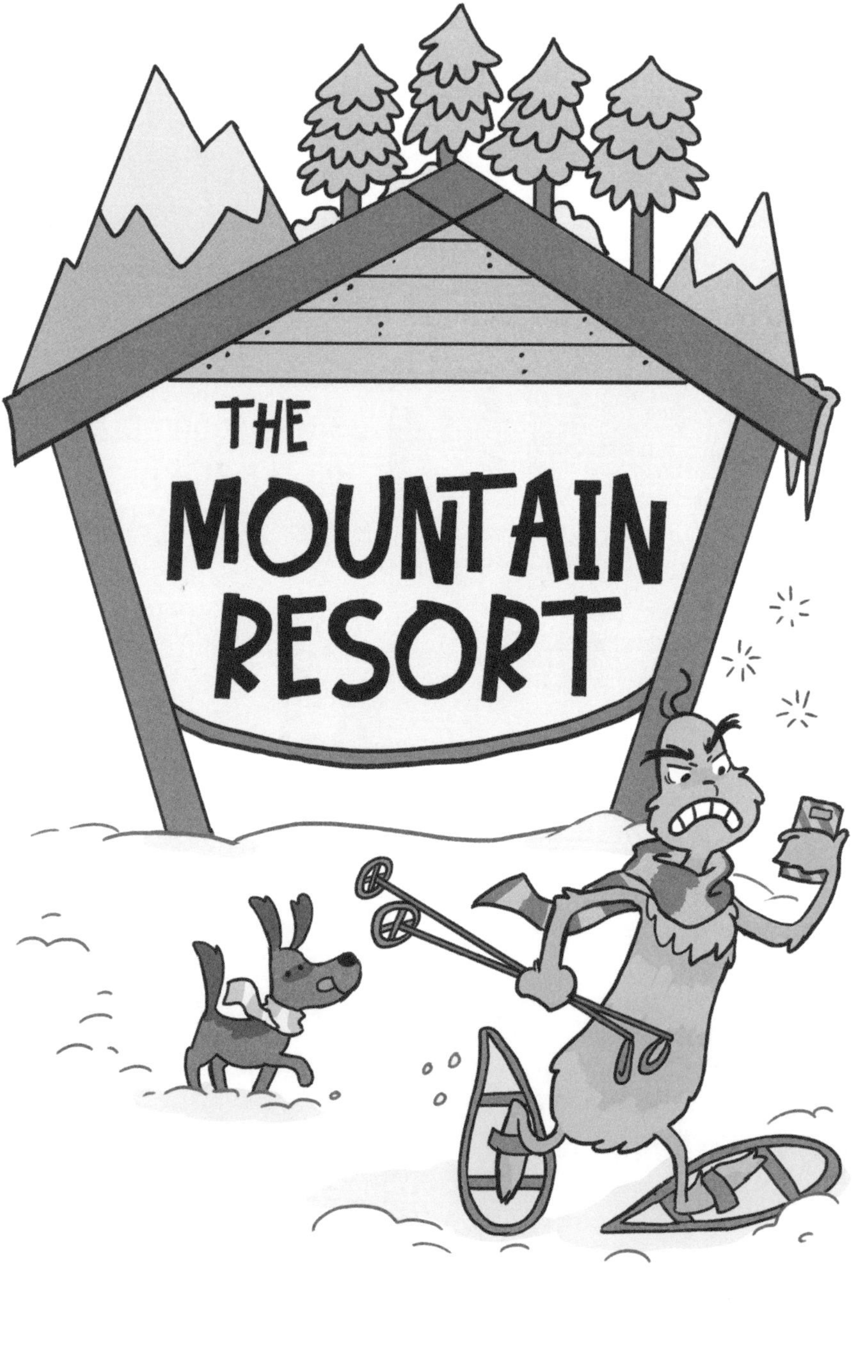
THE
MOUNTAIN
RESORT

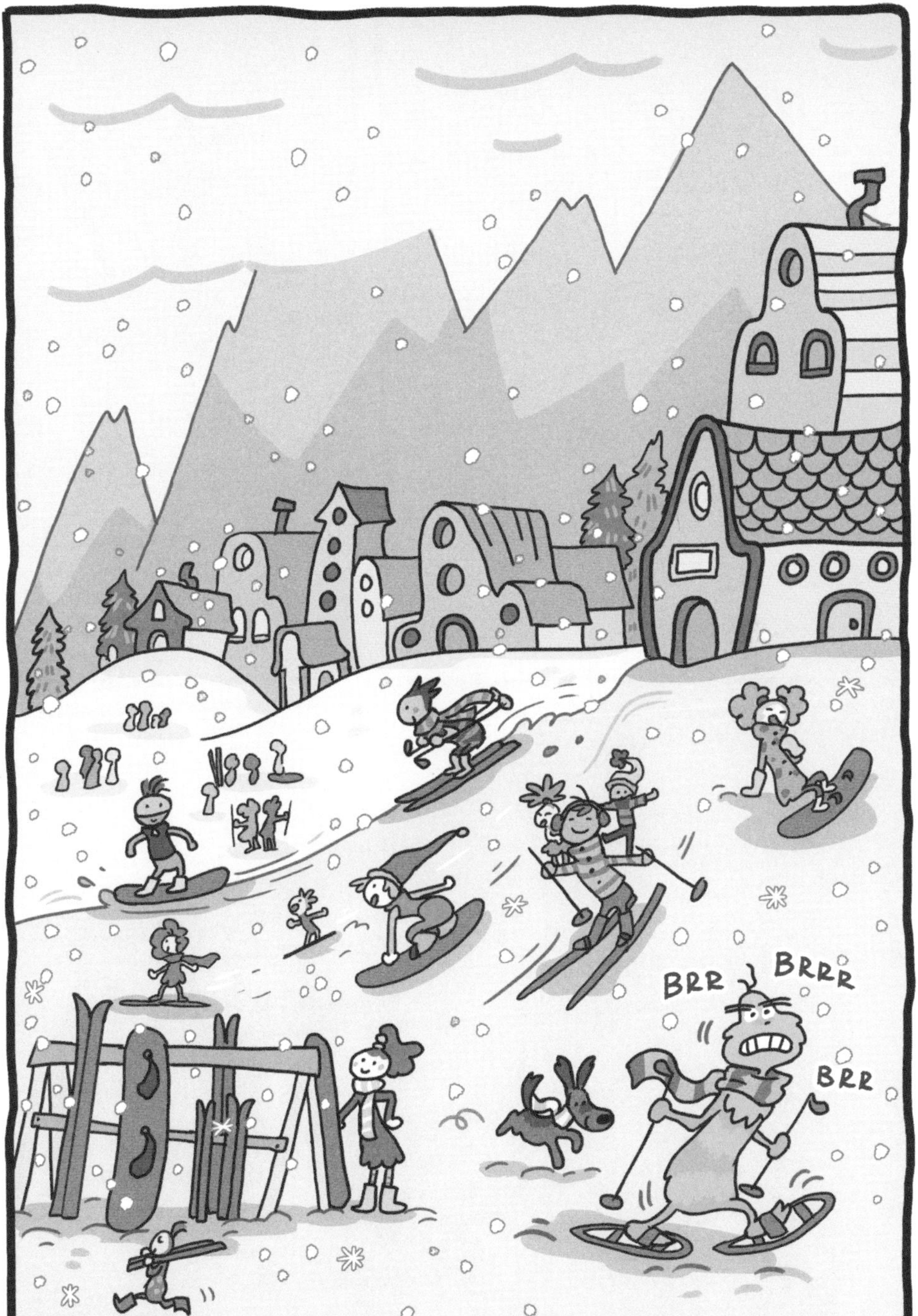
BRR
BRRR
BRR

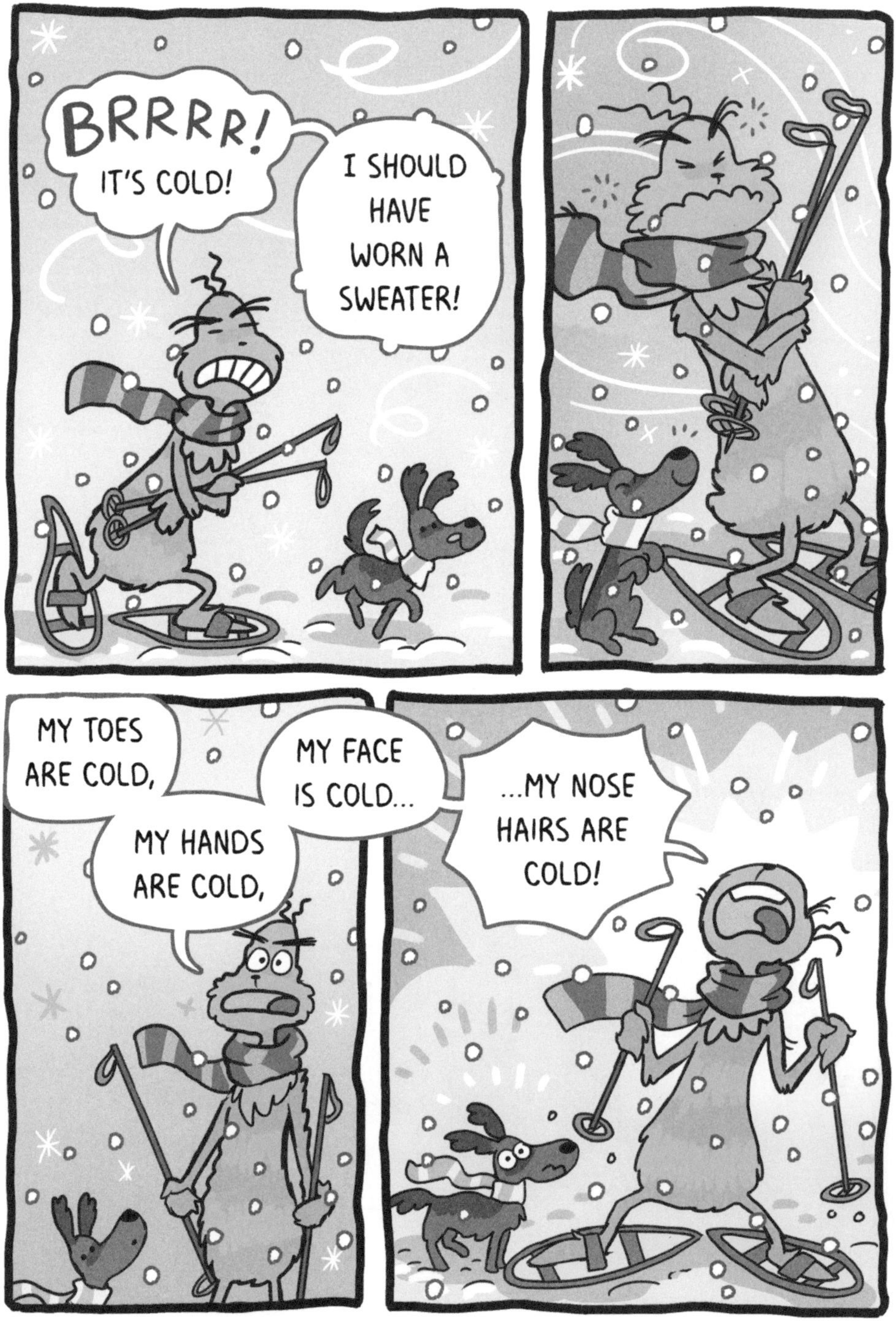
BRRRRR! IT'S COLD!
I SHOULD HAVE WORN A SWEATER!
MY TOES ARE COLD,
MY HANDS ARE COLD,
MY FACE IS COLD...
...MY NOSE HAIRS ARE COLD!

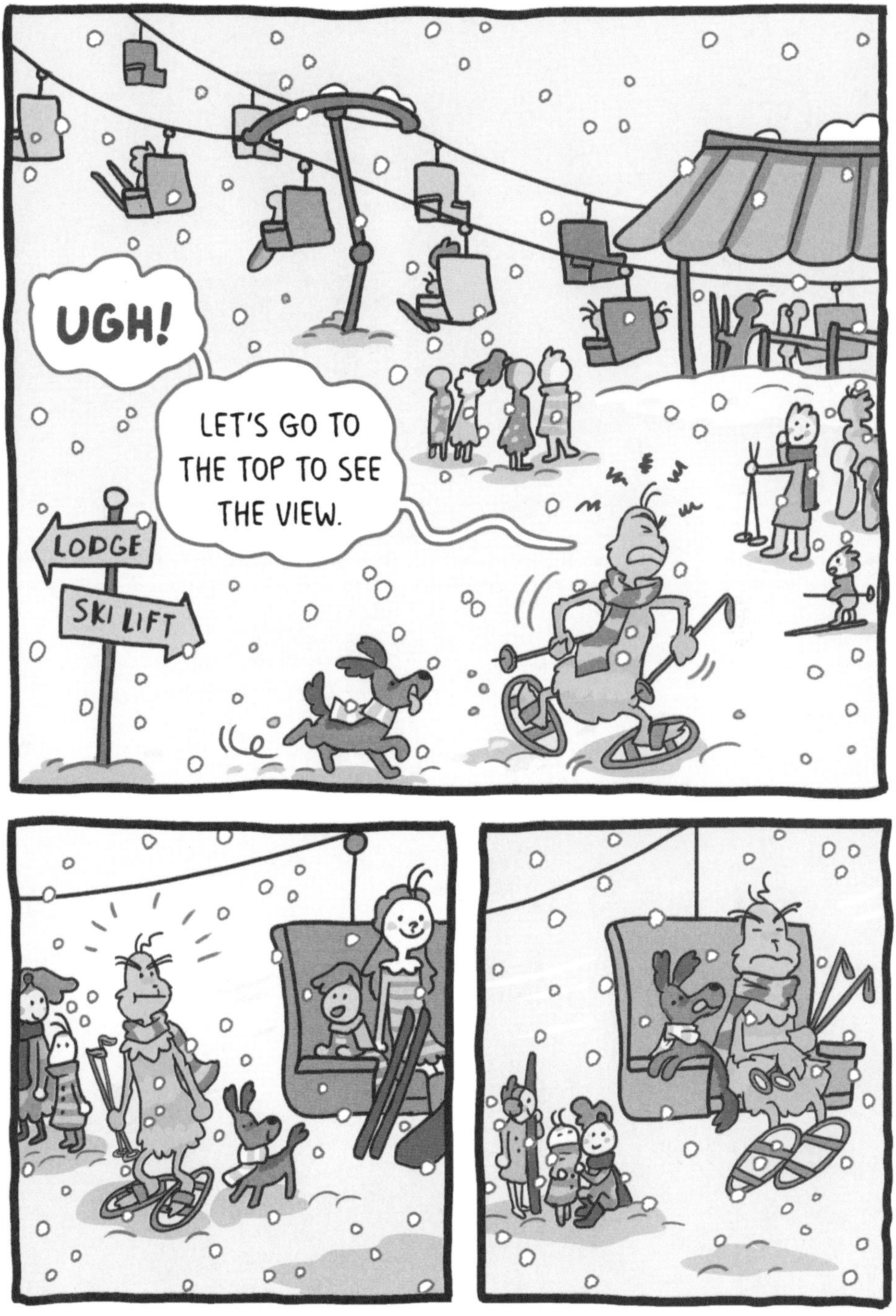
UGH!
LET'S GO TO THE TOP TO SEE THE VIEW.
LODGE
SKI LIFT

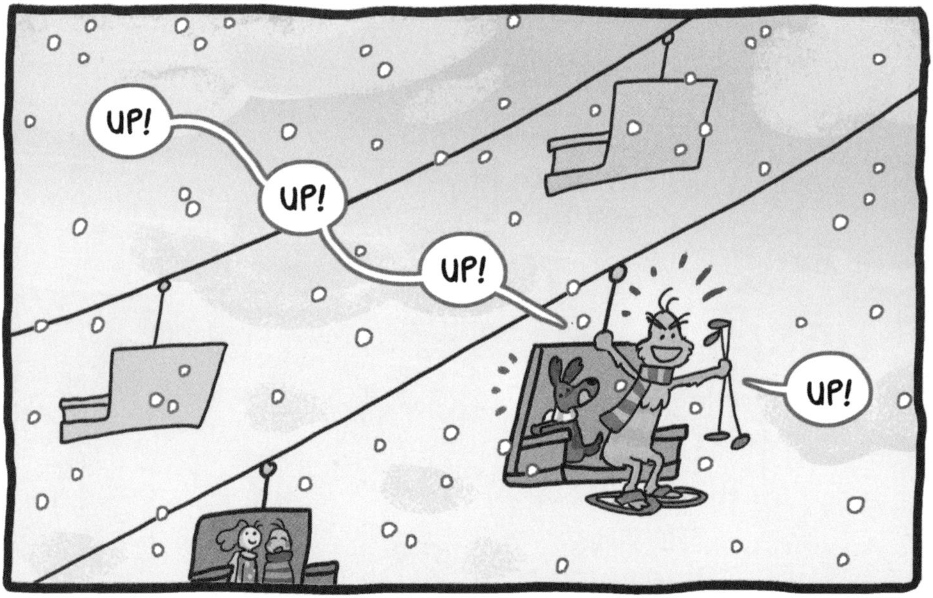
UP!
UP!
UP!
UP!

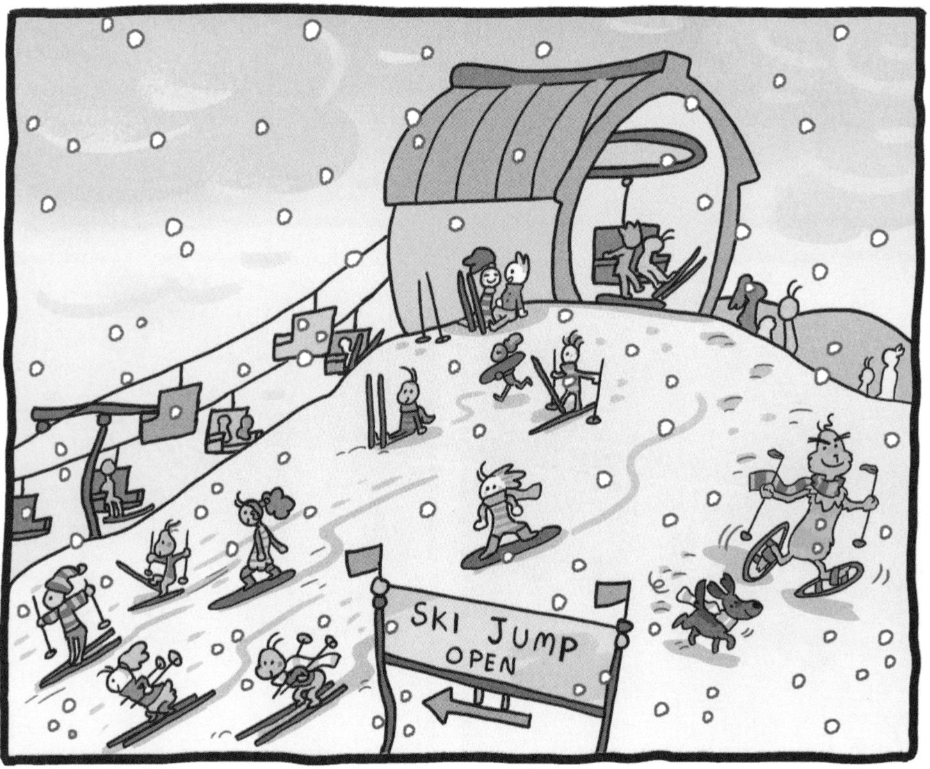
SKI JUMP
OPEN

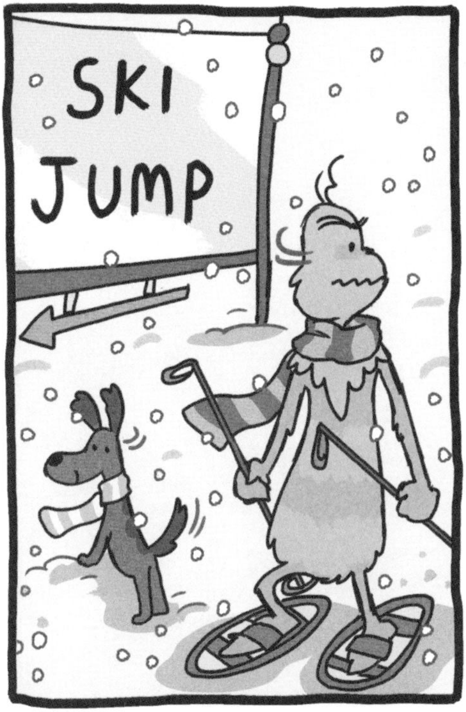
SKI
JUMP

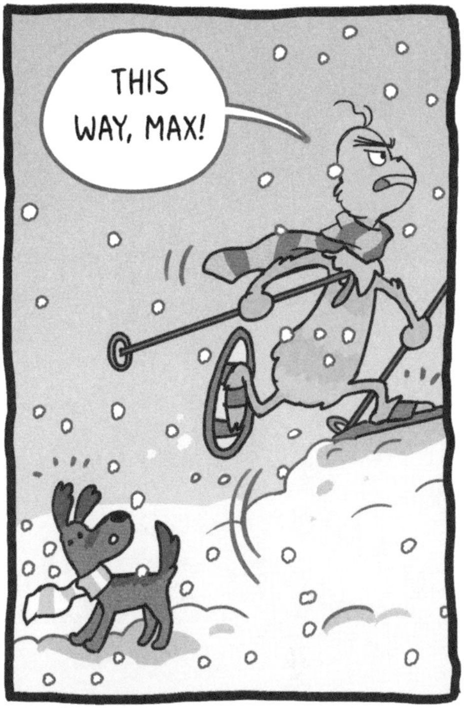
THIS
WAY, MAX!

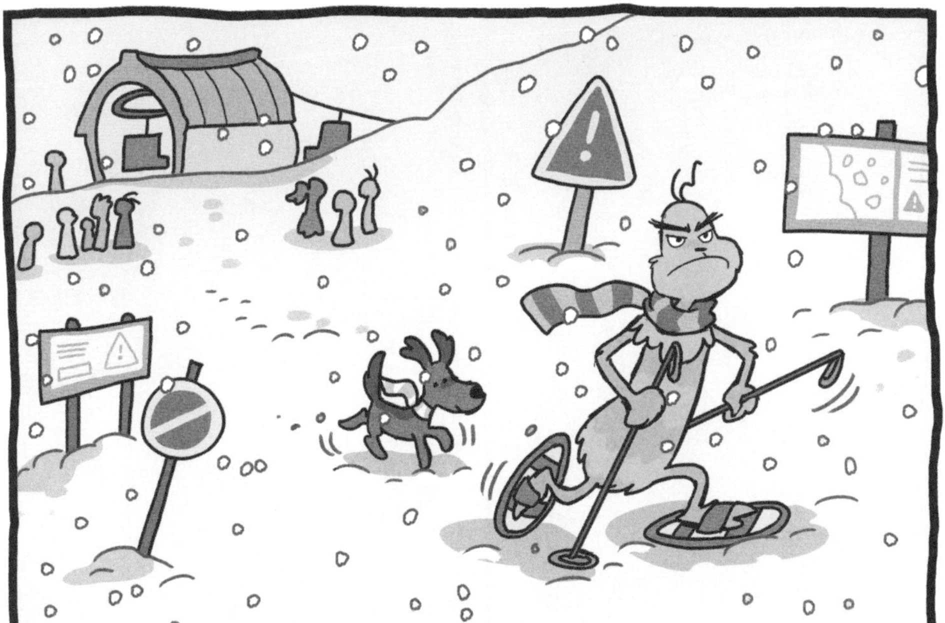

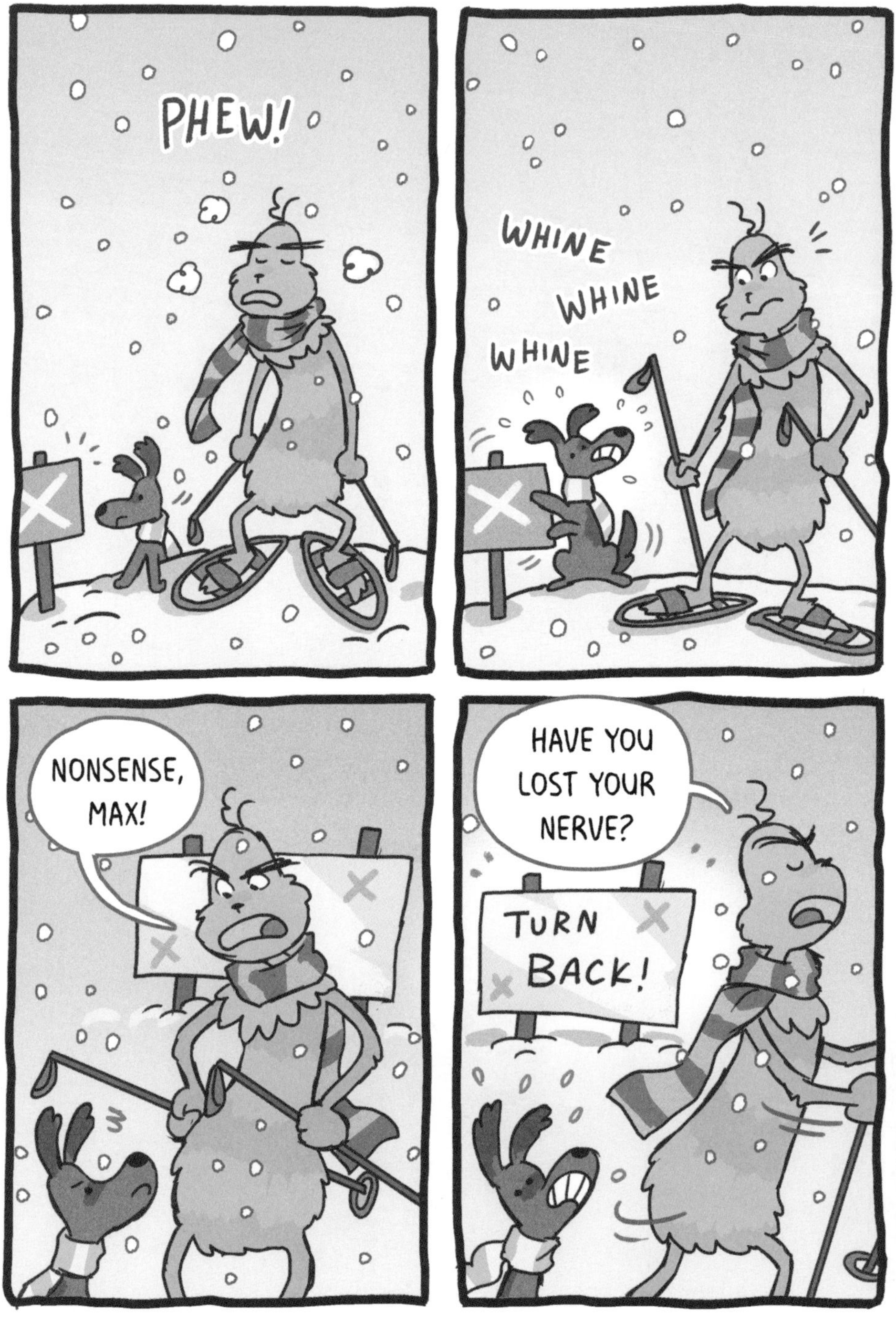
PHEW!
WHINE
WHINE
WHINE
NONSENSE, MAX!
HAVE YOU LOST YOUR NERVE?
TURN BACK!

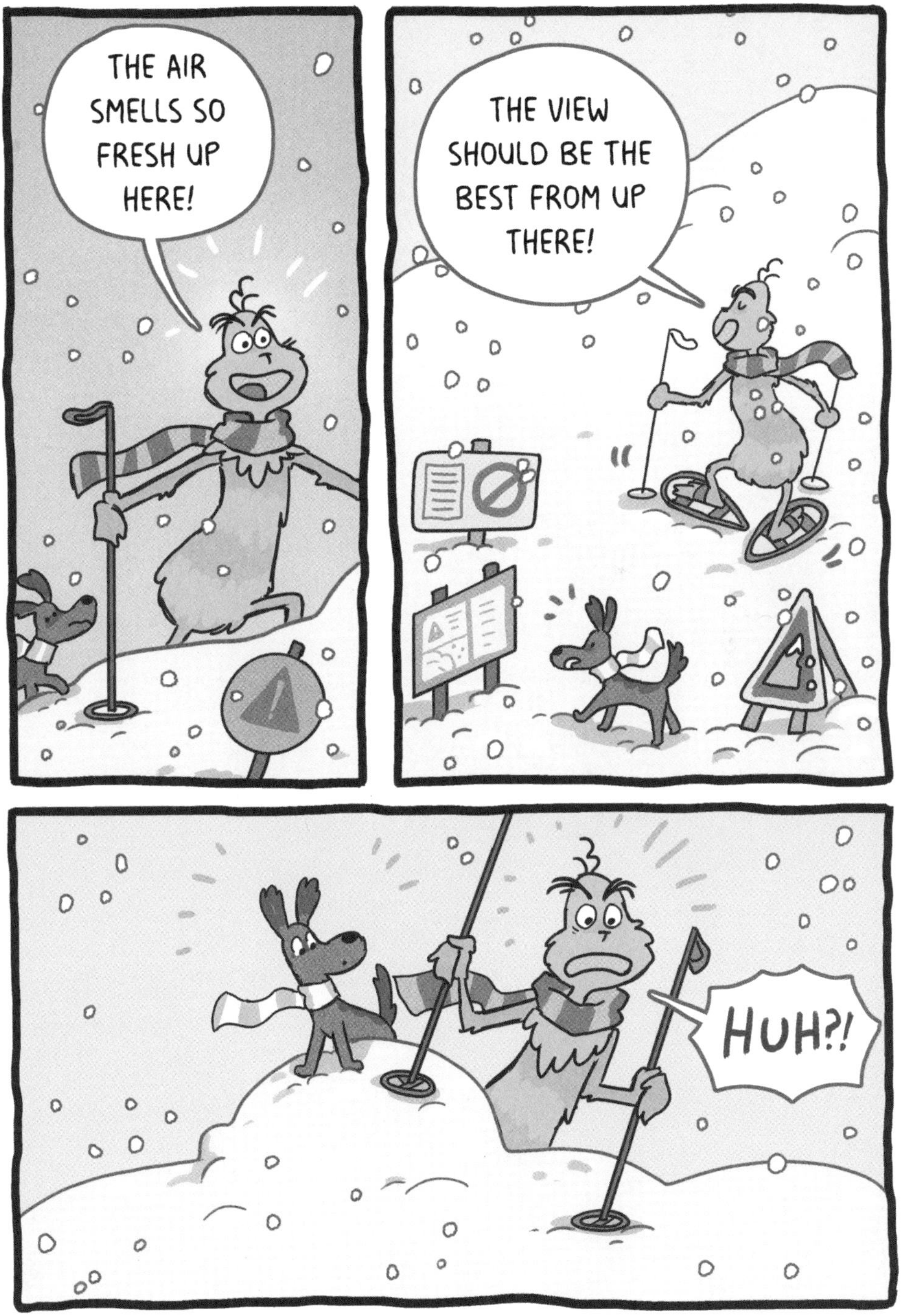
THE AIR SMELLS SO FRESH UP HERE!
THE VIEW SHOULD BE THE BEST FROM UP THERE!
HUH?!

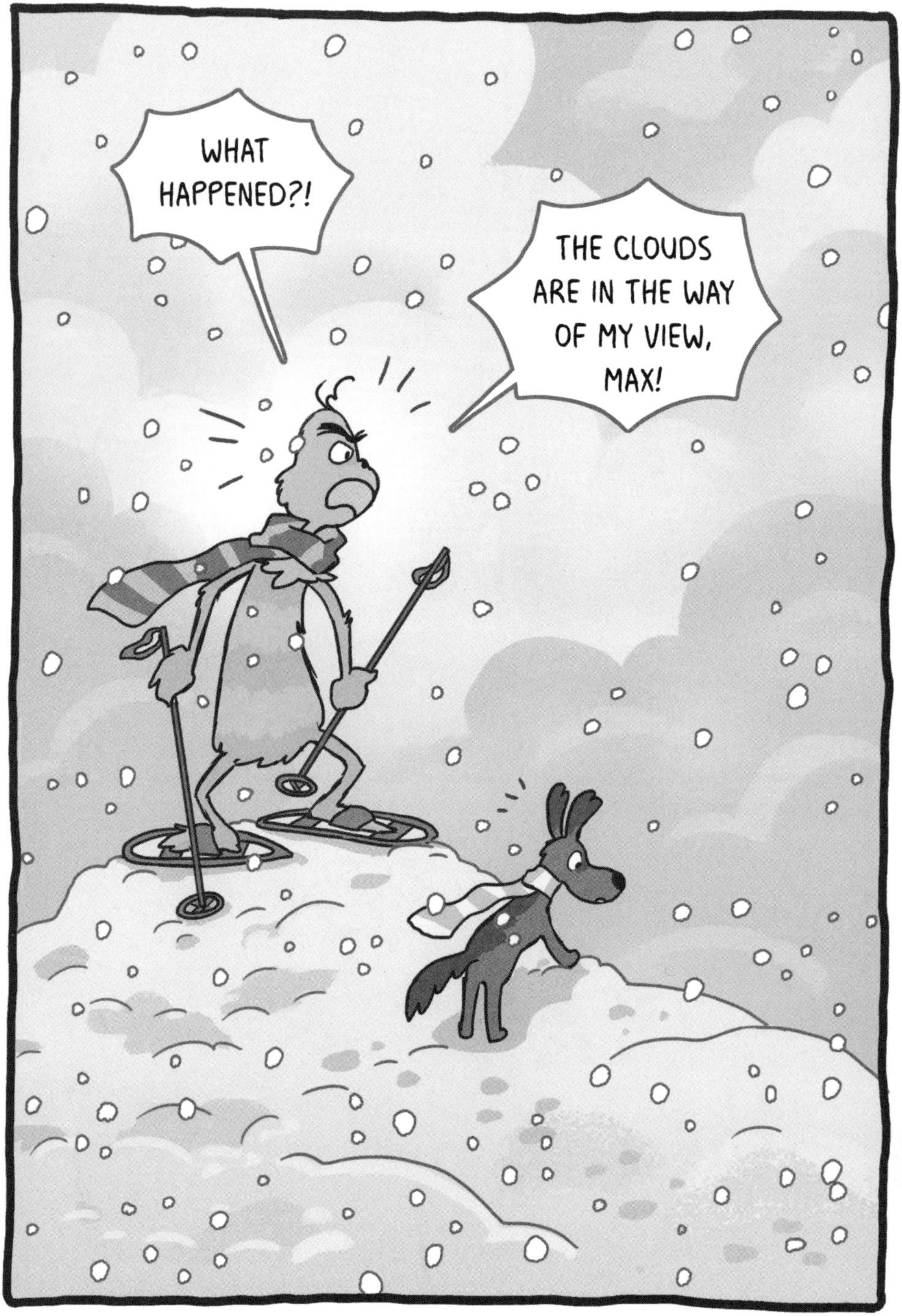
WHAT HAPPENED?!
THE CLOUDS ARE IN THE WAY OF MY VIEW, MAX!

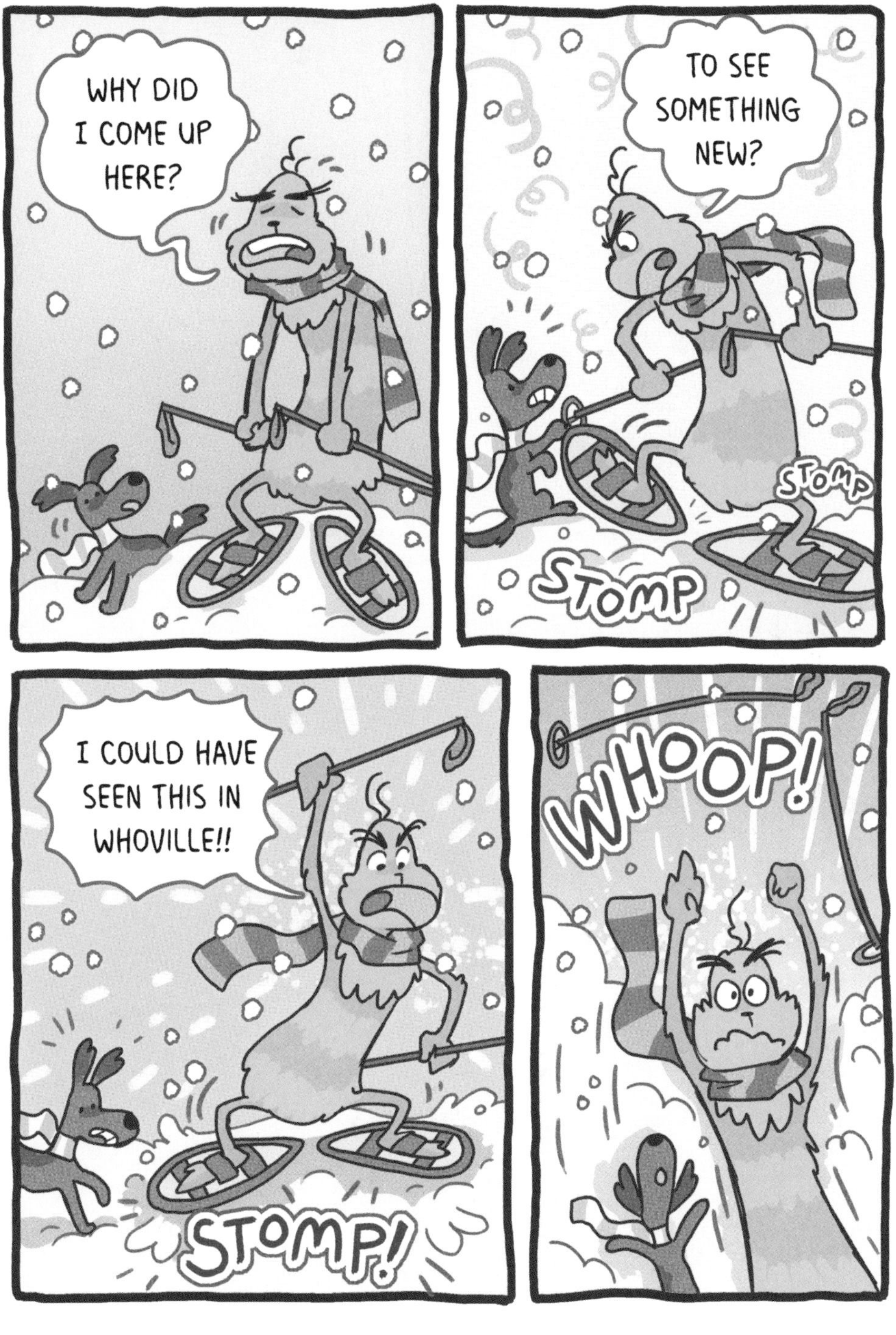
WHY DID I COME UP HERE?
TO SEE SOMETHING NEW?
STOMP
STOMP
I COULD HAVE SEEN THIS IN WHOVILLE!!
STOMP!
WHOOP!

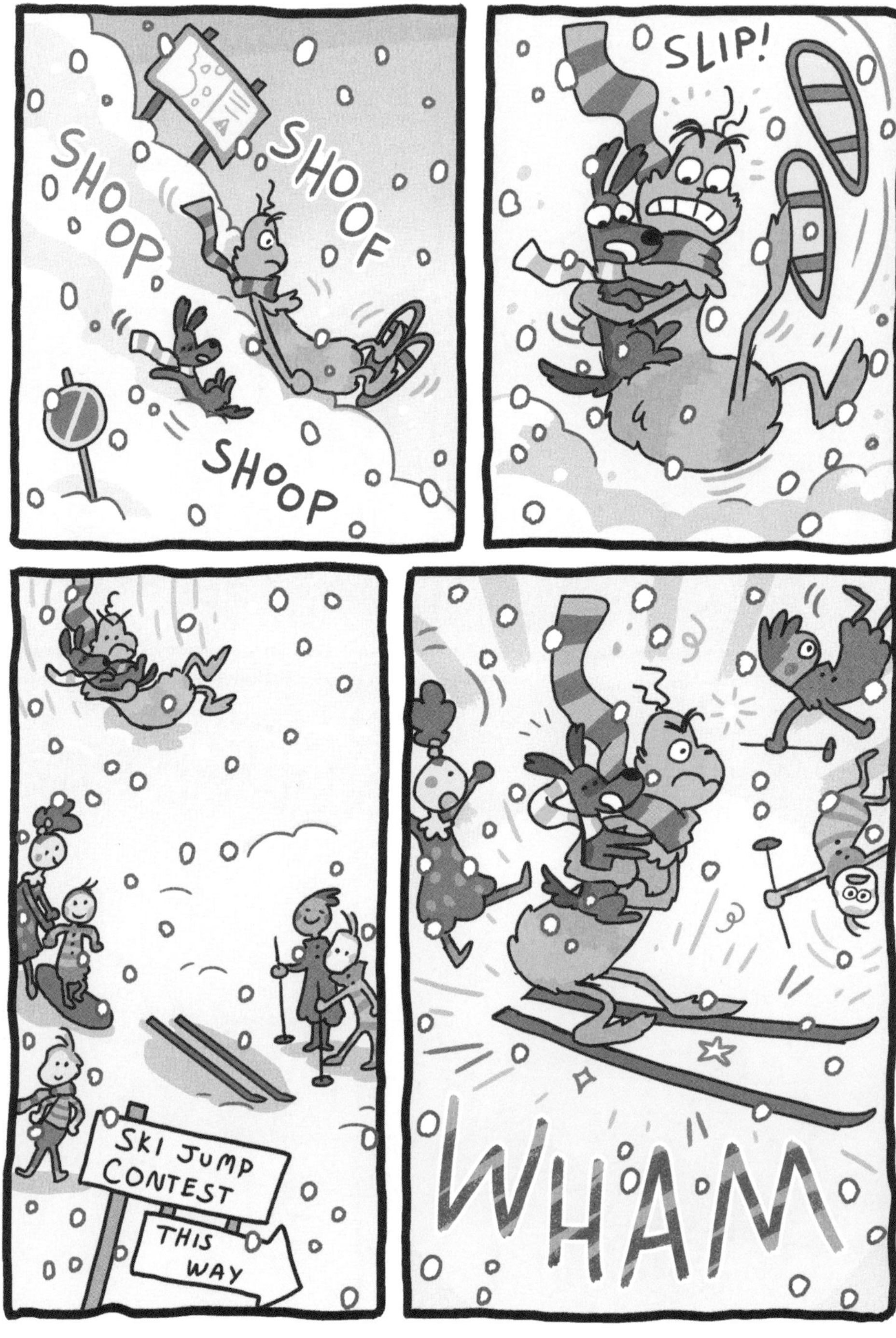
SHOOP
SHOOF
SHOOP
SLIP!
SKI JUMP CONTEST
THIS WAY
WHAM

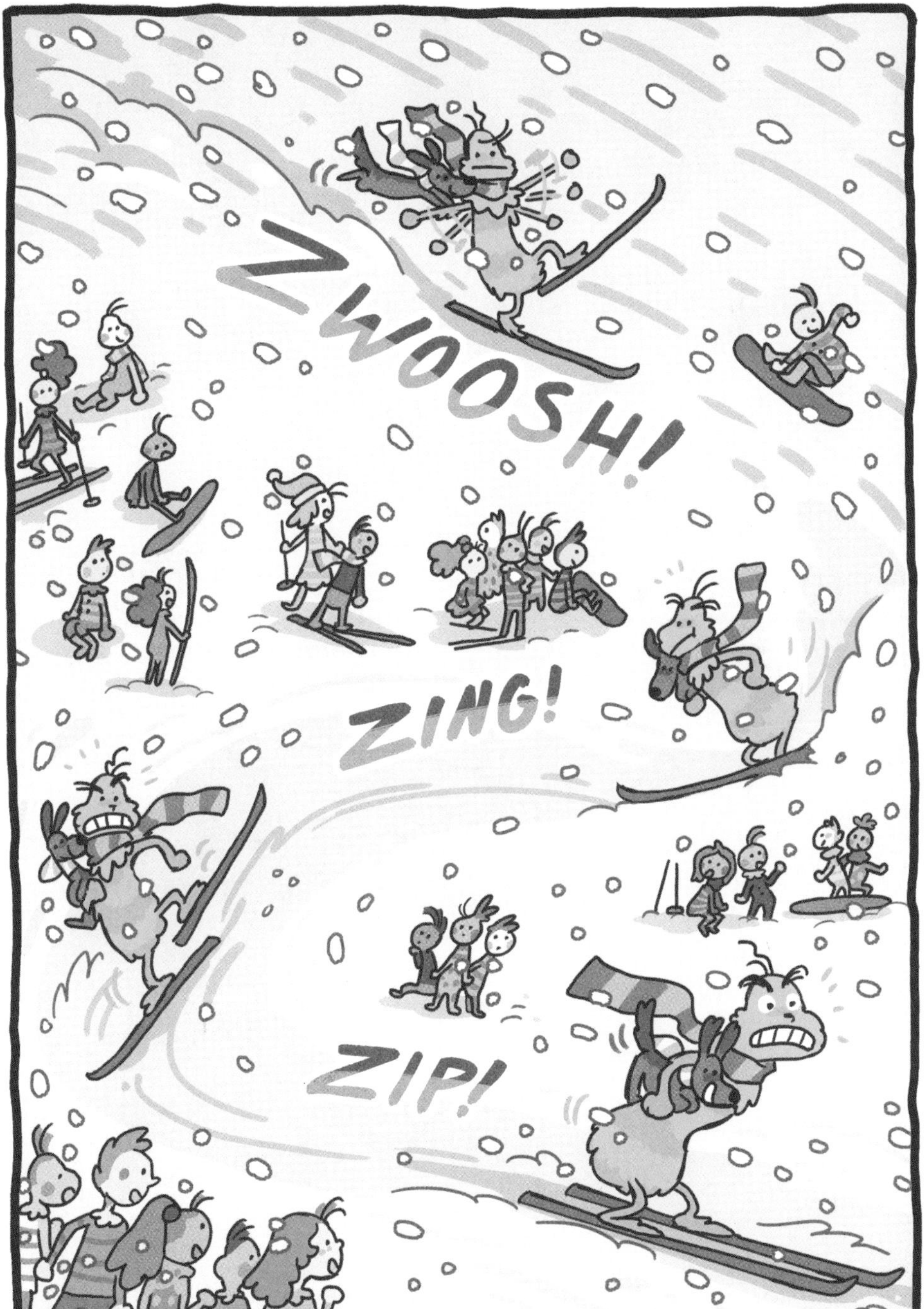
ZWOOSH!
ZING!
ZIP!

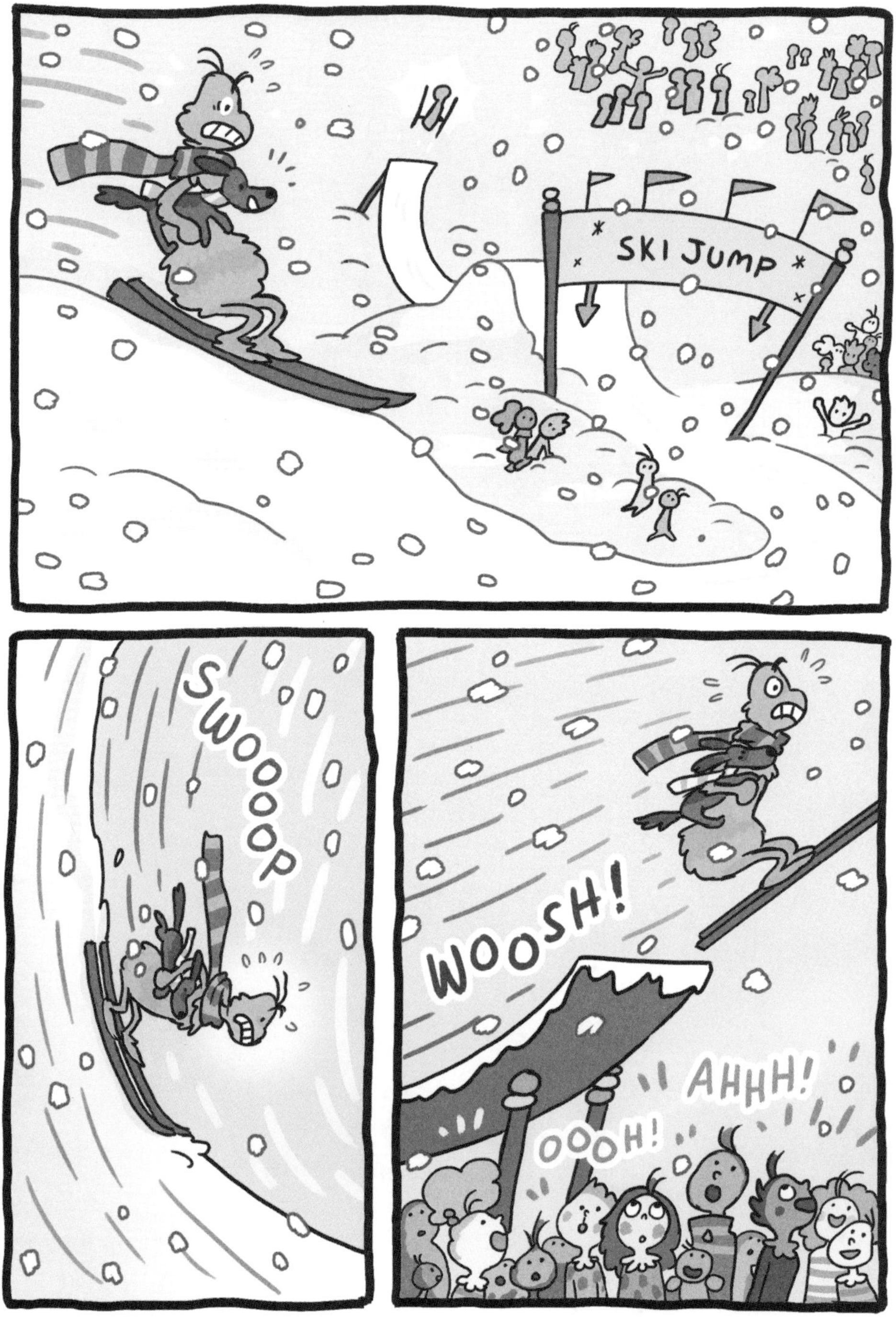
SKI JUMP
SWOOOOOP
WOOSH!
AHHH!
OOOH!

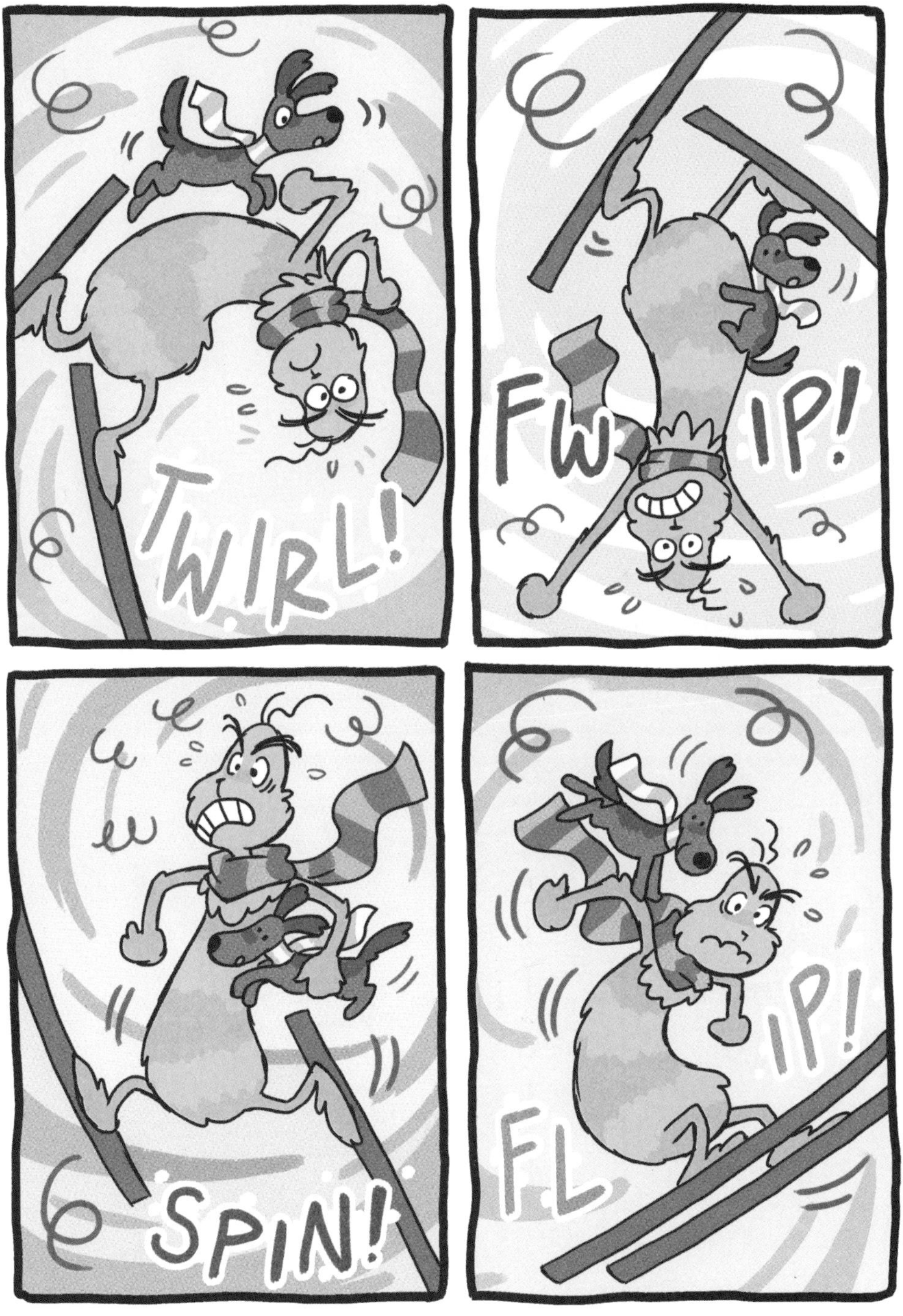
TWIRL!
FW IP!
SPIN!
FL IP!

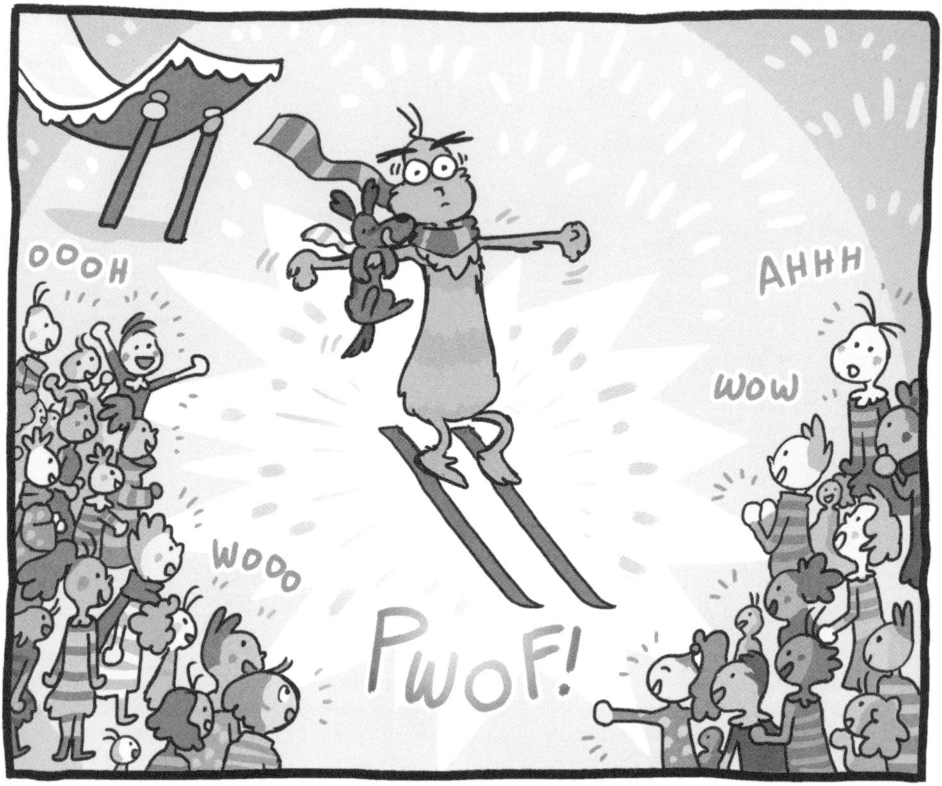
OOOH
AHHH
WOW
WOOO
PWOF!

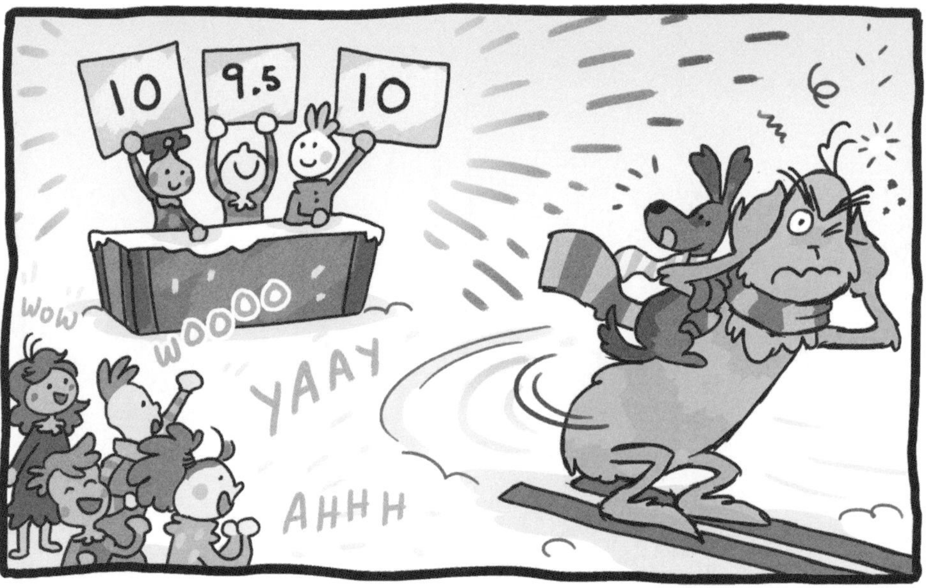
10
9.5
10
WOW
WOOOO
YAAY
AHHH

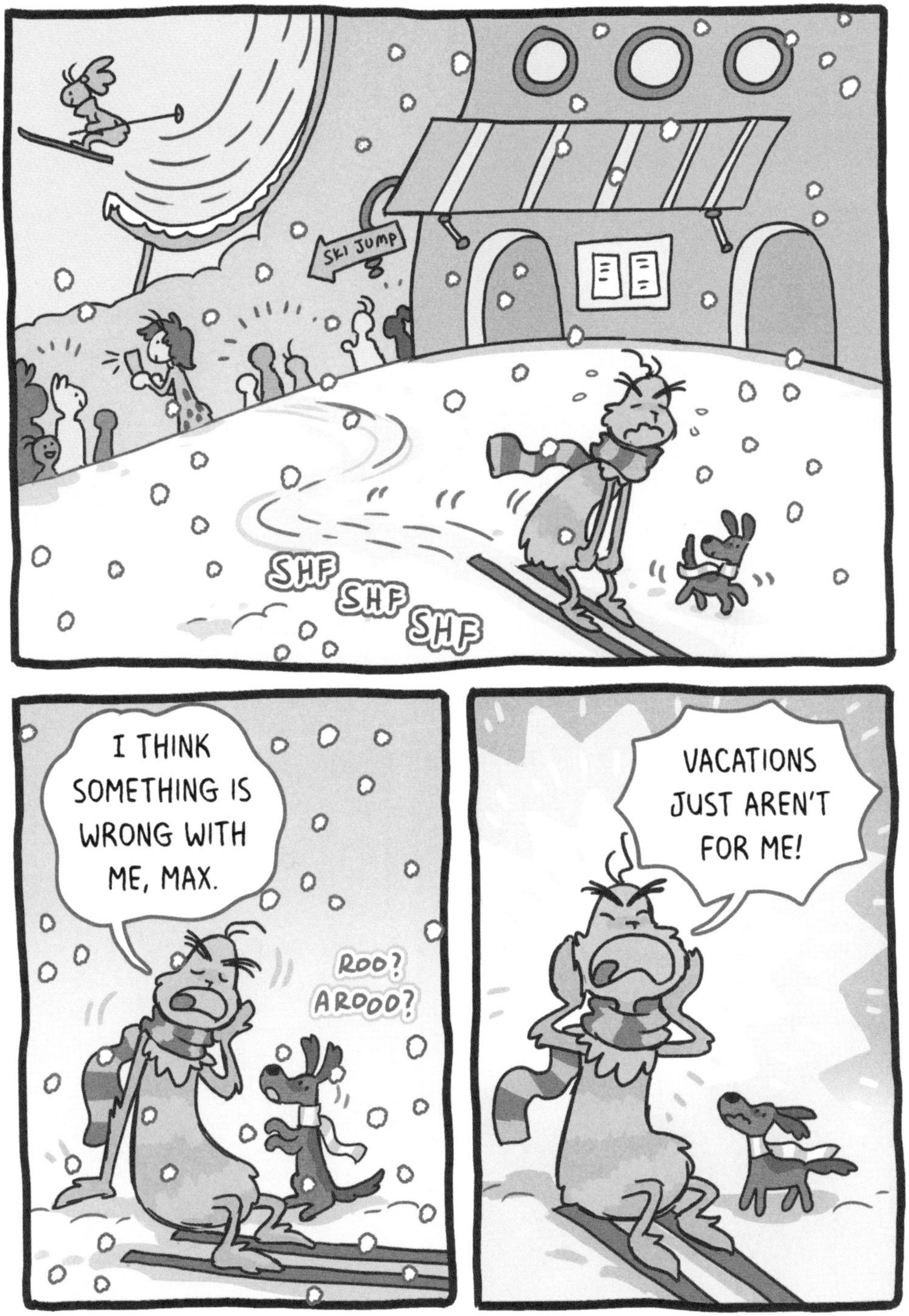
SKI JUMP
SHF
SHF
SHF
I THINK SOMETHING IS WRONG WITH ME, MAX.
ROO? AROOO?
VACATIONS JUST AREN'T FOR ME!

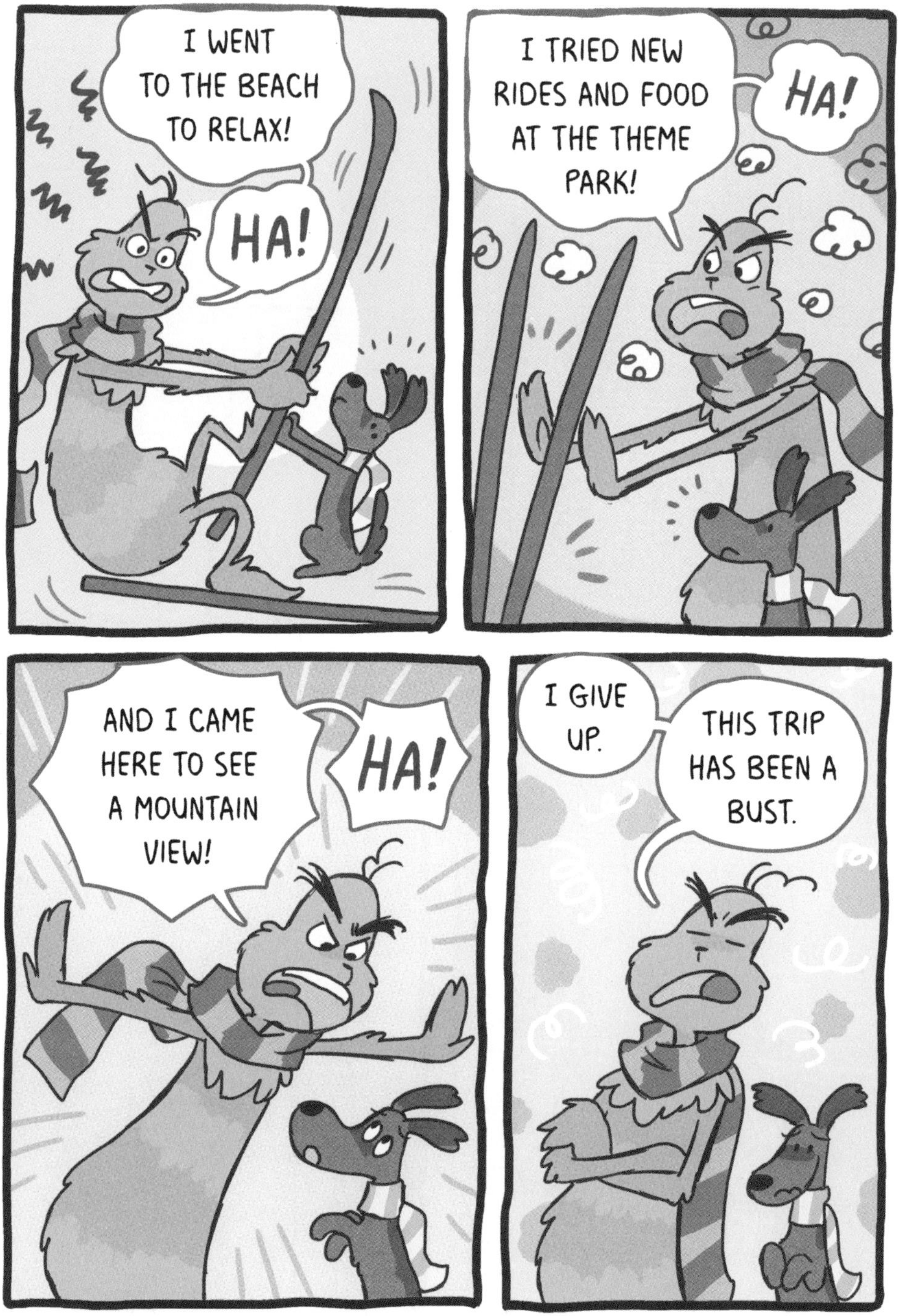
I WENT TO THE BEACH TO RELAX!
HA!
I TRIED NEW RIDES AND FOOD AT THE THEME PARK!
HA!
AND I CAME HERE TO SEE A MOUNTAIN VIEW!
HA!
I GIVE UP.
THIS TRIP HAS BEEN A BUST.

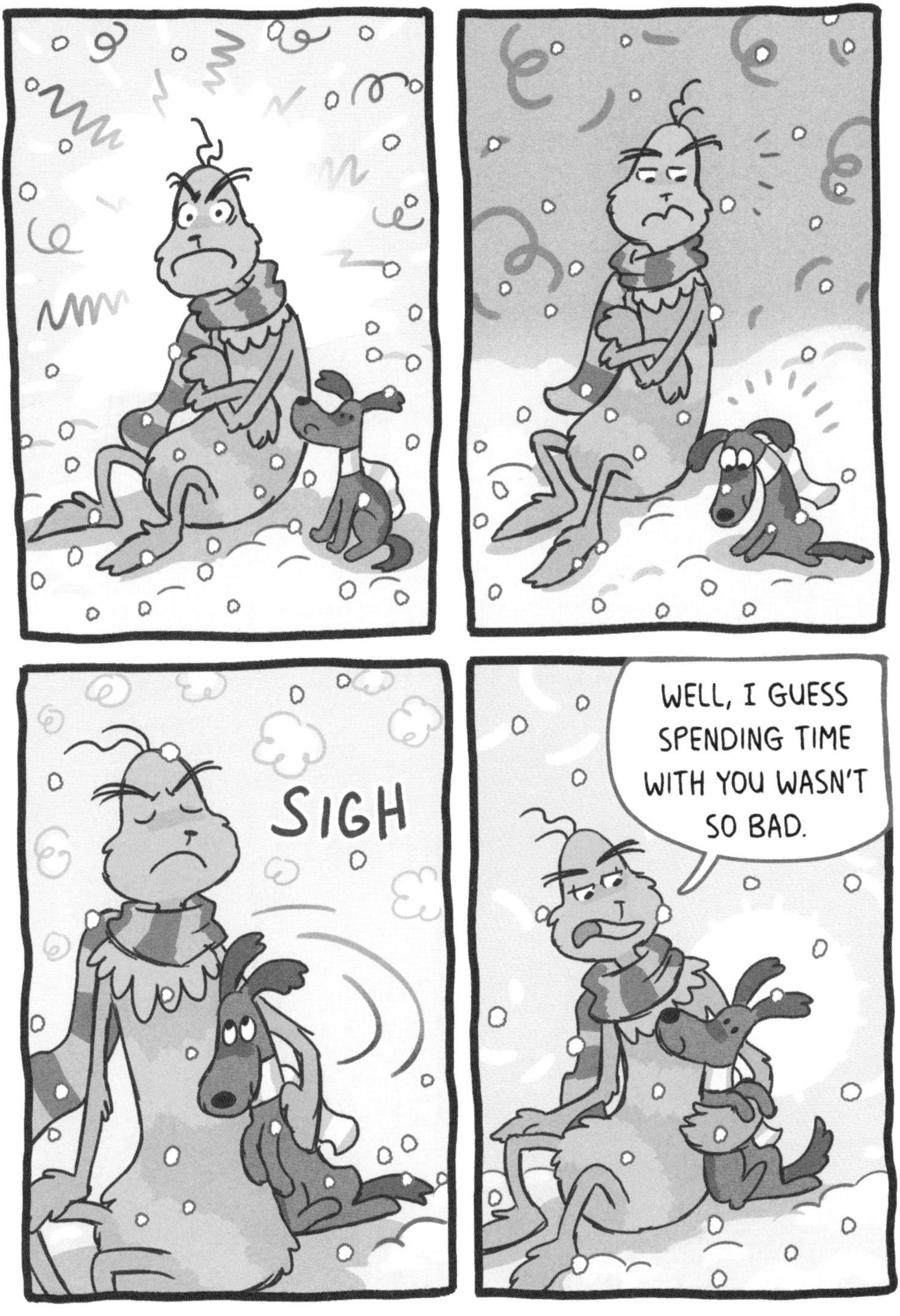
SIGH
WELL, I GUESS SPENDING TIME WITH YOU WASN'T SO BAD.

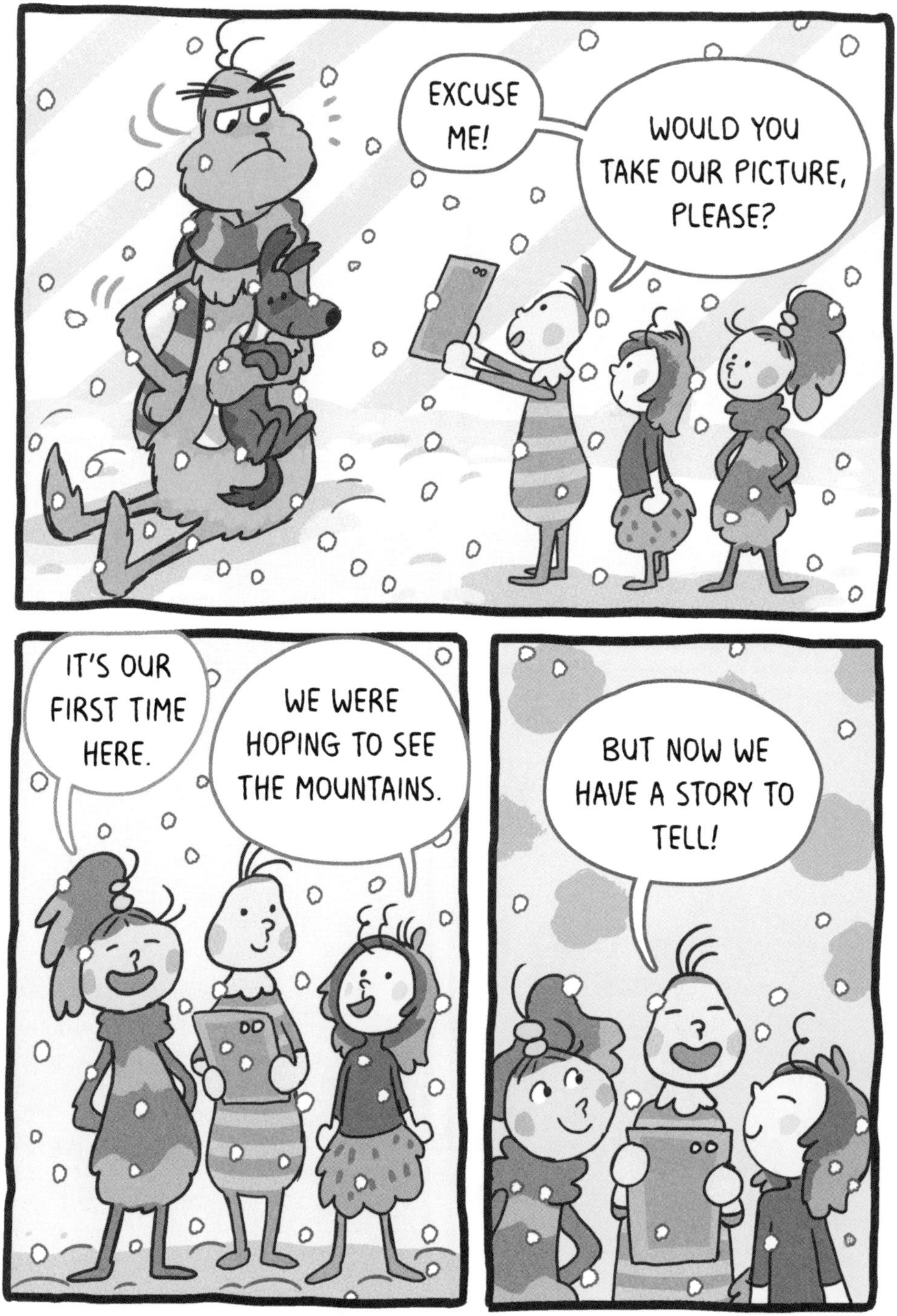
EXCUSE ME!
WOULD YOU TAKE OUR PICTURE, PLEASE?
IT'S OUR FIRST TIME HERE.
WE WERE HOPING TO SEE THE MOUNTAINS.
BUT NOW WE HAVE A STORY TO TELL!

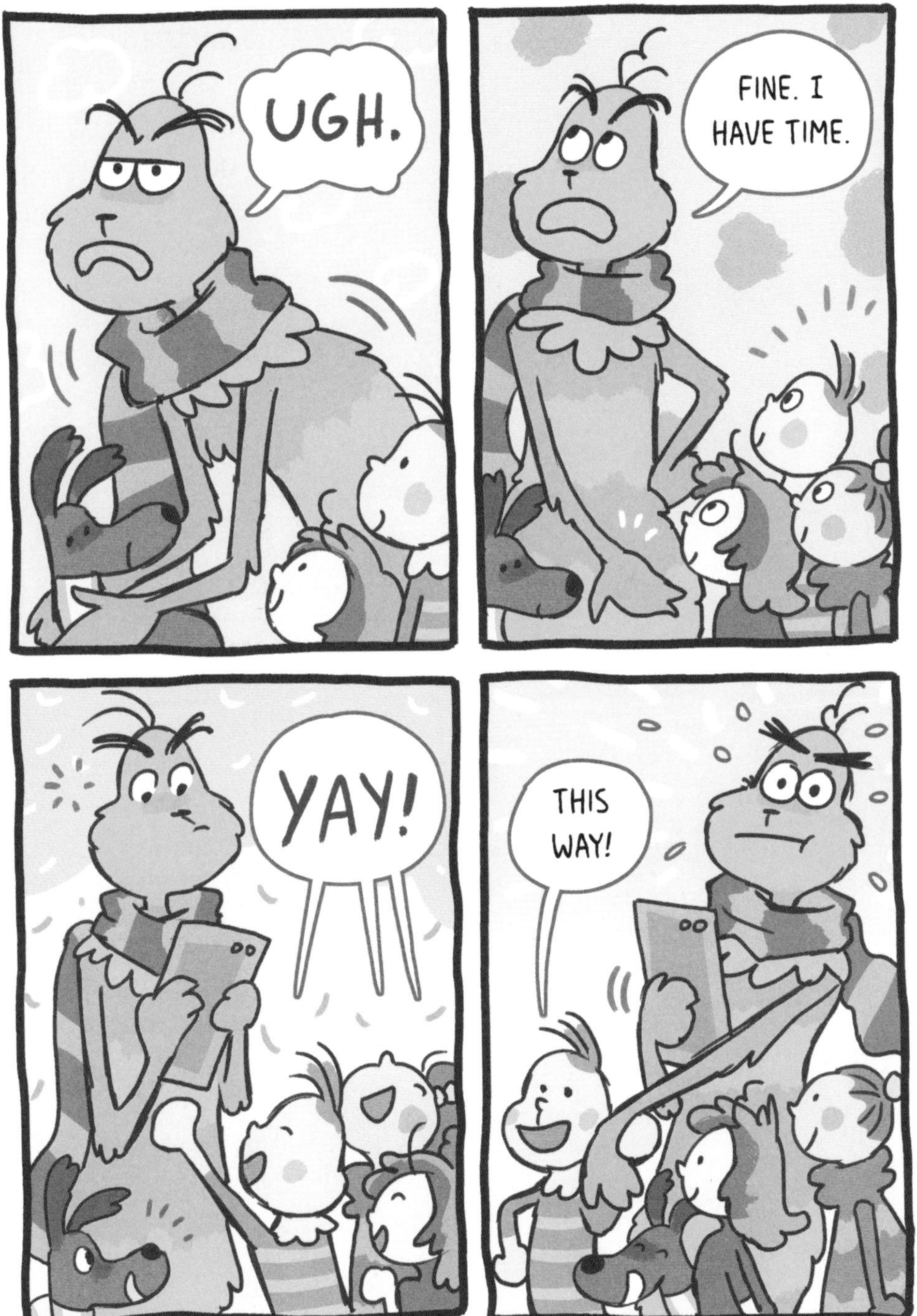
UGH.
FINE. I HAVE TIME.
YAY!
THIS WAY!

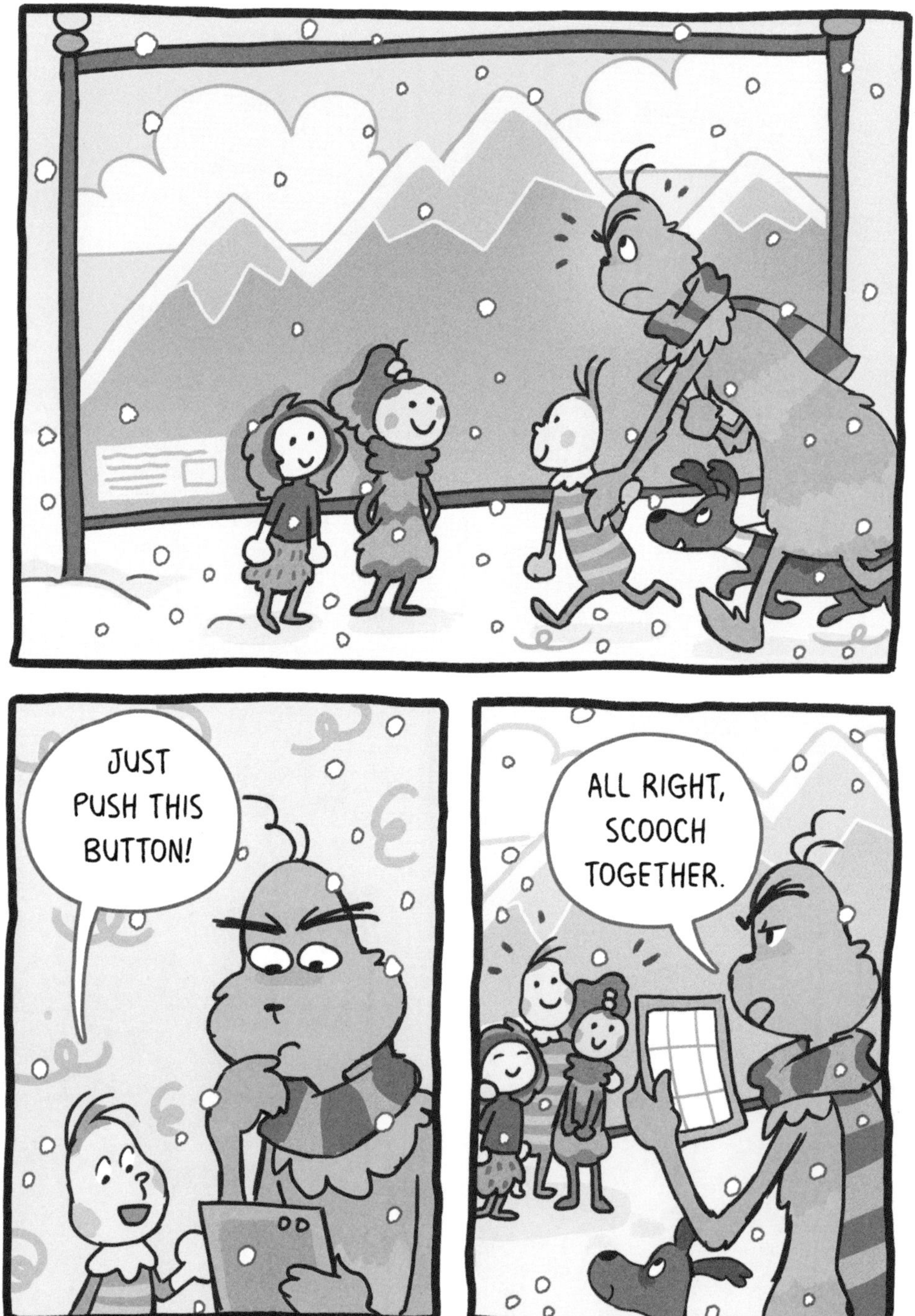
JUST PUSH THIS BUTTON!
ALL RIGHT, SCOOCH TOGETHER.

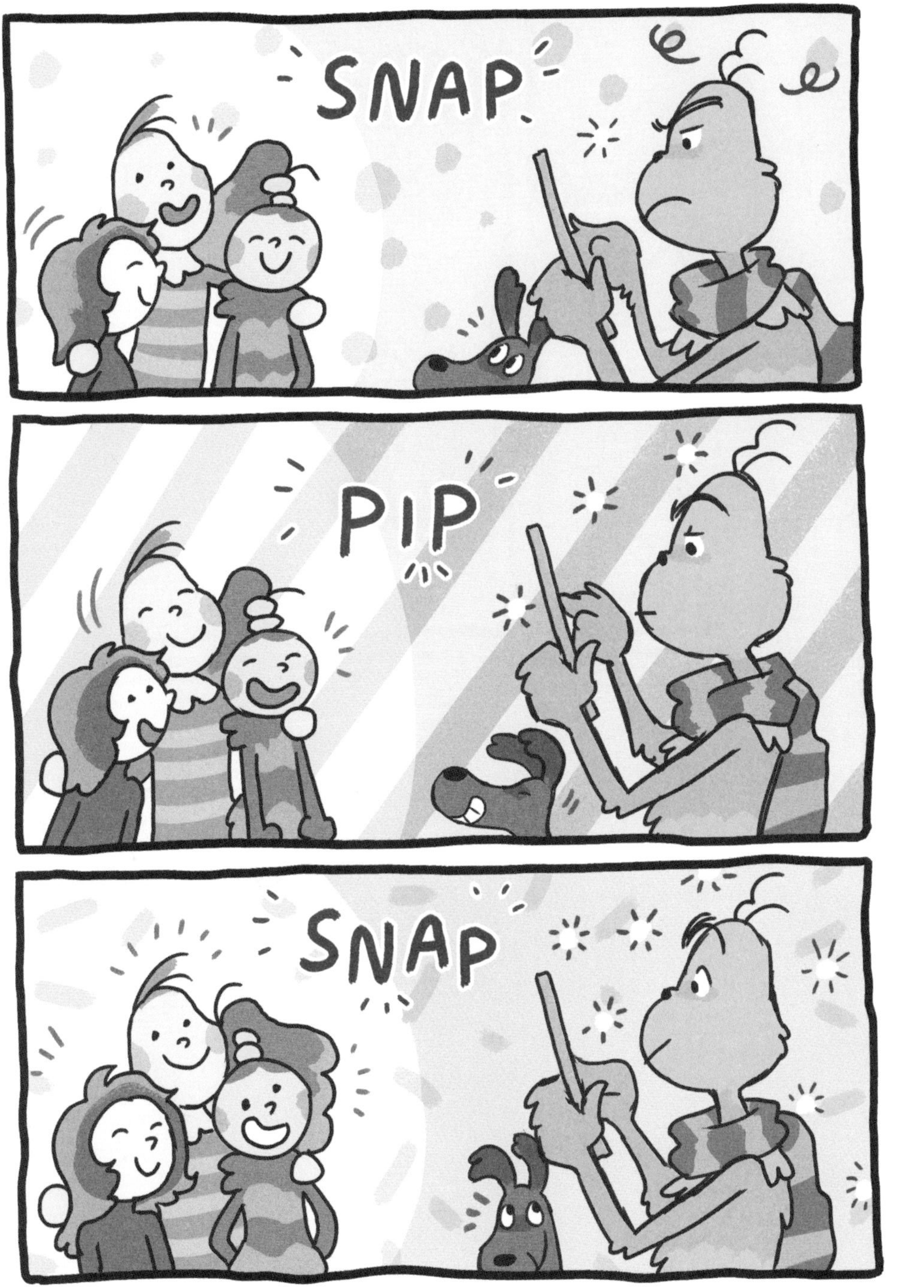
SNAP
PIP
SNAP

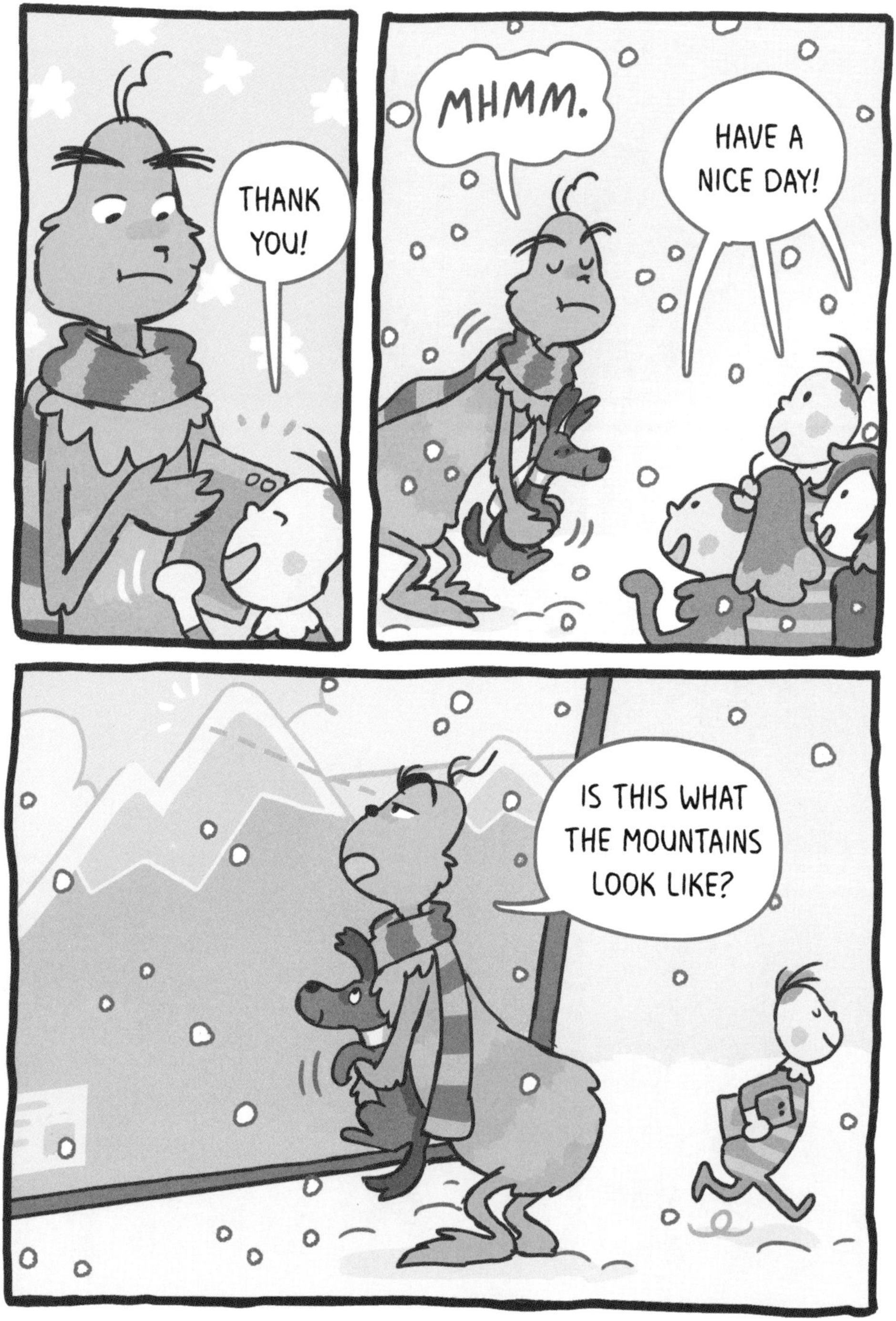
THANK YOU!
MHMM.
HAVE A NICE DAY!
IS THIS WHAT THE MOUNTAINS LOOK LIKE?

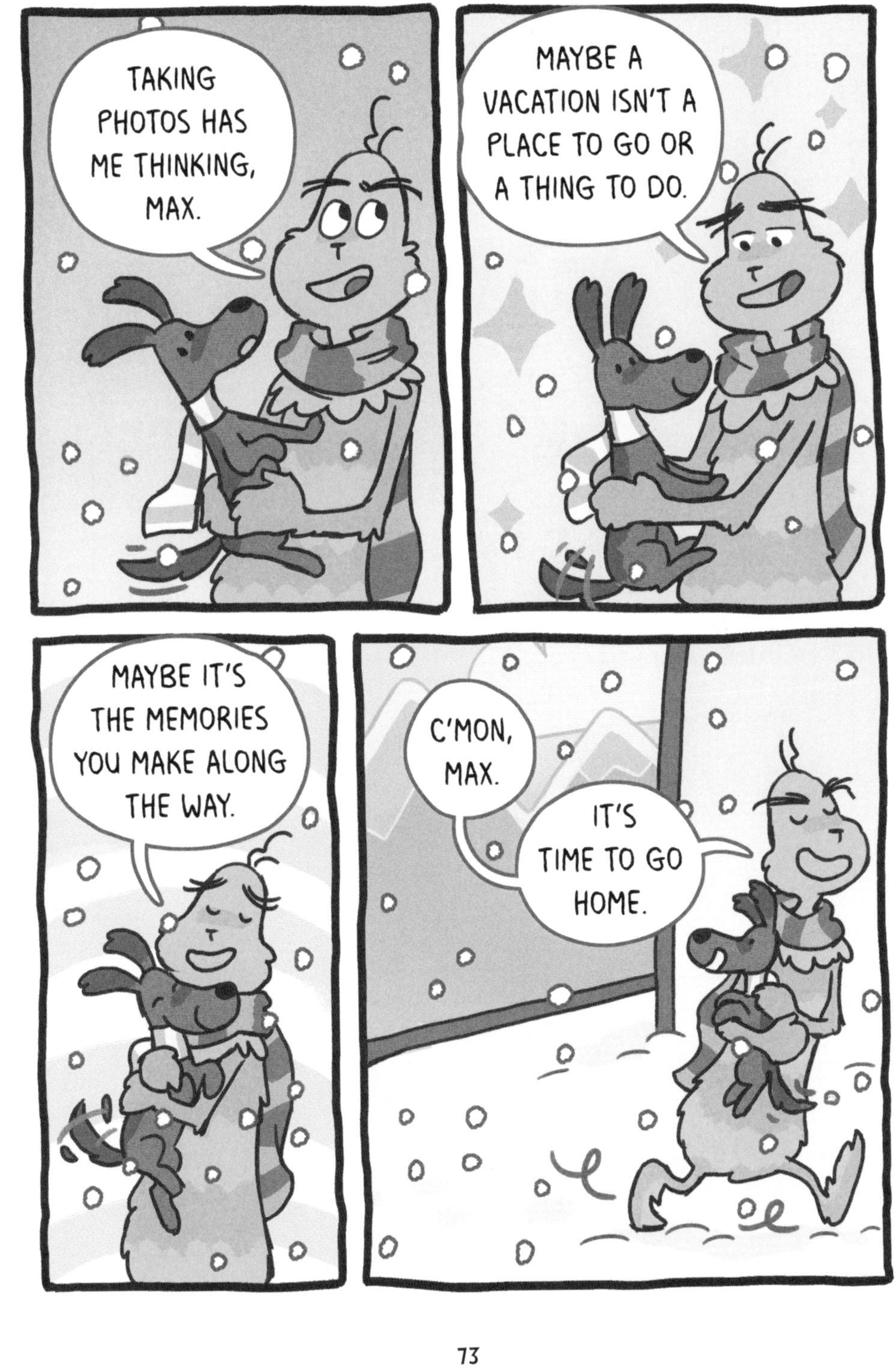
TAKING PHOTOS HAS ME THINKING, MAX.
MAYBE A VACATION ISN'T A PLACE TO GO OR A THING TO DO.
MAYBE IT'S THE MEMORIES YOU MAKE ALONG THE WAY.
C'MON, MAX.
IT'S TIME TO GO HOME.

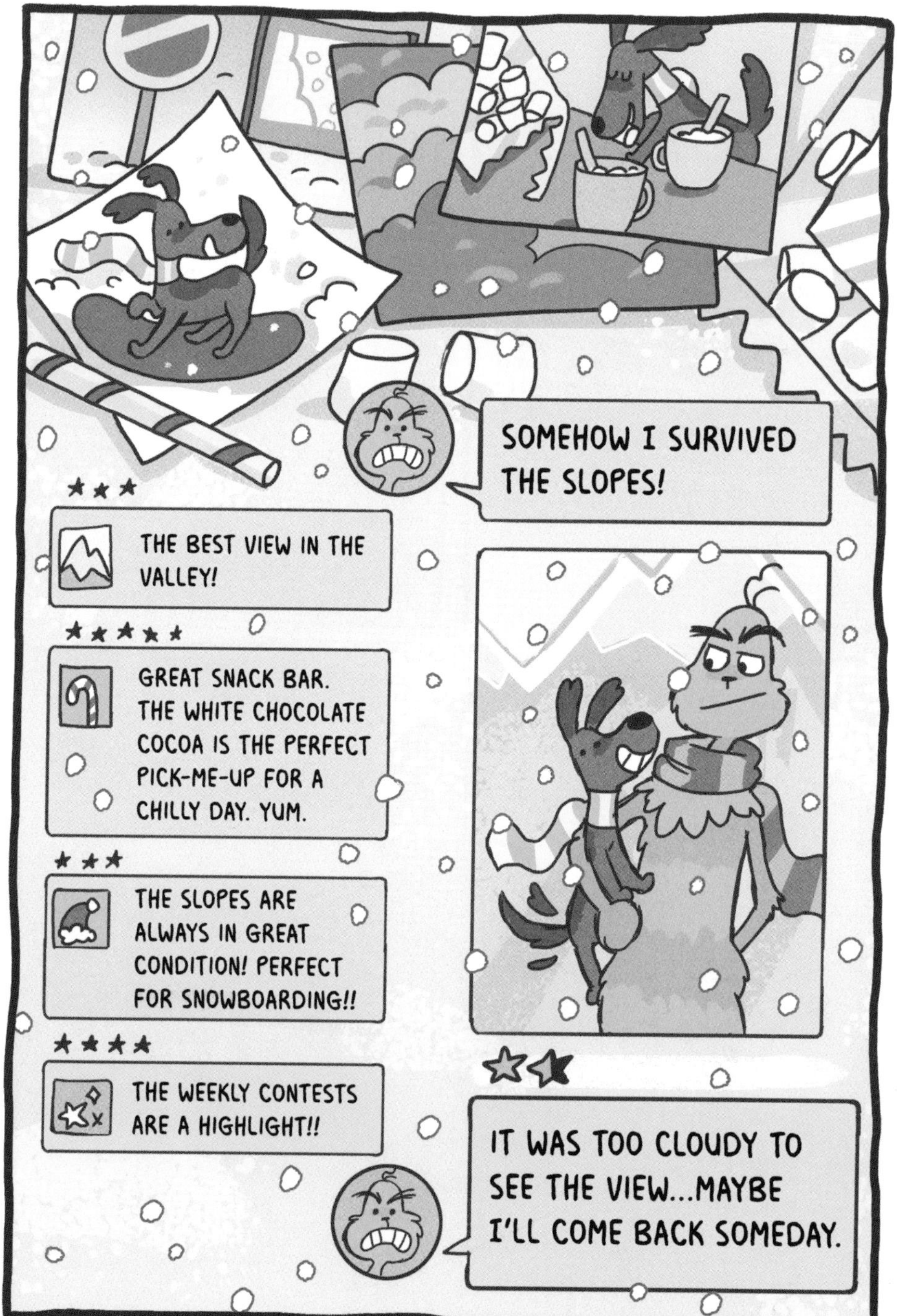

SOMEHOW I SURVIVED THE SLOPES!
THE BEST VIEW IN THE VALLEY!
GREAT SNACK BAR. THE WHITE CHOCOLATE COCOA IS THE PERFECT PICK-ME-UP FOR A CHILLY DAY. YUM.
THE SLOPES ARE ALWAYS IN GREAT CONDITION! PERFECT FOR SNOWBOARDING!!
THE WEEKLY CONTESTS ARE A HIGHLIGHT!!
IT WAS TOO CLOUDY TO SEE THE VIEW...MAYBE I'LL COME BACK SOMEDAY.

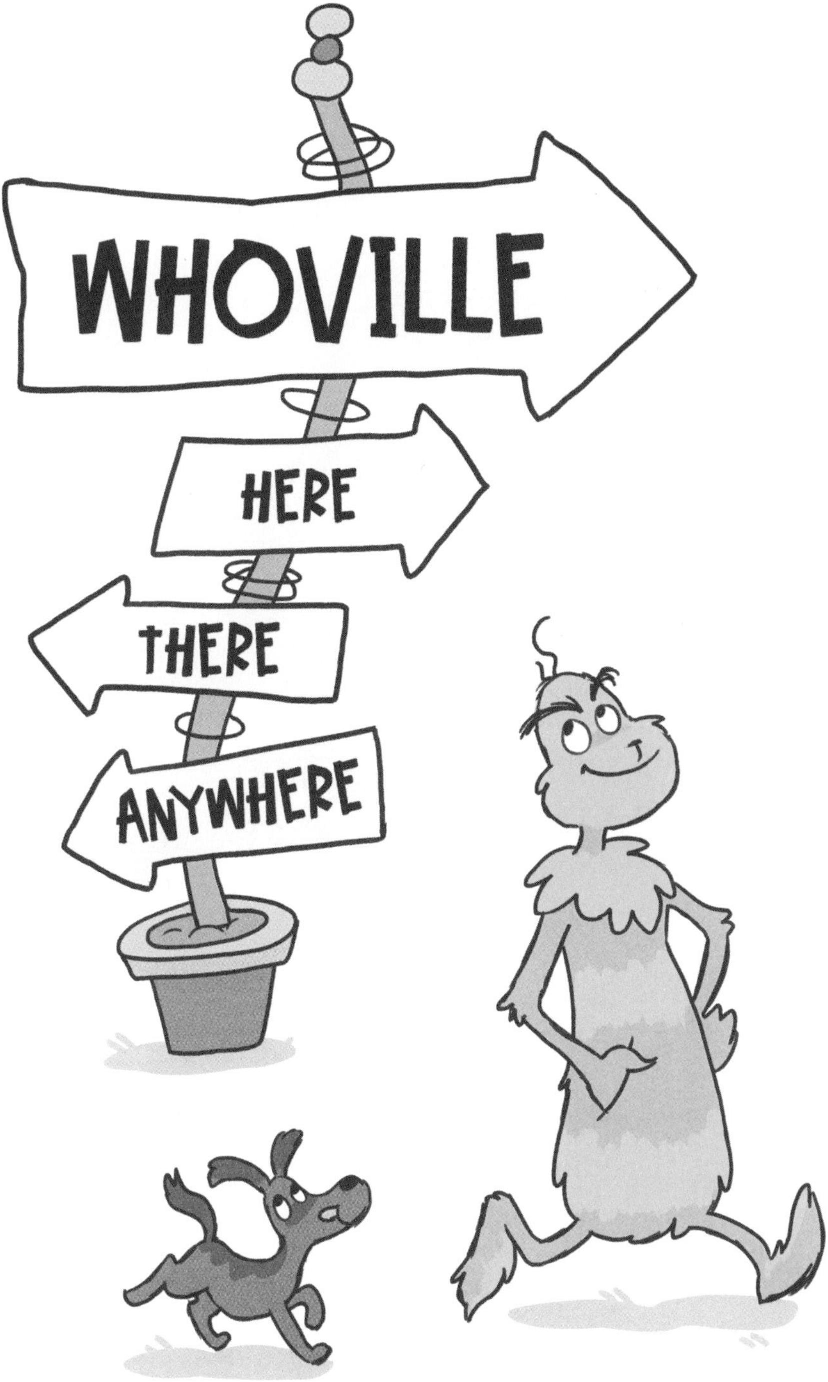
WHOVILLE
HERE
THERE
ANYWHERE

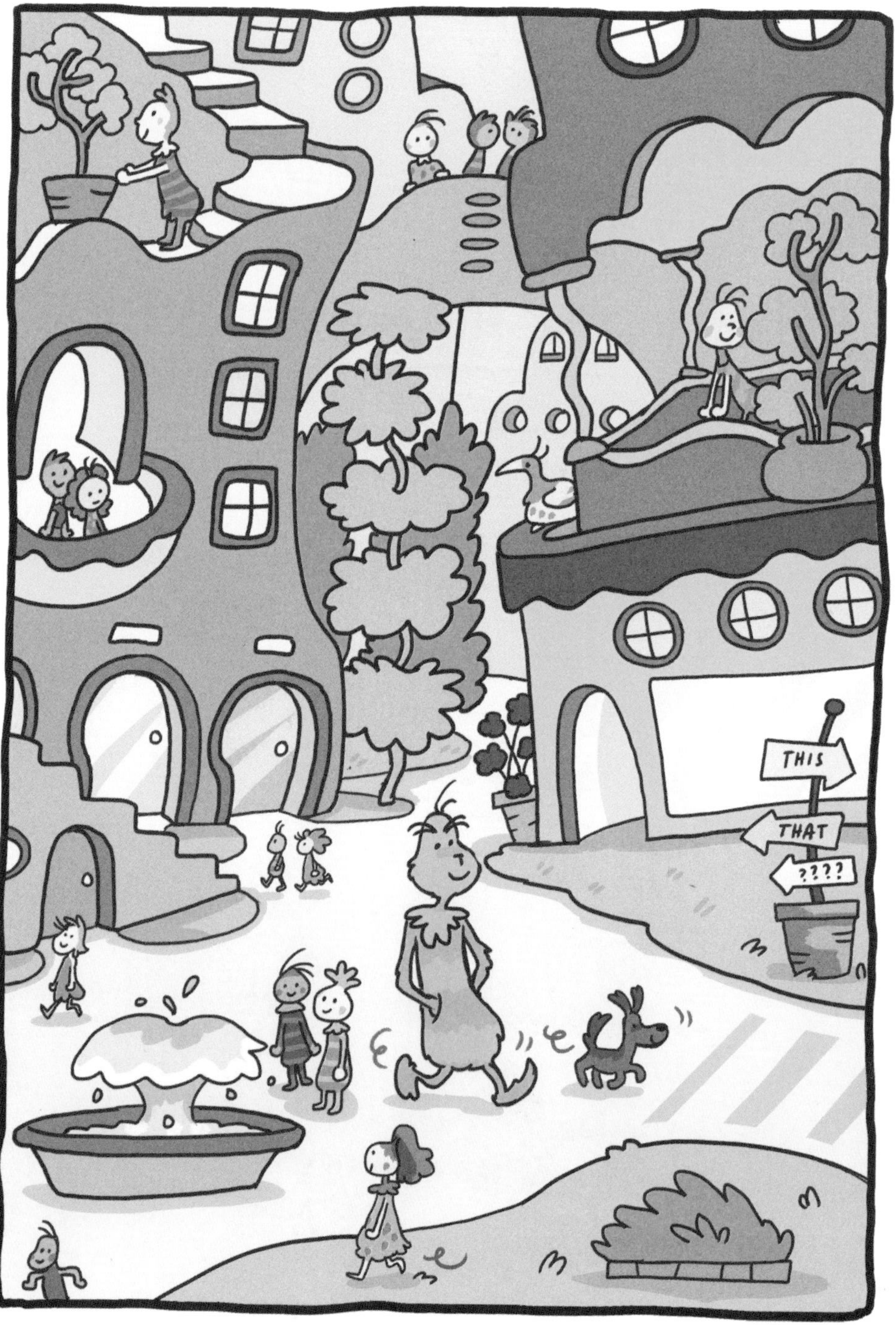
THIS
THAT
????

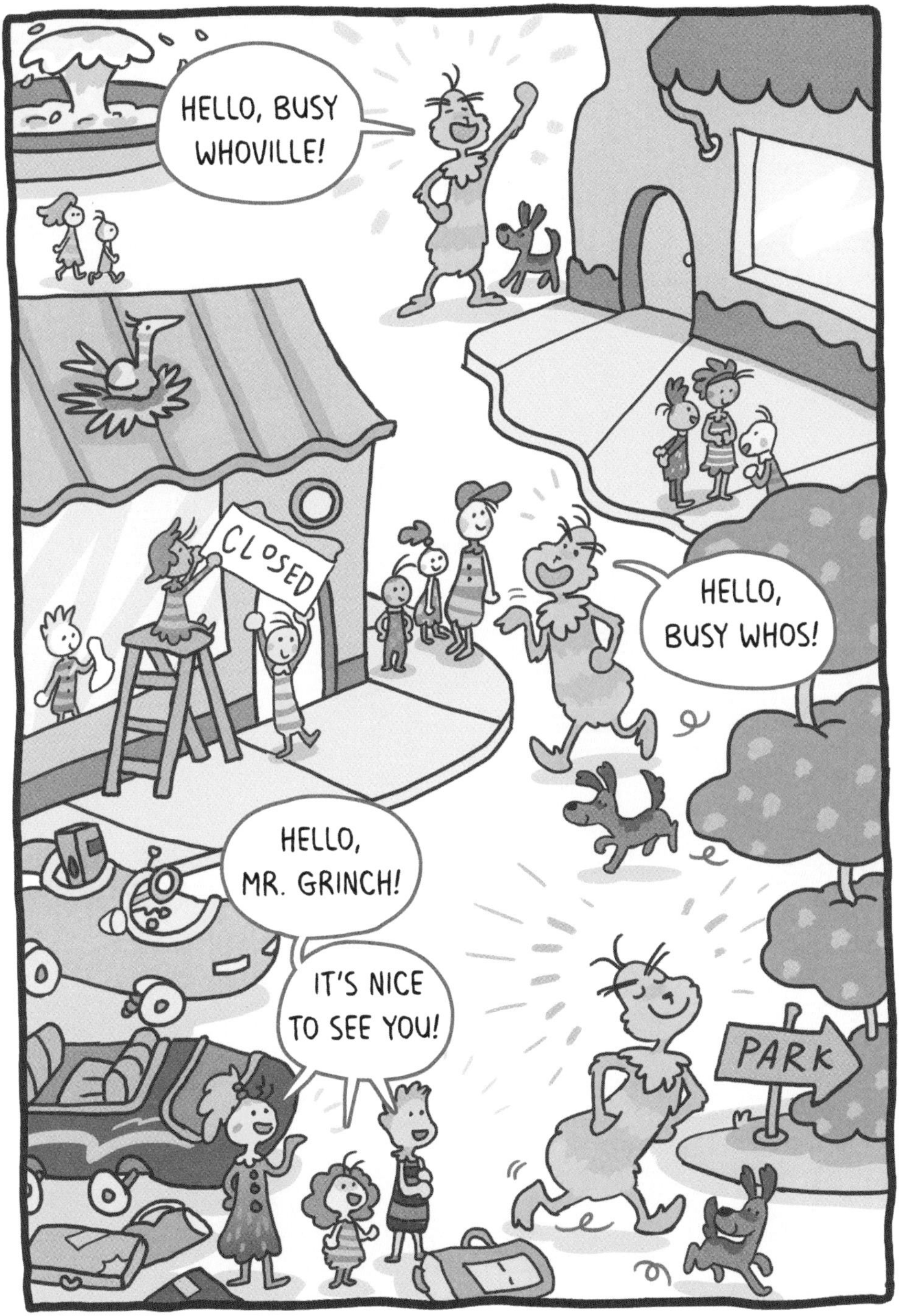
HELLO, BUSY WHOVILLE!
CLOSED
HELLO, BUSY WHOS!
HELLO, MR. GRINCH!
IT'S NICE TO SEE YOU!
PARK

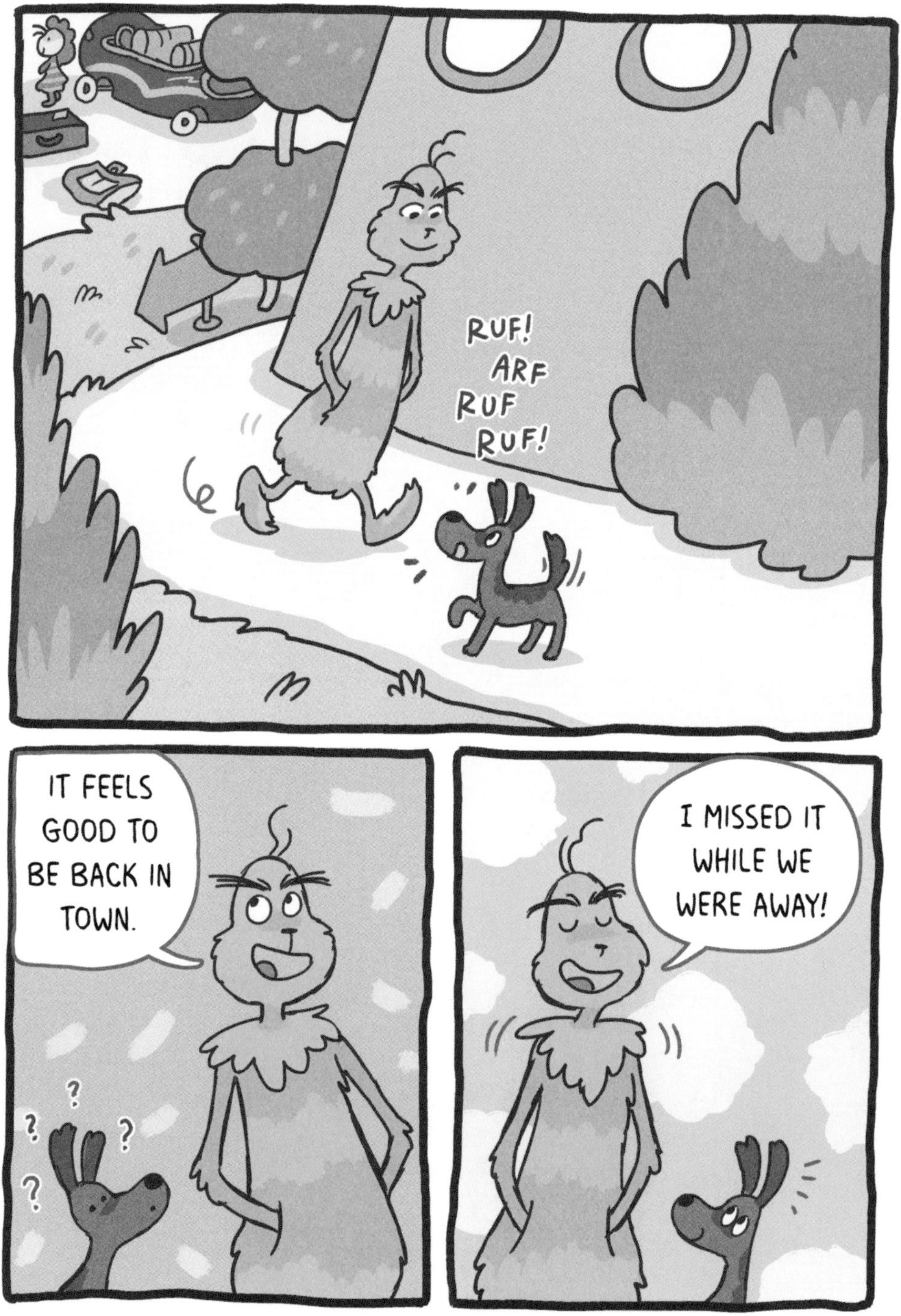
RUF!
ARF
RUF
RUF!
IT FEELS GOOD TO BE BACK IN TOWN.
I MISSED IT WHILE WE WERE AWAY!

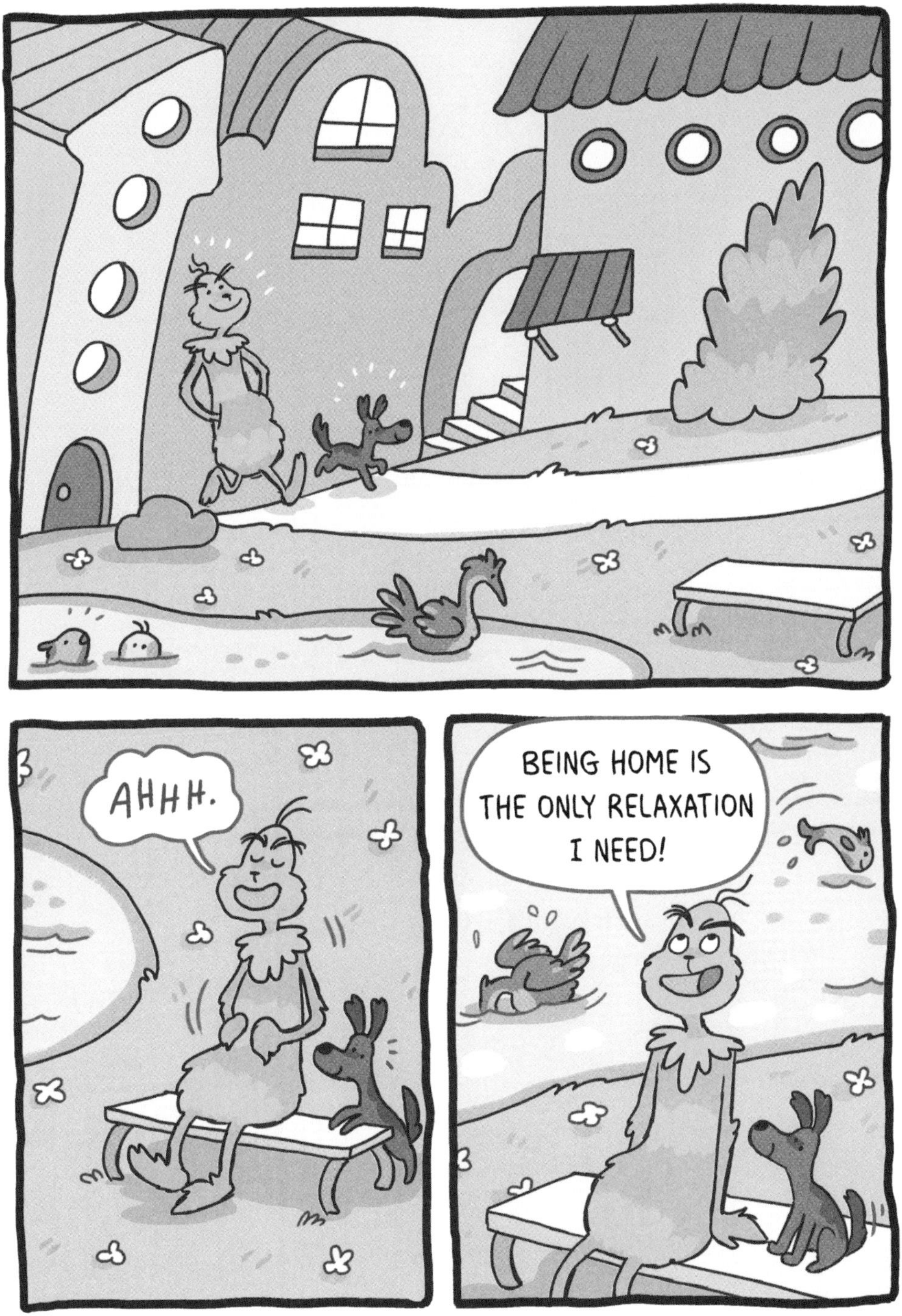
AHHH.
BEING HOME IS THE ONLY RELAXATION I NEED!

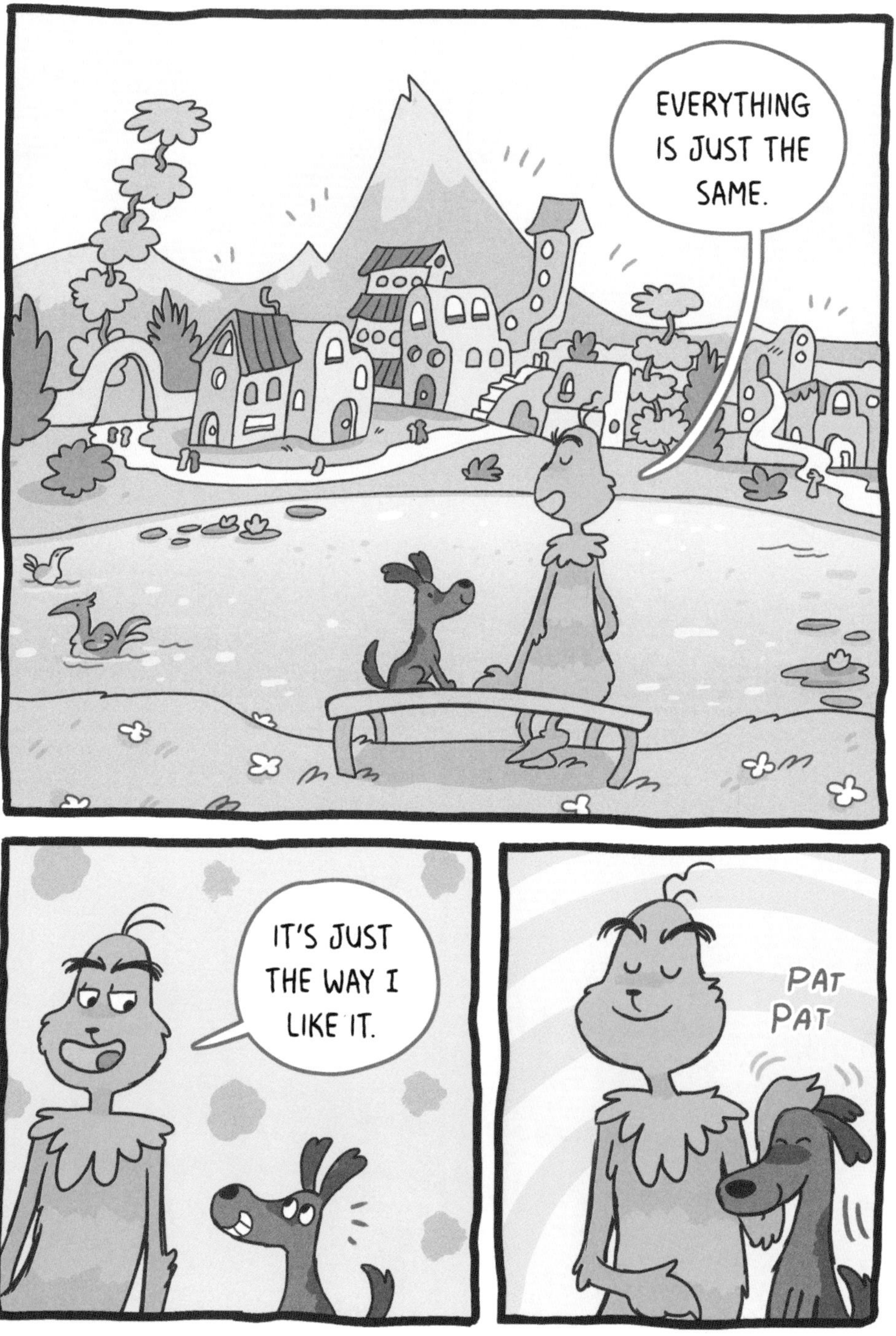
EVERYTHING IS JUST THE SAME.
IT'S JUST THE WAY I LIKE IT.
PAT PAT

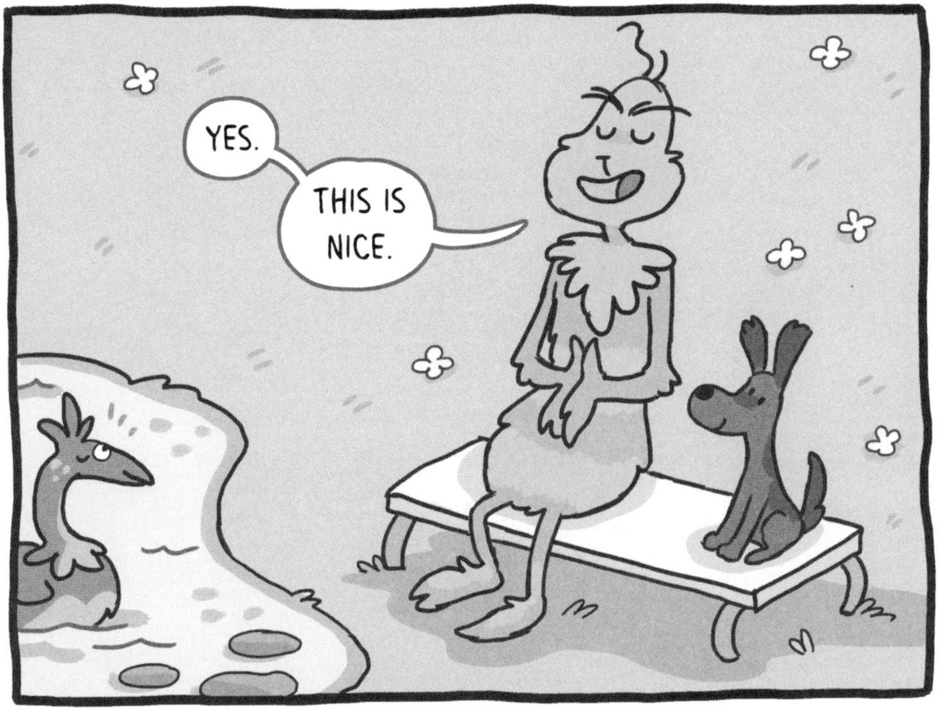
YES.
THIS IS NICE.

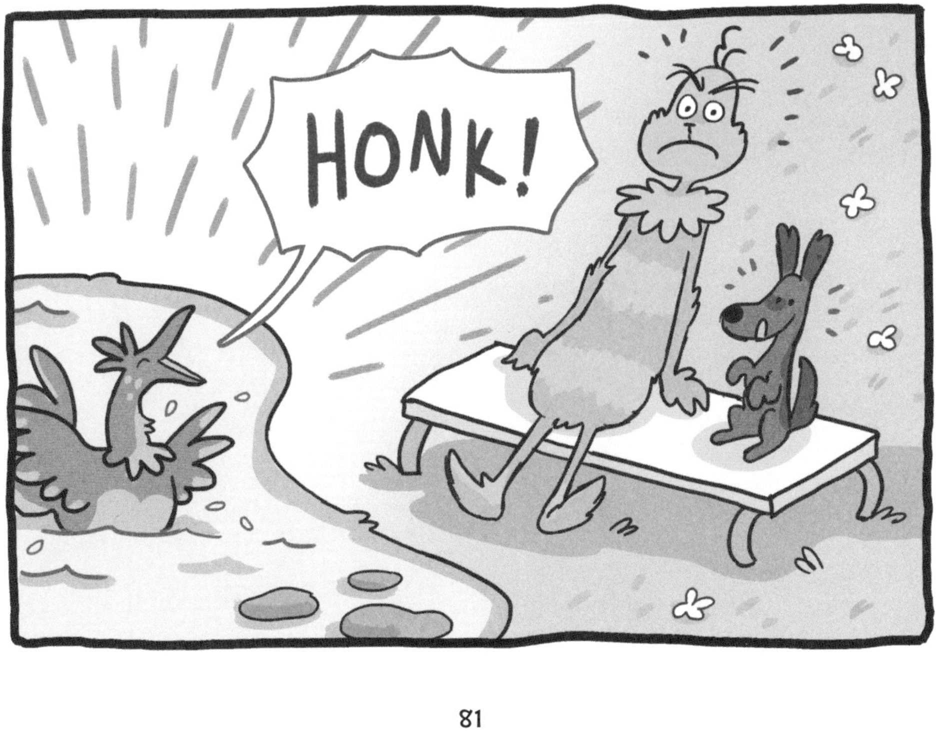
HONK!

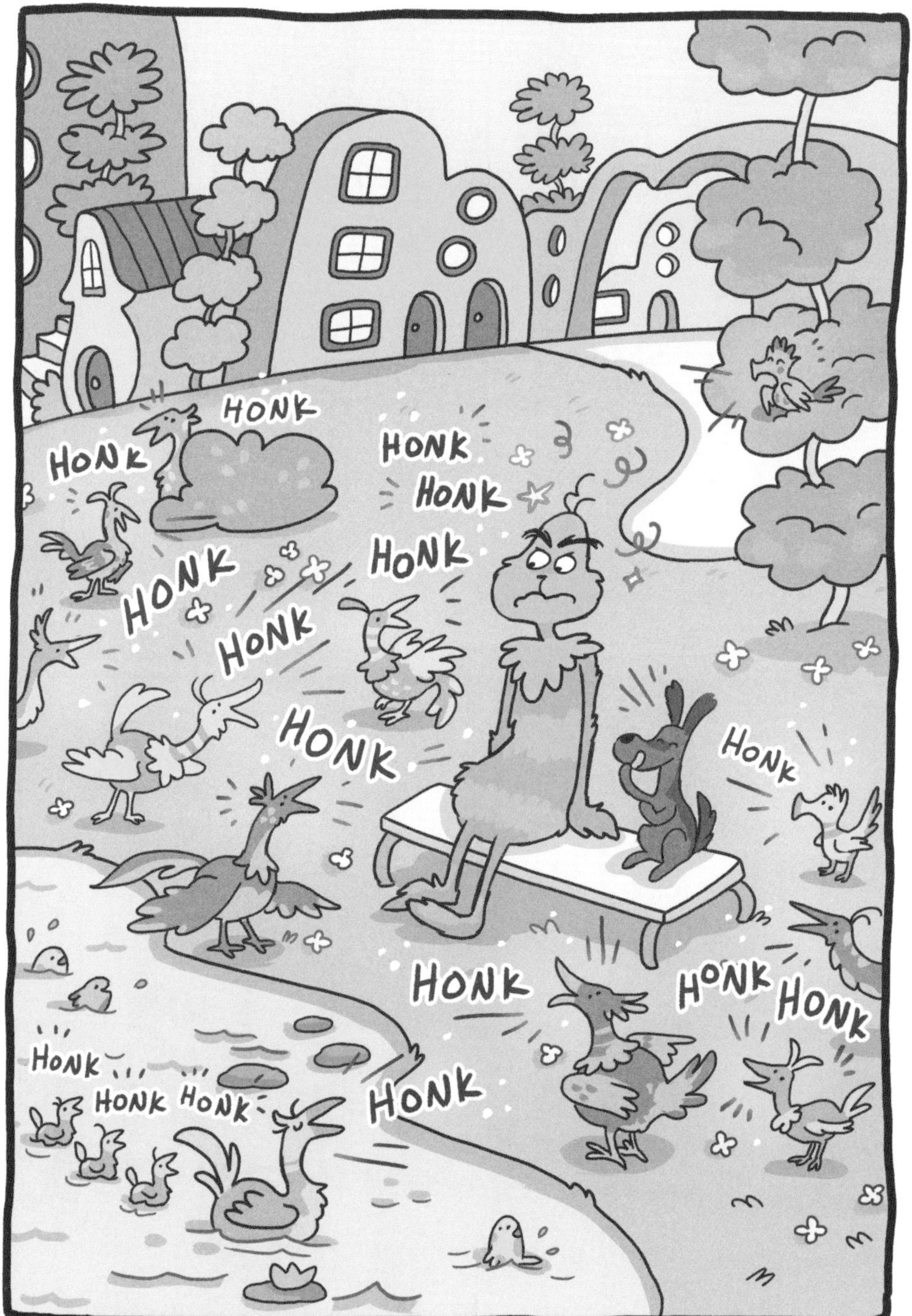
HONK
HONK
HONK
HONK
HONK
HONK
HONK
HONK
HONK
HONK
HONK
HONK
HONK
HONK
HONK
HONK
HONK

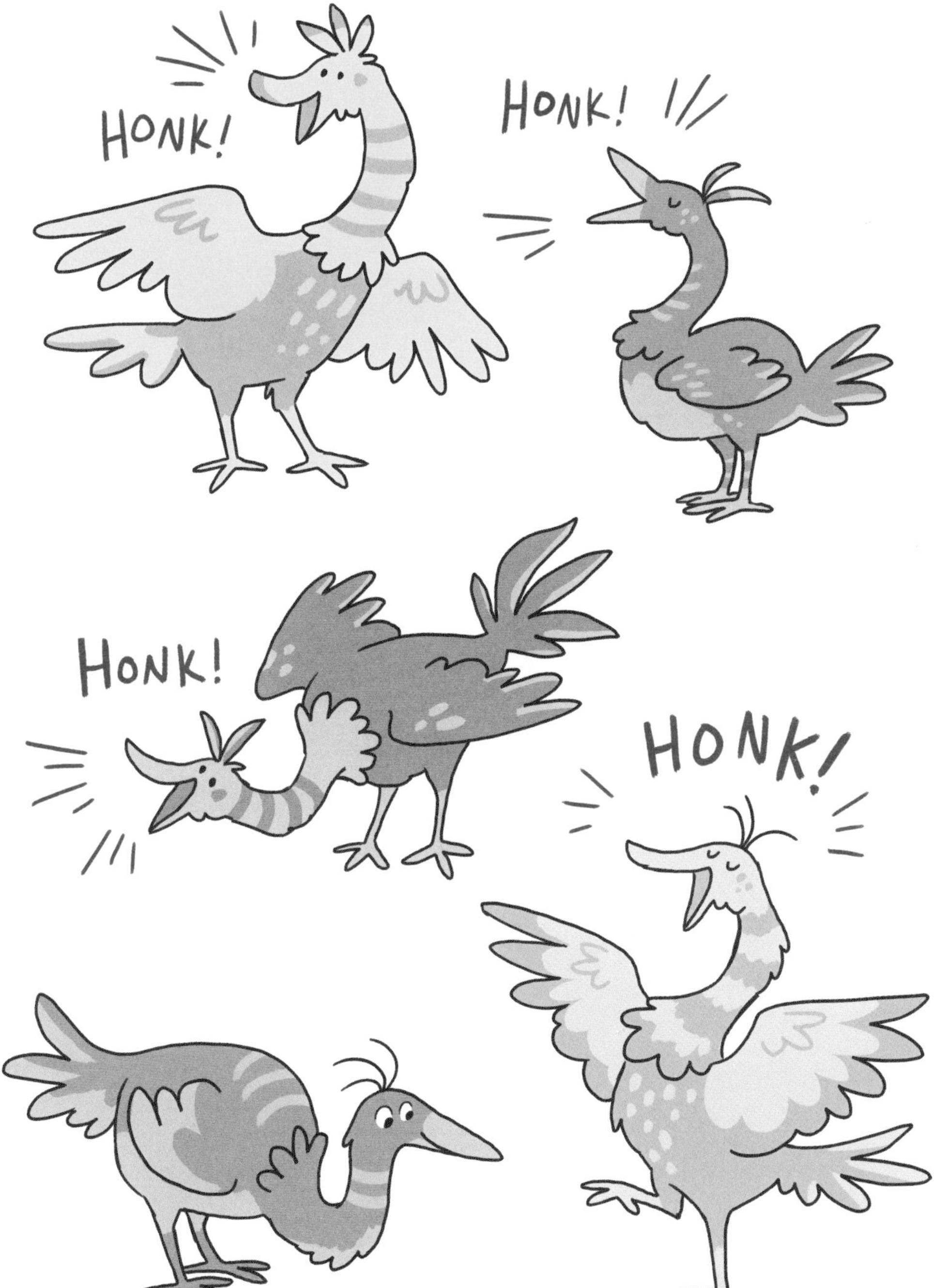
HONK!
HONK!
HONK!
HONK!

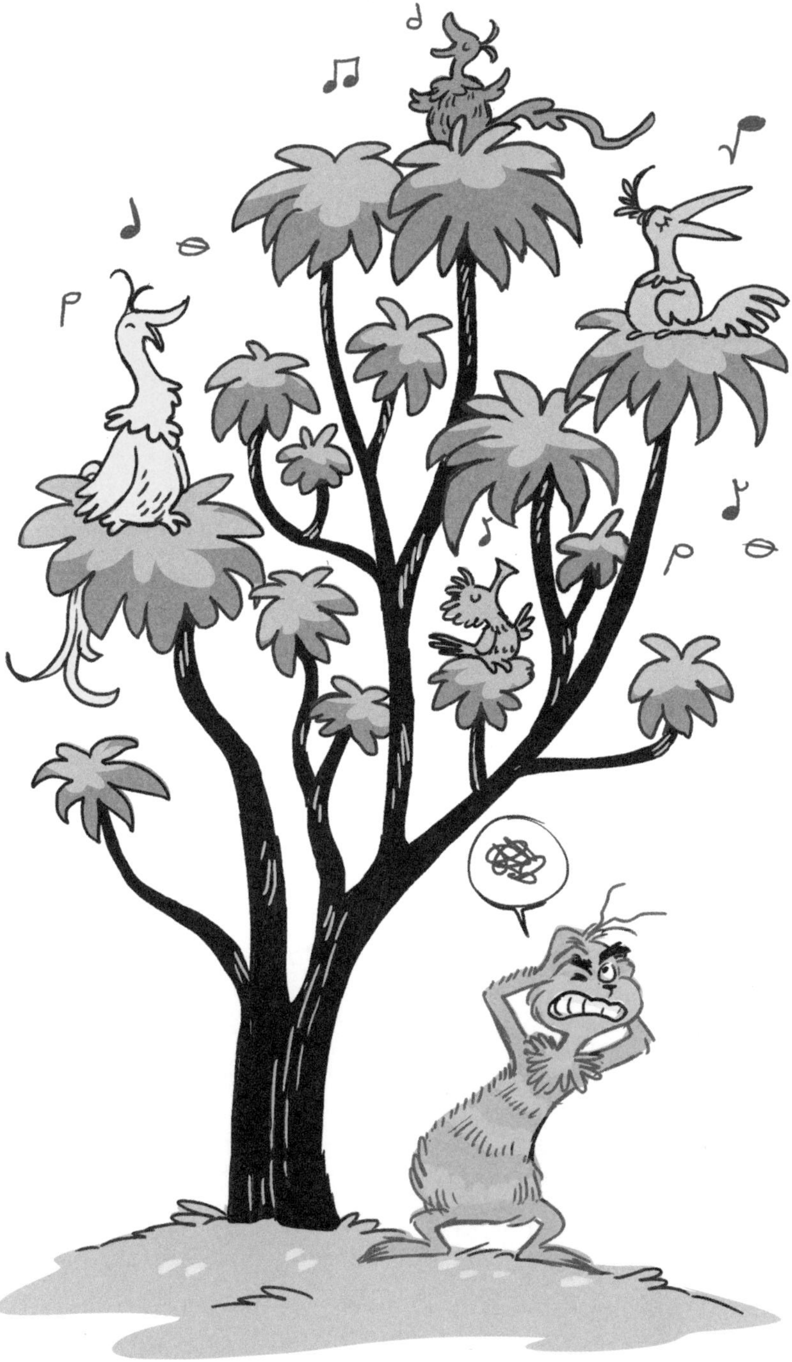

HOW TO DRAW MAX!

① DRAW TWO BEANS FOR MAX'S HEAD AND BODY.

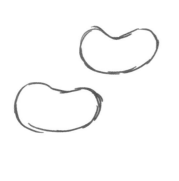

② DRAW HIS EARS, NECK, LEGS, AND TAIL.

③ CONNECT YOUR LINES! ADD A SWEET FACE.

④ CLEAN UP AND COLOR!

CHARACTER SKETCHES

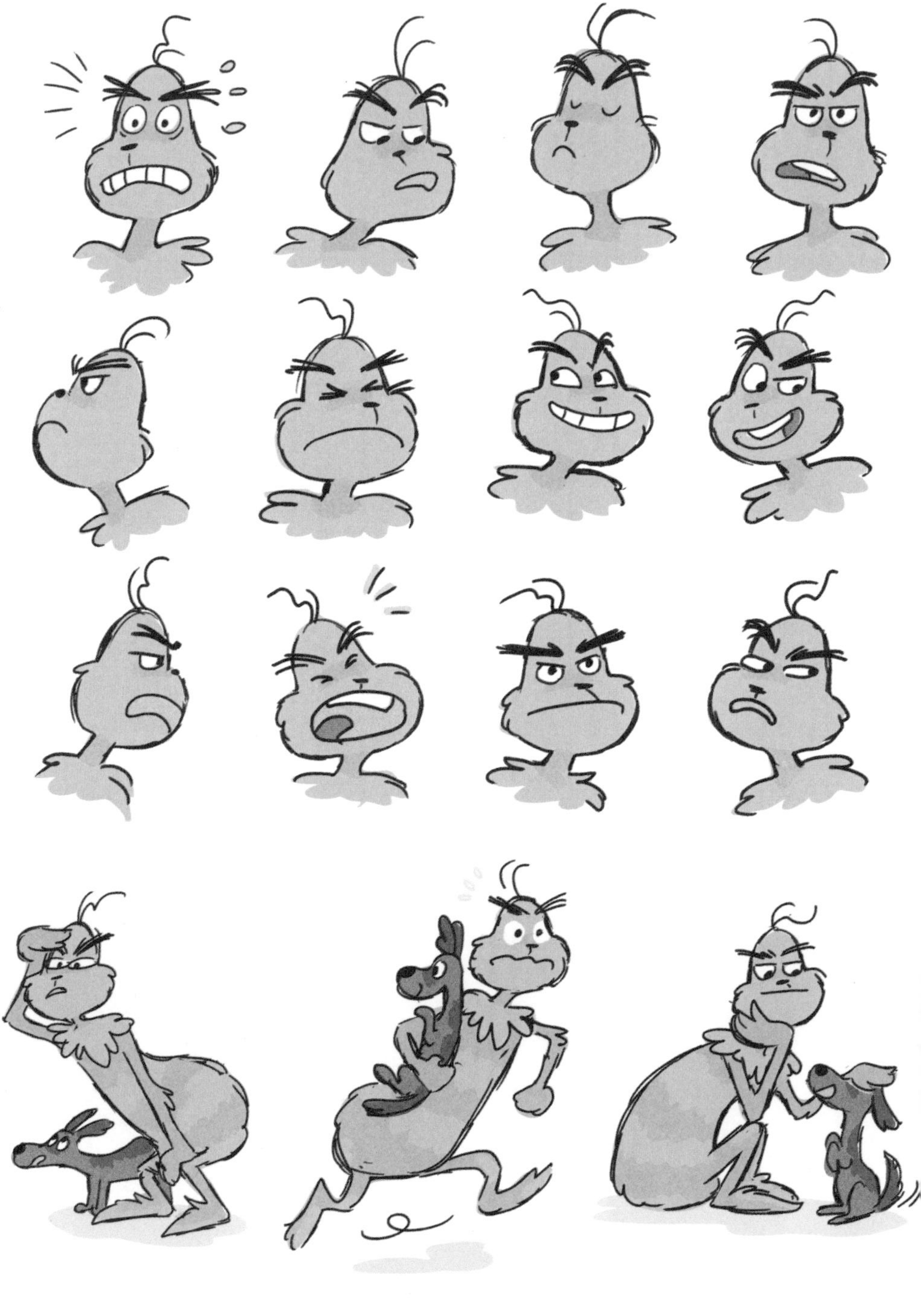

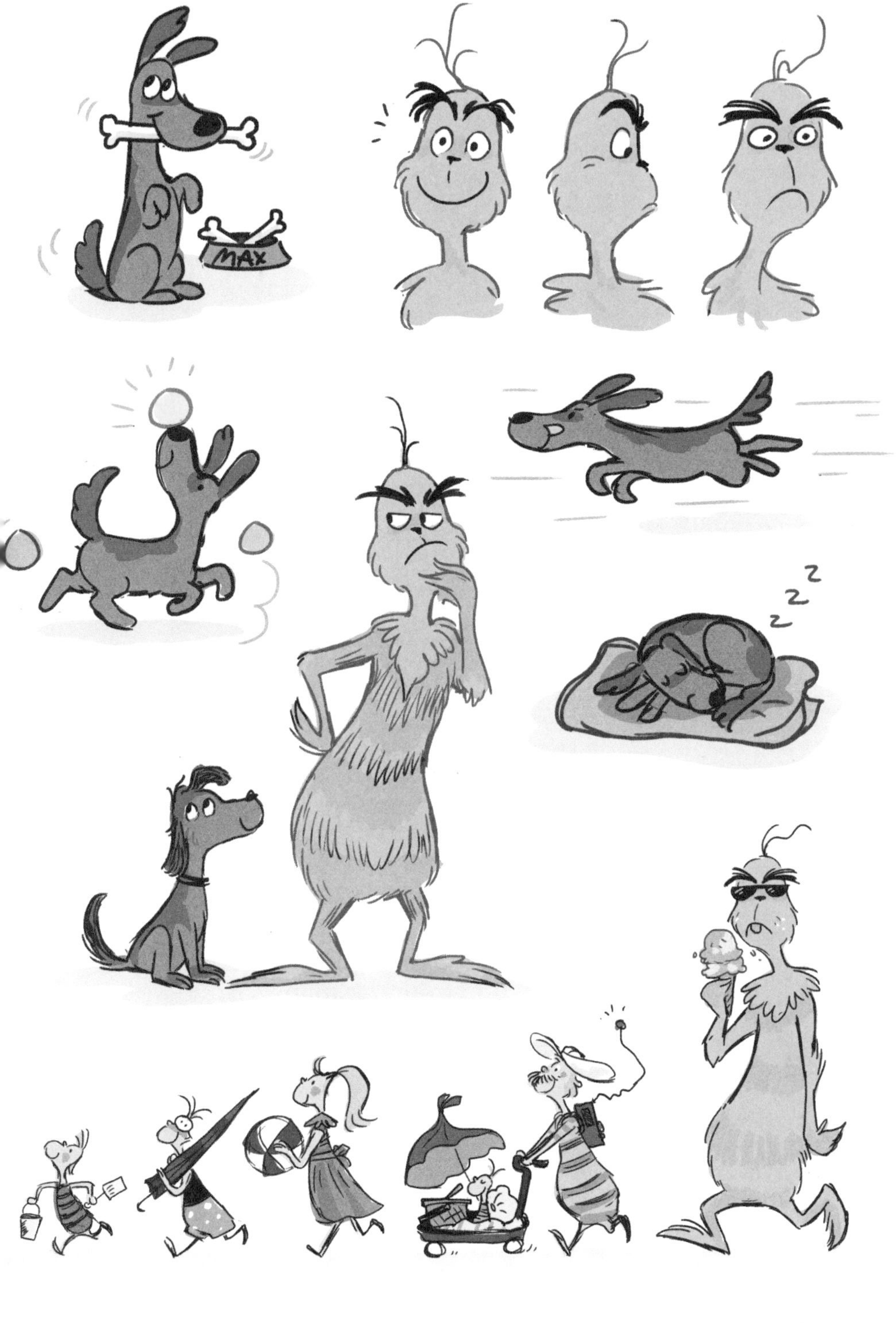
MAX
Z Z Z

KAETI VANDORN is an author and cartoonist. She grew up on the plains of Kansas, thrived among the woods of Alaska, and now lives on a big grassy hill in Vermont. If she wasn't a creative (and so wary of bugs), she would probably be a naturalist, studying the bizarre and wonderful creatures of the world.

Kaeti likes writing stories about little monsters having big adventures and has self-published her comics online since 2014. Kaeti is also the creator of the graphic novels *Crabapple Trouble*, her first published book, and *Monster Friends*, which was nominated for an Eisner Award.

The Grinch Takes a Vacation has been a challenge and a delight for Kaeti, who never dreamed of contributing to the Dr. Seuss library. She is not a Grinch, but she knows a handful of Grinchy people. Kaeti's ideal vacation would be a home-away-from-home situation—a leisurely trip visiting relatives, eating good food, and spending time in quiet, beautiful, and comforting places to kindle her imagination.

Visit proteidaes.com, proteidaes.tumblr.com, and @proteidaes on X/Twitter for more fun.

Discover Dr. Seuss's whimsical world like never before in all-new graphic novel adventures!

Presented by:

AWESOME COMICS!
AWESOME KIDS!